The Way You
Tempt Me

Also by Elle Wright:

The Wellspring series
Touched by You
Enticed by You
Pleasured by You

The Pure Talent series
The Way You Tempt Me

Published by Kensington Publishing Corp.

The Way You
Tempt Me

Elle Wright

Dafina
BOOKS

Kensington Publishing Corp.

www.kensingtonbooks.com

To the extent that the image or images on the cover of this book depict a person or persons, such person or persons are merely models, and are not intended to portray any character or characters featured in the book.

DAFINA BOOKS are published by

Kensington Publishing Corp.
119 West 40th Street
New York, NY 10018

Copyright © 2020 by Elle Wright

All rights reserved. No part of this book may be reproduced in any form or by any means without the prior written consent of the Publisher, excepting brief quotes used in reviews.

If you purchased this book without a cover, you should be aware that this book is stolen property. It was reported as "unsold and destroyed" to the Publisher and neither the Author nor the Publisher has received any payment for this "stripped book."

All Kensington Titles, Imprints, and Distributed Lines are available at special quantity discounts for bulk purchases for sales promotions, premiums, fund-raising, and educational or institutional use. Special book excerpts or customized printings can also be created to fit specific needs. For details, write or phone the office of the Kensington special sales manager: Kensington Publishing Corp., 119 West 40th Street, New York, NY 10018, attn: Special Sales Department, Phone: 1-800-221-2647.

Dafina and the Dafina logo Reg. U.S. Pat. & TM Off.

ISBN-13: 978-1-4967-2577-6
ISBN-10: 1-4967-2577-8
First Kensington Mass Market Edition: August 2020

ISBN-13: 978-1-4967-2578-3 (ebook)
ISBN-10: 1-4967-2578-6 (ebook)

10 9 8 7 6 5 4 3 2 1

Printed in the United States of America

For Jason, my husband and friend.
Your constant support means the world to me.
Love you!

Acknowledgments

Wow! What a blast! *The Way You Tempt Me* turned out to be one of my favorites. I had so much fun writing Xavier and Zara. There is just something special about a friends-to-lovers journey that sends a rush through my veins. And the colorful cast of characters . . . I found myself laughing throughout the process as I put their antics on the page. I really hope you loved them as much as I did. I appreciate all of your love and support.

Giving honor to God, Who is able to do anything. His Grace and Mercy brought me through. I am living this moment because of Him.

To my husband, Jason, I can't imagine my life without you. Thank you for *tempting* me all those years ago.

To my children, Asante, Kaia, and Masai, I love you all so very much. Keep being who you are. Keep God first.

To my family and friends, thank you for your unwavering support. My life is brighter because of you. Thanks for being #TeamElle!

To my sis, Sheryl Lister, you already know. I'm so grateful for you. Love you!

To my lit sistas, Sherelle Green, Anita Davis, and Angela Seals—let's get it. I can't wait to do more. Love y'all!

To my Book Euphoria ladies, you are #SoDope.

To #EllesBelles, my street team, thank you so much for rocking with me.

I also want to thank Beverly Jenkins for extending a lifeline that I'll always hold on to.

Special thanks to Priscilla C. Johnson and Cilla's Maniacs, A.C. Arthur, Brenda Kidd-Woodbury (BJBC), MidnightAce Scotty (MidnightAce Book Bar), King Brooks (Black Page Turners), Sharon Blount and BRAB (Building Relationships Around Books), LaShaunda Hoffman (SORMAG), Orsayor Simmons (Book Referees), Tiffany Tyler (Reading in Black and White), Shannan Harper (Harper's Court), Naleighna Kai (Naleighna Kai's Literary Café and Cavalcade of Authors), Wayne Jordan and Romance In Color, Radiah Hubert (Urban Book Reviews), and the EyeCU Reading and Social Network for supporting me. I truly appreciate you all.

Thank you to my readers! You're amazing! Nothing would be possible without you.

Thank you!

Chapter 1

"I've been here since day one. I've seen the strides made, the battles fought, the victories won, and the losses suffered. As one of this agency's first clients, I believe in my father's vision." Xavier Starks met his father's eyes and smiled. "And I can't wait to lead this company into the future."

"And you're sure about this?"

Xavier paused, mouth open, thumb on the presentation clicker. He glanced back up at the screen showcasing his hard work, the slide that he'd worked painstakingly on in an effort to garner applause. Or at least a smile. What he didn't expect was that particular question from his father. Because he was sure. He was definitely confident in his plan to take Pure Talent to the next level by spearheading a new sports division.

Dropping his arms to his sides, he sucked in a deep breath. "Excuse me? Of course, I'm sure. We talked about this. Sports will change the game, improve our bottom line. I envision a huge marketing campaign, the best sports agents, talented players. What's there not to be sure about?"

Jax arched a brow and glanced down at the small box sitting on the desk. The ring. The vintage marquise-cut diamond sparkled from the box, gleaming at him. His father pointed at it. "This."

Sighing, Xavier picked it up and closed the top of the box before he stuffed it in his pockets. "Does this mean you didn't hear a word of my presentation?"

"I heard you." Jax leaned forward, elbows against the oak desk. "Xavier, you came into my office and showed off this ring you purchased for Naomi. Then you went into your work proposal. Shouldn't we talk about this? You are my son. This is a big deal."

Xavier shrugged. "It is. Which is why I wanted to show you the ring first."

"A ring doesn't make a marriage, son. Are you sure you're ready for this?"

"Yeah, I'm ready. Dad, there is a board meeting in two hours. I need to table the discussion about the ring and focus on the work proposal I have to make."

Pure Talent Agency was founded by Jax Starks in 1989, after he had made a name for himself as a sharp, dedicated entertainment attorney for several African-American celebrities. He'd spent years building his brand, negotiating unheard-of deals in Hollywood for actors who had floundered under different representation. The first order of business was signing Xavier himself as the first child actor of the boutique agency.

With his father's vision and connections in the industry, Xavier landed a sought-after role on one of the most influential sitcoms of the 1990s. Every Tuesday evening, families of all backgrounds watched Xavier grow up right before their eyes as the sharp, inquisitive son of a fictional lawyer and his family.

It wasn't long before Xavier had decided he didn't want the life of red carpets and photo shoots. He didn't want to spend his school year with tutors, instead of teachers, and with costars, instead of his friends. Once he realized that acting was not for him, he'd gone to great lengths to distance himself from his squeaky-clean child star image, eventually settling into a career of his own within the agency as one of the best youth-performer agents at Pure Talent. Now he wanted—no, he needed—to take his career to the next level.

"Expanding into sports is huge for this company," Xavier said. "And I want to be the agent to helm this new venture. I've done the work, I've studied the market, I've made invaluable connections. This is exactly the type of project that I'm looking forward to sinking my teeth into."

Jax leaned back in his chair. "I agree. A sports division is the next logical step. I can definitely foresee us taking this company to a whole new level of success."

"Exactly."

"It's no secret that I'm getting older."

Xavier dropped his gaze. Over the past few

months, his father had been talking more and more about retirement, of traveling for pleasure, of enjoying dinner with X's mother without interruptions from clients and staff. As much as he understood the notion, he hated to think of his father getting older. In Xavier's mind, Jax Starks was still a force to be reckoned with in the industry.

"I have to admit that seeing you take the initiative on something like this makes me happy," Jax continued. "You've done a good job on the proposal, your presentation is thorough. I'm very interested in exploring this further."

"Thank you. Your faith in me means a lot, Dad."

"Have you thought about potential agents?"

Xavier finally took a seat. "I have some ideas. I can get you a list this afternoon, after the presentation."

"Great. I see no reason not to move on this quickly. I also have a few names."

Curiosity piqued, Xavier asked, "Care to share?"

"Not particularly."

Xavier barked out a laugh. "I'm not surprised." Without another word, Xavier closed his laptop and gathered his hard copy of the presentation.

"Are you sure?"

Glancing at his father, Xavier sighed. He'd been in this position with his father more times than not, hoping to distract from a conversation he didn't want to have. When he'd mentioned marriage to Naomi, both of his parents had reservations and had made it known in no uncertain terms.

He couldn't say that he blamed them. Naomi was

one of the hottest black actresses in the industry. Going out with her was inviting attention that he'd tried hard to avoid for many years.

"I'm sure," Xavier said finally.

"Why? Why is *she* the one?"

"We've been together for over a year."

"That's not an answer."

Xavier shrugged. "What do you want me to say?"

"I want you to tell me why you're proposing to a woman who spends more time on her phone than with you. What is it about her that makes you think marriage is the next logical step?" Jax stood to his full height and strolled over to the mini refrigerator he kept in the office. Pulling out two bottles of water, he offered Xavier one before twisting the cap off of his own. "Being married is much more than a high-profile wedding. I just want to be sure you're doing this for you—and not for an image you think you need."

"I don't need to get married, Dad. I want to. Naomi is talented, funny, adventurous, beautiful. We get along, we have fun together, we enjoy the same food and the same activities. She challenges me to . . ." *Watch reality TV and read fanfiction?* He scratched the back of his neck. "She's amazing."

His father leaned against the desk and assessed him with eyes that saw too much, way more than Xavier wanted them to see in that moment. "But you didn't mention *love*. Do you love her?"

"*Love*"? Xavier closed his eyes as the chorus to that damn Tina Turner song played in his head. The question in the song taunted him, because love hadn't been a part of his decision-making process. Of course, he cared for her, and he did love her. But not in a fiery, all-consuming "A Couple of Forevers" way. More like a "We've Only Just Begun" way.

Still, he couldn't bring himself to admit that to his father; he knew it would only make matters worse. Because Jax Starks fell in love with Ana Perry-Starks thirty-eight years ago and had never stopped being in love with his wife. Growing up, Xavier had watched his parents build an empire, all while demonstrating unconditional love to each other, even during the hard times. Marrying for anything other than love was a no-no to his mother and father.

"You know I have feelings for her. Otherwise, I wouldn't be doing this. I'm a grown man doing grown-man things. I know you think I'm being impulsive, but I don't take this lightly."

He'd thought about everything, weighed the possible pros and cons. In the past, Xavier had made very questionable decisions, based on emotions and appearances.

"I'm doing the right thing." Xavier stood, picked up his laptop. "Tonight is the night I will propose to Naomi. Everything will be fine. You'll see."

"Fine. If this is what you want, I'm going to support you."

"Thanks. I have to run an errand. I'll be back in an hour."

Xavier left his father's office and hurried to his own office to drop off his things. Grabbing his jacket, he told his assistant, Jennifer, to hold his calls; then he rushed to the elevator. He responded to a client while he waited for the car and sent a text to another. When the door opened, he stepped inside. As soon as he exited the elevator, his phone buzzed.

"What's the word, bruh?" Xavier breezed past a crew in the process of decorating one of the many Christmas trees that would adorn the lobby leading up to the holiday in a few weeks.

"Shit," Duke answered.

Since they were kids, Duke Young had been a constant in Xavier's life, since their fathers were best friends. They'd seen each other through stupid decisions, crazy exes, and even an overnight stint in jail.

"Is everything all set?" Xavier's phone buzzed, indicating another call was coming in. He glanced at the screen and hit IGNORE. His cousin, Skye, would have to wait.

"Who the hell do you think you're talking to?" his friend asked. "Of course, we're all set."

Voted one of the hottest chefs of his generation, Duke had blazed a trail in the culinary industry, winning multiple awards and turning the food game on its ears. He'd recently won a reality-television contest for best chef and was currently wielding all kinds of offers, from product endorsements to lucrative job offers to cookbook deals. He'd even managed to snag a deal as an underwear model.

"Did the florist come to the house?"

Xavier had spared no expense, hiring one of the top floral artists to decorate his condo for the proposal.

"She just left," Duke said. "But not before I got her number for tonight."

"You just make sure the entrée is on point, before you hook up with Samantha."

"I got you, bruh. You know that."

"Thanks, man. I need this entire thing to go off without a hitch."

"At least the food will be good." Duke laughed. "That is the only thing that I'm sure about."

"Shut the hell up, man." He'd heard all of his friend's reservations about Naomi and the proposal multiple times since he'd asked him to prepare the meal for the occasion. And after the conversation he'd just had with his dad, he didn't want to hear it again.

"I'm just sayin' . . . Despite the slammin' dinner, the whole engagement thing doesn't sit right with me. But it's your life."

"Exactly, so stop talking about it." The phone buzzed in his ear again. Xavier glanced at the screen. His father. Hitting IGNORE, he said, "Bruh, once you're finished, you can go ahead and go. I'll probably be done here a little early today, because I want to take care of some things at the house."

"I don't just cook a masterpiece and walk away. Part of my process is the presentation."

"For someone else, yes. But not for me."

Another call buzzed in his ear. Skye again. For a

second, he wondered if something was wrong. But he quickly brushed that worry off, because she would have sent a text.

Xavier stopped at a coffee kiosk in the lobby, while Duke ticked off all the details for the romantic date he'd planned tonight. He placed his regular order, but paused when the barista simply stared at him. He looked down at his suit to check for a stain or something. "Is something wrong, Rita?"

The petite woman quickly snapped out of her trance. "Uh, no. I'm sorry, X." She hurried to get his drink.

Frowning, he scanned the area and noticed that Rita wasn't the only one staring at him. Conspicuous glances from several people in the lobby got his attention. Stares and whispers weren't new to him. As a former child star with a hit show still running in syndication, being noticed wherever he went was commonplace. But not in the Pure Talent offices. And not the way the various staff members were watching him.

"X, what's up?" Duke asked, interrupting his thoughts.

"Nothing." He smiled when Rita slid a cup of coffee toward him. Meeting her gaze, he noticed her chin tremble, almost like she was going to break out in an ugly cry. "Are you okay?"

She dropped her gaze. "I'm okay, X. Are you?"

Tilting his head, he nodded. "I'm fine." He pulled out a twenty-dollar bill and set it on the counter.

Before he could slide it to her, she placed her hand on top of his. "It's good. Coffee's on me today."

"Okay," he murmured. "Thanks, Rita."

"Who the hell is Rita?" Duke asked.

Xavier blinked. Because for a second, he'd forgotten he was on the phone. "No one to you, bruh. Listen, what did you decide for dessert?"

Duke described a strawberry-and-chocolate torte that he was sure Naomi would love. Smiling, Xavier said, "Sounds like you have everything under control."

"I told you . . . I got this. This is what I do."

"X!"

Xavier turned toward the entrance of the building. Skye waved at him and rushed over to where he'd been standing near the small coffee kiosk. He held up a hand, signaling her to wait a second. Speaking to Duke, he told him to call if he had any issues and ended the call.

"What's up, Skye?"

Breathing heavily, like she'd been running, Skye ran a hand through her hair. "I've been trying to call you."

Xavier opened an e-mail and skimmed a message from one of his client's parents. "I was in the middle of something." He quickly typed out a response to the e-mail and hit the SEND button. "What's going on?" He read another e-mail and pondered the best way to answer the question posed to him.

Skye snatched his phone. "Listen to me."

Frowning, he wondered if he'd missed something. *Has she been talking?* "There's a lot going on. I'm actually on my way out to take care of something for the proposal tonight."

"X, I . . ."

He pulled the ring out of his pocket. "I forgot to show you the ring." He opened the box and smiled, anticipating her reaction.

Skye had been his number one supporter in everything he'd done in life. They'd grown up together, joined at the hip from the time they could walk. Their fathers were brothers and partners in numerous business ventures.

With a hard eye roll, Skye shook her head. "X, stop."

He paused, confused by Skye's reaction to the ring. He'd expected her to hype him up, coo over the size and shape of the diamond. "What? You don't think she'll like it? We talked about this. You told me marquise-cut was the way to go?"

"Will you just shut up about the ring?" Skye scanned the immediate area. "Too many people, too many ears," she mumbled, grabbing his hand and pulling him toward an empty conference room.

Once inside the room, she closed the door and the blinds and turned to him. "X, we need to talk."

Skye worked for Pure Talent in the public relations department. She knew how to handle all types of situations—good, bad, or catastrophic. Her specialty was putting a positive spin on everything, whether she was writing press releases, fine-tuning images, or managing crises. Right now, she was giving him "bad news" vibes. Soft voice, direct eye contact, and straight back.

He eyed her, waited for her to speak. Then he saw it. The slightest tremble in her chin. This was personal, not client related. "What's wrong?" he asked. "Did someone die?"

She shook her head.

"Accident?"

"Okay, I'm going to talk now." She sighed heavily. "And I need you to remain calm, no matter what."

Dread knotted in his stomach. The last time Skye had told him to remain calm, she'd informed him that their uncle had passed away suddenly. "I'm good."

Finally her shoulders relaxed. "You obviously haven't seen Page Six."

"No. Like I said, I've been busy. Why?"

She pulled out her phone. "There's something you need to see." Xavier took the offered device from his cousin and peered at the Page Six head-line. "I'm so sorry," she whispered.

The title of the article was the punch to the gut, the huge picture under the article served as the up-percut. The combination of both knocked the wind out of his lungs. He sat down on one of the empty chairs. Muttering a curse, he glared at the screen. He didn't need to read the article to know that he was screwed, that he had been screwed.

Still, he forced himself to look at the "happy couple" on the page. The woman smiled as if she'd recently descended from cloud nine, while the man held on to her waist as if he'd never let her go. It wasn't the type of picture taken without permission. The man and woman had posed for it, made sure the photographer caught her good side. The only problem? He was an asshole and she had recently been voted one of the "30 Hottest Women under 30" in *People* magazine. His woman, the woman he had planned to propose to that night. The title taunted him, and he re-read it three times in a row, just to be sure and maybe to will it away. He closed his eyes and reopened them. *Shit.* It was still there, still pissing him off, still taunting him: NAOMI MURPHY DUMPS XAVIER STARKS FOR PRO-BASKETBALL PLAYER ETHAN PORTER.

Chapter 2

"Damn, X. What number is this?"

Xavier glanced over at his friend Garrett Steele and watched as he ordered a cognac neat. Without answering, he turned his attention back to his own glass, half filled with the same amber liquor his friend had just requested.

"X?" Garrett called.

It wasn't Garrett's fault. He'd been sitting next to him for a good fifteen minutes, trying to engage. But Xavier wasn't ready to converse with anyone. Christmas music blared through the surround-sound speakers, laughter permeated the air around him, and his parents worked the room, as they did every year at this time. The annual Starks holiday party was in full swing.

It had been two weeks since he'd been dumped via tabloid, and Xavier had finally emerged from his cocoon of work, home, and takeout. But only because his father had sent reinforcements to force him to shower and put on his best suit for the occasion. His mother and Skye had appeared on his doorstep with a brand-new suit, shoes, and a veiled threat to "get your shit together, because that woman will *not* get another ounce of your energy."

Xavier finished his drink and tapped the bar counter, signaling to the bartender to refill his glass. "I'll drink until people stop staring at me."

Garrett snickered. "Man, this is not your first scandal, and I'm sure it won't be the last."

"If that's your attempt at helping the situation, you failed miserably."

"Shit, I'm done. I can't even muster the obligatory 'you're better off' speech. Because the whole thing is fucked-up."

"Exactly." Xavier picked up his glass and tipped it in his friend's direction. "The silver lining will reveal itself when I get over forking over twenty thousand dollars on that damn ugly-ass ring, ordering exotic flowers, and flying Duke here for a gourmet meal, only to find out that the woman I was supposed to propose to . . ." He shook his head. He couldn't say it out loud anymore.

After some prodding from Skye, he'd tossed a few glasses against his living-room wall. That shit didn't help. The only thing it did was shine a light on how incredibly oblivious he'd been. Naomi didn't love him, or even care that much about him. She'd used him from the beginning, and he'd helped her. His connections in the business, his father's name . . . everything about him fit into her plan for her career. He'd just been so preoccupied with his own career track that he'd failed to see she was playing him all along.

Now he was embarrassed, humiliated, tormented by the gossip and vlogs devoted to his pitifulness. His saving grace was that the downfall of his relationship only cost him money, and not his heart. Oh, and a little bit of his dignity and a possible client in Ethan Porter. Because at Naomi's encouragement, he'd approached the popular small forward about representation for the new division.

Xavier snorted. "She played me. Hell, they both did. This is some bullshit."

"Yeah . . . pretty much," Garrett agreed.

Garrett and X had attended Morehouse College together and pledged the same fraternity. X had often credited Garrett with helping him experience normal life, without cameras. He'd learned a lot about navigating the world simply by watching Garrett handle college without help from his mother or any support system capable of helping him adjust. There was only Garrett and his little sister, Maxine. So Xavier became their family.

"But you did dodge a bullet, man." Garrett clasped X's shoulder and squeezed. "I can't be upset about that. Just imagine how bad this could have been."

As usual, Garrett was right. Having this happen after he married Naomi or even proposed to her would have been so much worse. Still, it didn't dull the sting of being labeled everything from an abusive drunk to a down-low cheater to a swinger who wanted Naomi to be a part of his harem. Yes, the bloggers and vloggers had grasped at every straw in their haste to get more likes and subscriptions.

"You're right, bruh," Xavier conceded.

"Are you going to speak out? Tell your side of the story? I'm available to help."

Garrett owned his own crisis management firm and he specialized in making shit go away. But Xavier didn't need to hire out for this. As long as he kept his cool, it would blow over. At least that's what he told himself every time he had the urge to find Ethan Porter and pummel him to the ground.

He rubbed the back of his neck. "Nah, I'm good. My plan is to lay low right now."

"That's always a good plan in these types of situations. I'm sure Skye is working behind the scenes to turn the narrative and make Naomi the big bad in the relationship."

Xavier shrugged. "I really don't know. She's—"

As if on cue, Skye appeared out of nowhere, a bright smile on her face as she walked toward them. He picked up his drink just in time for her to snatch the glass from him.

"You've had enough." She quickly tossed back the drink. "People are pretending not to stare and are murmuring under their breath."

"Hello, Skye," Garrett said. "Merry Christmas."

With cool eyes, Skye glared at his friend for a moment before turning her attention back to him. "I hate that shit," she said without acknowledging Garrett's greeting. "Get up and mingle, X." She set his empty glass on the bar top and walked away.

Xavier eyed his friend. "My suggestion?"

"What?" Garrett asked, an edge to his voice that hadn't been there earlier.

"Maybe you need to handle your own business, instead of trying to get in mine."

Garrett stood abruptly, nearly tipping the stool over. "Man, shut the hell up."

Xavier tried hard not to laugh as his friend headed over to another group of people on the other side of the room, muttering a string of frustrated curses along the way.

Turning to the bartender, he ordered another drink.

"Son, are you going to sit here all night, babe?" His mother stepped up to the spot Garrett had just vacated. She perched herself on the empty stool and smiled at the bartender. "Justin, please make this his last one tonight."

"Justin, make this one a double," Xavier ordered.

The bartender's gaze darted back and forth from Xavier to Ana. "Sir, I . . ."

Ana patted the nervous bartender's hand. "It's okay. This is it for him. I'd like another glass of champagne, too."

Justin rushed away to pour the drinks, and Xavier's mother looked at him and smiled. Her eyes were sharp, all-seeing. Her beautiful dark brown skin seemed to glow in the muted lighting. Always stunning, she wore a long-sleeved, sequined emerald-green dress to match the occasion. The jewelry she wore sparkled like Christmas lights. It was no wonder she'd made a living as a model for the world's top designers. Her portfolio included print, runway, movies, and even her own calendar.

Her impressive career broke down barriers for many who had come after her.

He kissed Ana's cheek. "You look beautiful, Ma."

His mother straightened his tie. "As do you." Her Liberian accent was thick, soothing to him even at his age. "But I worry."

"Don't. I'll be fine."

She tilted her head and peered into his eyes. "Still, you're my son, my only child. I hate to see you this way."

He let out a deep sigh. "I already told you, I'm okay. Stop worrying."

She smoothed her hands over his shoulders. "I'll stop worrying when you stop sulking. Don't let that trollop win the battle."

Xavier chuckled at his mother's choice of words. "'Trollop'?"

She shrugged. "Well, that's the nice way of saying h—"

"Okay, Ma," he interrupted. "No need to bring out the big guns."

Gripping his hand, she tugged him to his feet. "Let's go talk to Stewart and Victoria." She grabbed her champagne glass and directed him to grab his tumbler. "It's been a while since they've seen you."

Xavier let his mother lead him over to Duke's parents. He greeted Stewart with a man hug and Victoria with a kiss on the cheek. Jax met them over there and told a story about his latest endeavor to steal a new client from one of his competitors. Jax and Stewart had been friends since they were kids growing up in the same Ann Arbor, Michigan, neighborhood. Their bond had never waned, and their families had remained close friends.

Skye joined them, and soon Xavier was glad that his mother had forced him away from the bar. Victoria shared the latest adventure of one of her eight children, Dexter. Then she begged Xavier to help Duke find some direction.

Xavier held up his hands in surrender. "Hey, you know Duke does his own thing. I have no influence."

"Seriously, Xavier." Victoria wrapped an arm around his shoulder. "I need him to get his shit together."

They all burst out in a fit of laughter, partly because Victoria didn't curse, but mostly Duke was the one who always made her break the no-cussing rule she'd always tried to live by.

"Damn it," Skye murmured.

Silence descended on the room and Xavier watched everyone's attention veer to the door to where Naomi and Ethan had just entered the room.

"What is she doing here?" Ana asked between clenched teeth. The smile she wore never wavered, even though Xavier knew it was hanging on by a thread. "Jax, did you invite her?"

Jax gave Ana a sidelong glance. "As a client of the agency, she received her invitation weeks ago, just like everyone else."

"The nerve," Skye whispered. "I'll handle this."

Jax gripped Skye's hand, preventing her from kicking the duo out. "Leave it be."

With a sympathetic glance X's way, Skye relented and stayed put.

"Are you okay, son?" Jax glanced at Xavier with narrowed eyes.

The challenge in his father's eyes told Xavier he'd better be okay. Jax Starks had always maintained control, even in the most stressful situations, and had implored Xavier to do the same. It took Xavier leaving the Los Angeles party scene before the lesson finally took. That didn't mean his infamous temper never got the best of him again. It just meant that he did a better job of walking away from situations that tested him.

"I'm cool," he answered.

Naomi's eyes lit up when she noticed their group. With her arm wrapped around Ethan's, and as if she hadn't just dumped him without telling him, she sauntered over.

In the background, he heard the faint whispers and felt the weighted stares on his neck. And he tried to ignore them. He really did. Even when Naomi hugged him like they were old friends. Even when Naomi introduced Ethan to everyone, as if he didn't cheat with her knowing she was with Xavier. Even when Naomi pulled out an embossed envelope and handed it to Jax. But when his father opened the envelope and read the words out loud, that's when Xavier lost it.

"A wedding invitation?" he roared, not even caring about the scene unfolding in front of all his parents' guests.

"Babe, please," Ana said, her voice calm. "This is not the place."

Xavier closed his eyes tightly, willed the rage that seemed to coat his insides away. But it was no use. He was pissed, and nothing anyone could say would make it better. "You bring this shit here? Like you didn't play me for the whole world to see? What the hell is wrong with you?"

Ethan stepped forward, ice in his eyes. "Watch who you're talking to?"

It wasn't in Xavier's nature to back down, so he glared at Ethan and took another step closer. "And what are you going to do about it?"

"You don't want to start with me, X." Ethan moved even closer.

"Get the fuck out of my face," Xavier warned.

"Maybe you should have been mowing your own lawn. Then we wouldn't be in this situation."

Before Xavier could think about the consequences, he shoved Ethan away from him and right into the dessert table. Ethan stood promptly and rushed him, knocking Xavier on his back. He wasn't sure how long they were fighting, or how many punches he'd delivered. But soon Garrett had his arms wrapped around X, holding him back, while Jax and Stewart, along with Naomi, were huddled over Ethan, who was on the ground.

Xavier slowly regained his focus, and scanned the room, noting all the disappointed and horrified faces staring back at him.

Skye stood in front of him, arms crossed and frown deadly. "Xavier, you're out of control. Get out of here. Now." She pointed toward the hallway leading to the kitchen.

Dropping his head, Xavier did as he was told and left the room. *Shit.*

Zara Reid had spent the better part of her day with one of her clients and his family, engrossed in the nuts and bolts of a brand-new, multimillion-dollar contract with the Atlanta Hawks. In the end, it was time well spent, because they left happy and she left with the honor of representing another talented young black athlete.

After a long day, she'd arrived at the Starkses' home just in time to see Xavier beat the crap out of Ethan Porter, someone she'd been following for years and hoped to add to her client roster. She assumed the fight stemmed from the fact that his girlfriend had unceremoniously dumped her friend X without so much as a "good-bye, sucka." And she hated to see Xavier go out like that.

As she stood at the entrance to the kitchen, she wondered how to approach one of her oldest friends. Should she pretend she hadn't seen him engage in the battle for Naomi Murphy, in front of a slew of important guests and associates of Mr. Starks and the Pure Talent Agency. *Or should I give him a high five, because the asshole deserved it?*

Before she could make up her mind, X looked up and met her gaze. He blessed her with one of his beautiful smiles. "Zara? When did you get here?"

"Just in time to see the show." Spurred into

action, she walked over to the sink and grabbed a towel. She walked over to the freezer and scooped several ice cubes, dumping them onto the white cloth. Zara took a seat next to him at the kitchen table. "You need to put ice on that hand."

Xavier set his bruised hand atop the towel. "I thought Skye would appear with a first-aid kit, but she abandoned me." He chuckled. "Guess I deserve to be left alone."

"She's staying far away from you right now." Zara giggled, thinking about her run-in with Skye in the hallway. Her best friend had given her a quick hug before she bolted back into the ballroom, muttering dirty curses along the way. "I saw Garrett leave." Zara wrapped the cloth around X's knuckles.

"He went to help settle things down." He winced when she twisted his wrist to finish wrapping his hand up.

"Never a dull moment at the Starks holiday soiree."

He grinned again, allowing her a glimpse at the dimple on his left cheek. "Right."

She stared at him. The subtle gold pattern in his jacket matched his skin tone perfectly. His brown eyes were just as intense as they'd always been. And he smelled divine, like sweet apples and rich wood. One thing was for sure—Xavier Starks had grown into his looks. Sure, for years his face had been papered over the walls of teenage girls, but back then, he was just X. He was her annoying, cocky, smart but stupid, asshole-tendency neighbor. And now he was . . . still all of those things probably, with a hint of "fine as hell."

"Stop staring at me, Zara," he grumbled.

"You're staring at me, too," she responded.

"It's been a minute."

"Well, we're both extremely busy."

"Too much to do, so little time."

"Exactly. Then, there's the whole living two-thousand-miles-apart thing."

He chuckled. "Ha. Right."

Before Jax Starks had moved the headquarters of his company to Atlanta, the Starks family resided in the Los Angeles neighborhood of Brentwood. And Zara lived right next door with her father, pro-basketball player Alexander Reid, and her mother, Regine. She and her siblings had been introduced to Xavier and Skye on the day she and her family moved into her childhood home—the rest was history.

"I know I messed up, Zara," he admitted softly.

Sighing, she finished her work. "I'm not here to beat you down. I'm just here to help."

He dropped his head. "I tried hard to just let it go. But . . ." He shrugged. "I don't know. It's whatever. I knew better, and I let them take me there."

"I get it. I really do. I just wish you'd done it after the party, outside. Far away from your parents. The Youngs. The agency. The town."

He laughed. "Thanks for not beating me down."

"I'm just sayin'." She bumped his knee with hers and winked at him when he met her gaze. "I probably would have done the same thing," she admitted.

"If I recall correctly, you have done the same thing."

"Oh, God," she grumbled. "There is a time limit on these things. After twenty years, you're not supposed to be able to bring that stuff up."

"I'm sure Judy would rather forget about that fight. You mopped the floor with ole girl."

Zara rolled her eyes. "That will teach her *not* to proposition someone else's homecoming date. Women everywhere should consider that beatdown a public service. I'm sure it prevented her from becoming some man's side chick."

X barked out a laugh. "You're silly."

She sighed. "Seriously, I think you are right to feel devastated by this. It sucks to be hurt by the person you love."

Xavier traced an invisible pattern on the table with his healthy hand. "I wouldn't say that."

Frowning, she asked, "Why not? You were going to propose, right? At least that's the impression I got from Skye."

"I was."

"That's awful. I know how it feels to have your heart broken."

"Not so much my heart. More like my pride."

"Wait, now I'm confused. You were going to propose, but you weren't in love with her?"

"No, Zara," he said, his voice even.

Her name on his lips had never made her feel like *this*. The low, husky tremble of his voice, the smell of cognac on his breath, the way his fingers were moving against the table, almost put her in a trance. Her stomach tightened. *It's hot in here all of a sudden.*

Swallowing, Zara said, "No?"

"No," he repeated. "Getting into a fight at my father's annual holiday party wasn't the only mistake I made. Marrying Naomi would have been epic."

"So, why propose?" *Is that my voice? High-pitched, unsure . . . flirtatious? Damn it, no.* She wasn't supposed to be flirting with him. They were friends. *Just* friends. And she didn't melt in the presence of any man. She was strong, self-assured. She got shit done.

"I thought I knew the answer to that question." He shook his head. "I didn't. Because Naomi is not the one."

Zara sucked in a deep breath. *Okay, so I'm melting a little. Why?* She didn't know because that had never happened before. Maybe it was his voice? Or it could be because she hadn't had any in a long time? And he *was* hot—so hot, she couldn't keep her eyes off of him.

In the back of her mind, she knew she should look away. She didn't. She couldn't. It was his eyes, the way he stared at her like she was the answer to that question. Even though common sense told her he was simply being X. And she was Zara. He'd always been an intense person, and she'd always been . . . *Why is he looking at me like that?*

"How do you know?" she whispered.

"Xavier?" Jax called from the doorway.

Jumping to her feet, Zara shouted, "Okay, I'm going to go. I have to . . ." She rested her palm against the table to steady herself. "I have to get the hell out of here," she added under her breath.

Jax approached her and pulled her into a hug. "Zara, it's good to see you. I'm glad you made it."

She smiled at her surrogate uncle and mentor. "You as well. I'm happy to be here."

"I saw your father a few weeks ago. He mentioned he would be in the States next month."

Zara resisted the urge to roll her eyes. Her father had been promising he'd be home for eight months. It had been three years since she'd seen him. Once her father hit fifty, he'd decided that life was too short to be tied down to one place and one woman. And after the divorce, he'd made it his mission to travel to all the places he'd wanted to see. Without them.

"That's good," she lied.

Jax nodded, patting her back affectionately. Fatherly. Something she'd missed. "How long are you in town?"

The change in subject was welcome. "Until tomorrow morning."

"I've actually been meaning to contact you for some time. Just to check in, see how the agency is treating you."

Zara couldn't deny the influence Jax Starks had on her life. She'd modeled her career after his. She'd interned with Pure Talent every summer as a teenager, learning from him, watching him in action with his clients and his staff.

"Things are good. I'm up for partner."

"Great." He frowned slightly. "We should catch up. How about we set up some time after the holidays?"

Zara eyed Xavier, who'd been watching their interaction quietly. Meeting Jax's waiting gaze again, she nodded. "Sure. I'll call."

"Sounds good. Now, if you'll excuse me, I need to talk to my son."

"Sure," she said. A little too loud for her taste. "I'll . . . join the party." *If there is still a party to join.*

Zara hurried toward the door. Unable to resist, she turned back and nearly tripped over nothing when she met X's waiting eyes. The smirk on his full lips told her he'd caught that. But she wouldn't give him the satisfaction of showing him that she liked that damn smirk. Tipping her head toward him, she mouthed "Good luck" before she left the room.

Chapter 3

Zara glanced at her watch for the umpteenth time since she'd arrived on the top floor of her office building: 1:25. The CEO of Huntington Sports Agency had another meeting, which ran over, pushing her scheduled one o'clock meeting back.

Jeffrey Huntington was never late. He may have been a jerk most days, a male chauvinist pig every other day, but he made it a point to be prompt. She'd seen him walk out of meetings to make it to another on time. In the ten years she'd worked for the agency, he'd remained aloof and unavailable, but he was consistent and direct. She didn't have to worry about him working behind her back. Every unpleasant thing he'd said about her had been to her face. And she appreciated it—even when it felt like a slap to the face—because it had made her better. And it made her one of the best agents at the company.

"Zara, stop pacing." Jeffrey's executive assistant, Alma, leaned back in her chair. "You already have more than enough steps to meet your daily goal."

"Girl, I didn't even realize I was doing that." Zara stopped in front of the desk and picked up one of Alma's paperweights. "Is this new?"

"Yes," Alma chirped. "I picked it up on my trip to Alaska."

The polar bear stared back at Zara and she set the potential weapon down. "I've never met anyone who collected paperweights."

Alma winked. "Just like you've never met anyone who was attracted to Richard 'I am not a crook' Nixon." She waggled her eyebrows.

Zara giggled, recalling the day that sweet, motherly Alma admitted she'd fantasized about the thirty-seventh president. It was akin to her own mother mentioning that she once imagined Billy Dee Williams in place of her father during sex. Yeah, that was really a conversation.

"At least you're not fantasizing on that current president. I might have to end our work friendship."

Alma waved a hand of dismissal. "I like handsome and debonair, not orange."

One of the things Zara loved about Alma was that she wasn't one of those people who got offended when called on their privilege. They'd had many heated debates and still remained cool, sharing walks during lunch and even meeting for dinner after work several times.

"Anyway"—Alma leaned forward—"are you ready to get that promotion, girly?"

Zara felt her face heat up. "I'm nervous. He's been in there a long time. Who is he with?"

The older woman rolled her eyes. "Damn Larry, the kiss-ass."

"Stop, Alma." Zara bit her lip to contain her laughter. "Larry isn't that bad."

"When he's not here, he's great!"

"I think he's cool."

"Whatever," Alma grumbled. "You're only saying that because you think he's hot."

"No comment."

"Hot" was the right adjective to describe Larry Boston. The Brooklyn native had swagger in waves and knew how to talk to women in a way that made panties melt off—not that Zara had any personal knowledge of this phenomenon. They'd attended Yale Law School together and struck up a conversation after a particularly hard exam on torts. He was the coolest, popular with everyone in his class, and a natural bullshit artist. He'd even recommended her to Jeffrey. Their friendship was unconventional, considering Larry asked her out on a date at least once a week, and liked to tell her crazy stories about his racist family. Zara had never dated a white man before, and wasn't sure if she wanted to. But she did put him in the friend category. They'd worked several deals together, and he'd gone to bat for her more times than she could count.

"Besides, we're friends," Zara added. "He's good people."

"Normally, I don't doubt your intuition, honey. But we'll have to agree to disagree about kiss-ass Larry. I told you already—"

"That you don't trust him, and I shouldn't, either," she finished for her buddy. "I know. We've had this conversation so many times, I've lost count."

Alma folded her arms across her chest. "I just feel like I owe you my opinion. I am your elder."

Zara laughed then, and didn't even bother to hold it in. "You're not that much older than me, Alma."

"I have a child your age, girly. So, *yes*, I'm that much older than you."

"Oh, please. You're young at heart."

"My heart might be young, but these knees are old as hell."

Giggling, Zara shook her head. "You're too much."

Laughter from behind Jeffrey's office door drew her attention there. Seconds later, the door opened. Jeffrey and Larry emerged, all smiles and hand-shakes.

Jeffrey clasped Larry's shoulder fondly. "Son, I can't wait to see your proposal in action. With the rising unrest in this country, positioning ourselves as an agency that is invested in diversity, equity, and inclusion is just what this company needs. We'll schedule a meeting to make the big announcement to the team. Partner."

Zara blinked. *Partner?*

"Thanks, Jeff," Larry said. "It's time to step into the future. We can't survive without making changes to the culture. We start here at Huntington, and the rest will follow."

With narrowed eyes, she crossed her arms over

her breasts. *That. Bastard.* Larry wasn't racist, but he certainly didn't make diversity, equity, and inclusion his mission. That was all her. Her idea to take Huntington to the next level. And he'd just stolen it.

Vaguely she heard Alma next to her muttering curses about kiss-ass, pansy-ass, stupid-ass entitled assholes. If she wasn't so furious, she'd be laughing at the incognito lesson on how to call someone an "ass" in as many ways as possible without drawing attention to themselves.

Larry's eyes widened when he noticed her standing there, and he quickly averted his gaze. "I have a call to take in five, Jeff. We'll talk later?"

"We definitely will." Jeff glanced at her. "Zara, step into my office."

She followed Jeff into his office, glaring at Larry the entire way. Once inside, Jeff directed her to have a seat.

"It's not good news, Zara," Jeff said, not even giving her a chance to sit, so she didn't. "I wanted to give you the promotion because your work is impeccable. But I have a slew of producing agents and I want someone who will bring something new to the fold. Fortunately for Huntington Sports, I believe Larry has what it takes."

"Jeff, I have worked my ass off for you. Seven years and I've brought clients you would have never represented otherwise, had I not been here. I overheard your conversation with Larry, and I hope you know that his ideas are *my* ideas. He just got to you first."

As if she'd not spoken a word, Jeff eyed the computer and typed furiously on his keyboard. "Zara, I know you're upset. Like I said, I value your contribution to the team, but it's not your turn. Maybe once Peterson retires, you'll have your chance." He glanced at his watch. "Now I have a two o'clock that I can't be late for. Have Alma put you on my calendar for tomorrow? I'd like to discuss your role in Larry's new plan for the company."

Ain't this about a . . . "I'm not available tomorrow." *There.* She'd managed to say it without screaming at the top of her lungs.

Jeff peered up at her. "Excuse me?"

Swallowing, she tugged at her suit jacket. "Since it's obvious that you don't appreciate me enough to even listen to me, I can't be bothered with a meeting tomorrow or any other day. Let's see how many of *my* clients stay with you when I leave. I quit."

Turning on her heels, she walked out—without slamming the door behind her. *Okay, you got this, Zara.* She ignored Alma's pleas to stop and hurried through the hallway, down the stairs to the fifth floor, where her office was.

Once inside, she closed the door, willing not a single tear to fall. Not until she left the building. She made quick work of packing up her things, stuffing everything into her briefcase and her large handbag. There wasn't a lot there: only small trinkets given to her by clients, awards, and a picture of her, her mother, and her sister at the Eiffel Tower in Paris. She purposefully kept her office bare, just in case she had to leave in a hurry. It was no secret the sports business was cutthroat. She had to be able to leave without making multiple trips.

The click of her office door sounded, and she looked up. "Get out."

She unlocked her computer and saved her current files to the flash drive she kept in the USB outlet. That flash drive held all of her contacts, every single contract she'd negotiated, and each e-mail she'd sent and received. She'd made it a point to back up to her personal drive every night, because . . . well, because of snakes like Larry.

"Zara, wait." He stepped forward.

"If I were you, I'd stay far away from me right now." Zara opened her e-mail one last time, noticing a new e-mail from Jax Starks: **Have you thought about my offer?**

One line, one question, from the man she'd admired since she was a kid. The answer was yes. The call she'd had with Jax after the new year had been enlightening. They'd caught up on work, she'd told him about her plans for Huntington, then he offered her a job. She'd thought about his offer to come to Pure Talent to help with the new sports expansion. She'd gone over every pro and con she could think of. She'd invested time into her current agency, and didn't particularly want to move to Atlanta, even for a short time to get acclimated to the company. Her family was in Los Angeles. And then there was him.

Super. Fine. Xavier. With his soulful eyes, hard body, and knowing stare. They'd never been more than friends, so the last few erotic dreams she'd had about him had been out of order. But something had changed in that bite-size interaction during the holiday party. Something had tripped her over into the "damn, I'm in trouble" zone. Could she ignore the sparks and settle into a job at Pure Talent, knowing she'd see him every day? Could she risk their innocent, side-hug, comfortable friendship for unsettling emotions that flared up for no apparent reason other than the fact that she might have been in the longest sex drought in history?

Zara hit the REPLY button and sent her response to Jax: Thanks for the offer. When do you want me to start?

"Can we talk?" Larry asked.

She eyed him. "You're still here?"

"Yes, I'm not leaving until you talk to me?"

"You know, maybe I expected too much from you all along. I thought we were better than that. I thought *you* were different from everyone who doubted me. But you're not. You never were."

"Will you let me explain?" he shouted.

"Explain what? How you took my idea and passed it off as your own? What about how you're a selfish, kiss-ass, pansy-ass, stupid-ass, entitled asshole?" *Thank you for the lesson, Alma.* "Better yet, how about this? I don't care about your explanation, because I don't care about you. You and Jeffrey Huntington can go to hell."

"You don't mean that. You can't quit your job."

"I said what I said." Once the last file downloaded, she pulled her thumb drive from the laptop and wiped it clean. She picked up her briefcase and her purse and stalked toward the door, stopping only because he blocked her way. "Move."

Larry lifted his hands in the air and stepped aside. "Zara."

She closed her eyes, halting in the doorway. "Larry, stop. Stop trying to explain, stop acting like you care. There really is no need to pretend anymore. I'm out."

Deciding to quit her job on the fly had zapped all of her energy, but she'd done it. And she couldn't say that she regretted the choice to leave Huntington Sports behind. Yet, with all that bravado she'd displayed in front of Jeffrey and Larry, she felt a well of panic creep in once she'd stepped outside the office. She made it to her car just in time for the first tear to fall. Then the dam broke.

"Thanks, Christian." Zara kicked off her shoes. "I knew I could count on you. Call you tomorrow."

She ended the call, tossed her phone on the sofa, and plopped down on the plush cushions. That was the last call she'd make today. Her agenda for the evening consisted of wine, pajamas, more wine, and her DVR. Twenty episodes of *Say Yes to the Dress* lay in wait for her.

Over the last few hours, she'd contacted all of her clients to let them know she'd be moving to Pure Talent. Out of her twenty-eight active clients, twenty-four had agreed to move with her, including the new NBA-bound client she'd just signed. Most had commented on how excited they were for her, and several mentioned that there was no way they'd stay with Huntington if she left. In the end, everyone who'd decided to follow her had remarked that her drive and dedication to them made the move a no-brainer.

Growing up the daughter of Alexander Reid had given her name recognition when she broke into the field. Her first client? Her college boyfriend, who went on to become one of the highest-paid rookies in the league. Although that relationship crashed and burned after he entered the NBA, the connection had helped Zara amass several new clients. So, when her younger brother, Zeke, signed with the Kings, she was well-versed in contract language and . . . *I can't think about him right now, because I'm already on an emotional trip.*

Basketball was her thing, though. Zara knew how to handle a ball, had spent years practicing, playing in youth leagues, and attending top basketball camps. An injury in high school had effectively ruined her plans to play college ball and eventually go on to play for the WNBA. But she still loved the game, loved the sound of shoes squeaking on the court and balls swishing through the hoops. She enjoyed the crowd, the stadium food, and the smell of popcorn and peanuts floating through the air. Most of all, she thrived on the fast-paced, unpredictable rush of her job.

Although she didn't need a law degree to do her job, she'd decided to follow her initial plan and get her Juris Doctor. Once she obtained her license to represent players in the league, she created her own company and worked for herself, until she joined the Huntington team. Becoming part of an agency had made sense to her, because of the support the established company could provide.

It was during her time there that she decided to become a certified MLB agent and snagged baseball's Christian Knight. The genuine good guy had become more than a client. She considered him one of her best friends, which is why she'd saved his call for last. And true to form, he'd offered his unwavering support and planned to visit soon.

Zara picked up her phone and ordered dinner via DoorDash—orange chicken, with shrimp fried rice and extra egg rolls, from her favorite Chinese restaurant. She quickly changed into her pj's, grabbed the bottle of red from her wine rack and a glass, and settled in on the couch.

Her doorbell rang right before the first bride said "yes" to a ten-thousand-dollar gown. She pushed the pause button and hurried to the door. Peering out of the glass, she grumbled a curse. "Go away," she shouted.

"If you don't open this door, I'll just use my key. I was just trying to respect the boundaries by ringing the bell."

Zara swung the door open. "I canceled dinner because I didn't want to be bothered."

"I'm not doing this with you." Her sister pushed past her and walked into the house. "You can't call me in the middle of my workday, tell me you quit your job and are moving to Atlanta, without expecting me to come here and talk you out of it. Besides, I'm the oldest."

"By eleven months, Rissa. That's not enough time for you to be so damn bossy all the time."

"Whatever. It still counts." Larissa dropped her purse on the floor next to the couch. "I figured you ordered Chinese, so I added my order to yours." She strolled into the kitchen, like she belonged there and grabbed another wineglass. "We're spending time together tonight. Whether you want to or not."

"You're ridiculous. There is such a thing as wanting to be alone."

"Why? So you can wallow?" She filled her glass with the red wine that Zara wanted to drink by herself. "Not going to happen, sista."

"Okay, we're not friends. So, why are you here?"

Larissa laughed. "I don't have to be your friend. I'm your big sister."

Frustrated, Zara crawled back onto the couch and buried her head in one of the throw pillows. "Go away."

"Never."

"Ugh, you get on my nerves."

And it had been that way since they were kids. Why her parents decided it would be great to have children one year apart was beyond her? Three children back-to-back: Larissa, Zara, and Ezekiel. The thought of her brother, Zeke, once again caused a familiar pang in her gut, one that hadn't gone away in the four years since he'd died.

"Zara, look at me."

She met her sister's concerned eyes.

"I'm worried about you. Not because you quit your job, not because you're moving, but because you cried."

It was true. She'd phoned her sister to tell her the news earlier and could barely get it out through the uncontrollable sobs and hiccups. Which was so unlike her. "Don't remind me." Zara closed her eyes and prayed that she wouldn't cry another tear over this situation.

"Seriously." Larissa scooted closer to her. "I think you're reacting to the stress of losing the promotion, and Larry, and . . . not having sex for so long."

Zara's eyes popped open. "What?"

"It's been a long time. Did you know that sex has many health benefits?"

"Oh, my God. Shut up, Rissa!"

"It counts as exercise and it lowers your blood pressure. It's a natural stress reliever."

"What does my sex life have to do with losing my job?"

Larissa placed a hand on Zara's knee and squeezed. "You're so tense. I wonder if you would have chosen to walk away if you were getting busy with someone."

"I'm not having this conversation. Again, why are you here? Because you're certainly not helping me feel better."

"Okay, fine. I'll just sit here and watch this crappy show with you and eat. But if you need any assistance in the orgasm area, I can hook you up."

Zara threw her pillow at her sister. "You're not pimping me out to one of your little friends."

"No, I wouldn't do that," she said with a giggle. "I was talking *sex toy*."

Shaking her head, Zara sat up and poured a healthy glass of wine. "And I'm not calling Paityn." Especially since she'd already purchased a few products from their childhood friend, who'd recently launched a very popular sex product business.

"You're so stubborn."

"Rissa, can you just be a sister and hug me?" she said with a grunt and a pout. "That's what I really need right now."

Strong arms wrapped around her in an instant, pulling her close. And Zara let her sister hold her. "I'm sorry, sissy. I know you had your heart set on making partner. But there is a bright side."

"What's that?"

"You have a chance to step up your game and work under your mentor to expand his company. Talk about résumé builder. You're only making yourself more marketable." Larissa worked in human resources for a Fortune 500 company in the area. "That's something in itself."

"I don't want to move."

"I know. Trust me, the thought of you not being ten minutes away is stressing me the hell out. But you *will* take your ass to Atlanta and you'll rock this job like you've done everything else in your life. Of that, I'm sure."

Zara pulled back and gave her sister a wobbly smile. "I guess you *are* my friend."

Larissa giggled, then wiped a tear from her cheek. "I guess I am. Love you."

"Love you, too."

Chapter 4

The Pure Talent offices were as beautiful as any Zara had ever seen—floor-to-ceiling windows, open meeting spaces, state-of-the-art equipment, and a gym. And that was just on the first floor. Jax and Ana Starks valued work-life balance and had created a workplace that people wanted to go to in the mornings. Generally, employees could work from anywhere in the building, and there were several shared spaces and plenty private "cubbies" to accommodate them. Every floor had a patio, where staff could relax, and on the fifth floor, there was a "cloud" room, where people could nap. There was a café on the lobby floor and a heavenly coffee kiosk that served the best coffee smoothie she'd ever tasted. People greeted her with smiles, welcoming her to the fold with offers to show her around or help in any way they could.

The hiring process had been smooth and hassle-free. Jax and his team provided a list of condos and apartments in the area the day after she accepted the offer. It had taken three weeks for Zara to find a rental, located within walking distance of the Peachtree offices, near Midtown. Her only requirements were lots of windows, outdoor space, and a private entrance. She didn't want it to feel like a stuffy high-rise condo, but more like a home.

It had taken five days for her to drive to Atlanta from California, because she wanted to take her time. She'd shipped most of her things ahead, and just wanted time to unwind before she had to move in and unpack. Larissa had insisted on riding with her, so she wouldn't be on the road alone. Initially, Zara had balked at the idea, because . . . *hello, alone time!* But she'd enjoyed the time with her sister. No telling when they'd be able to see each other again. Zara's schedule always remained jam-packed with meetings, games, phone calls; she didn't expect it would be much different at Pure Talent. The job was the same.

"Hey, Z-Ra!"

Zara smiled at Skye. Her best friend was the only one in the world that called her by that name, and it was only because Zara had insisted she would be the next She-Ra, Princess of Power. "Hey, boo."

Skye hugged her. "I've been waiting on you to finish that tour, so I can show you to your office." She pulled back. "Let me look at you. You look fine and fabulous, as usual."

"Girl, it was a struggle. But speaking of fine and fabulous, you are wearing that dress."

Skye had always marched to the beat of her drum as far as fashion. The black tie-neck shift dress fit her slender body like she'd had it custom made. A pair of black pumps showed off her long legs. Zara had always considered her best friend one of the most beautiful people she'd ever met, with her smooth mocha skin and dark brown hair. Her mother was Marisol P, top Filipina fashion designer. And Marisol had definitely influenced Skye's distinct sense of style. Even when her friend went simple, she looked glamorous.

"I'm glad you didn't go with blue," Skye told her.

"Really?" Zara smoothed her hair back. Navy blue was her go-to color, other than black. But she'd decided to shake things up. After trying on a dozen outfits set out by Larissa, she'd chosen a burgundy pencil skirt paired with a beige loose-fitting cowl neck sweater and beige pumps. "I was thinking I should have worn a coat." Although it wasn't cold in Atlanta, it wasn't the sixty-nine-degree weather she'd left behind in Los Angeles.

Her friend waved a dismissive hand at her. "You'll be fine. Fifty-eight degrees isn't freezing cold. We're not in Michigan."

"You're right." She fiddled with her watch. "I haven't been nervous to start a job ever. Not sure why this is different."

Skye motioned for her to follow her. A plethora of paintings lined the walls leading to the bay of elevators. Zara couldn't help but stop and admire a few of the pieces along the way.

"What time is your meeting with Uncle Jax?" Skye

asked, typing something on her phone. "I wanted to take you to lunch."

"He mentioned he would be in touch, once I settled into my office."

"I made sure IT hooked you up with three monitors and a new laptop. We're phasing out Dell and moving to HP. Oh, your assistant will start tomorrow. I was hoping Bethany would come with you. But I get it. It's a big move. Anyway, you'll love Patrice. She's one of the best."

Zara nodded. Before she left L.A., she'd made it a point to send her assistant and Alma thank-you gifts for being so supportive. She'd offered Bethany a job with her, but the twenty-four-year-old recent graduate didn't want to leave her boyfriend behind.

"I trust your judgment," Zara said.

Inside the elevator, Skye glanced at Zara. "It's going to be okay. I promise."

"I know." Zara offered her friend a smile, which she knew wouldn't pass for genuine. "It's just a lot. A month and a half ago, I had a job, a home I loved, and family nearby."

Her mother had cried a river of tears when she'd broken the news of her impending departure. The next day, the same crybaby who'd begged her not to move, announced she was moving to Paris in the fall.

"I still can't believe Ms. Regine," Skye said with wide eyes. "Moving to Paris? That's crazy."

"I know. Shocked the hell out of us."

The elevator opened and Zara followed Skye

down the hall. "Maybe Rissa will decide to leave the West Coast behind and give the South a try."

Zara giggled. "Yeah, no. She's not leaving Rick." Her sister had been in a relationship with Urick Roberts for years, and had no intention of moving anywhere without him. And since he was recently elected to the City Council, there was no chance of him relocating. "Besides, she's taken fifty million selfies of her surprised look in anticipation of a proposal."

Skye waved at several people gathered near the patio door. "I can't believe they're still together."

"I can. He's good people, though. Definitely good for her."

"Well . . ." Skye stopped in front of room 150-C and slid the glass door open. "Here we are."

Stepping into the bright office, Zara gasped. "Oh, my," she breathed. The space was huge, bigger than any office she'd ever had. "How?"

"Uncle Jax thought you needed space. So I worked it out."

Zara pointed out the large floor-to-ceiling windows, where she had a view of Downtown Atlanta. "I'm . . . I . . . I don't know what to say."

She twirled around, trying to take in everything from the desk situated to her right, to the large flatscreen television mounted on the wall to her left, to the brown couch and glass table.

"Sit down, and tell me if you like that chair," Skye said. "If you don't, I'll get you another."

For the first time since the New Year, Zara smiled.

Then she hurried to the chair and plopped down on it, swinging it in full circles, until she felt like she would fall off. Zara next spent a moment opening and closing drawers, testing out the lever that transformed her desk to a standing position. She stood, walked over to the window and peered out. "This is perfect."

"Glad you love it. There's a conference room next door. You can use it anytime. Just add your name to the shared calendar. Melvin from IT will walk you through your initial log-in. I have him scheduled to come at three. It shouldn't take more than half an hour. I've also taken the liberty of programming a few important numbers into your phone—mine, Uncle Jax, and X."

Zara gave her friend a sidelong glance. "How is he?" They hadn't talked since that nice-turned-awkward moment in December. "I've been meaning to call and check on him, but . . ."

"Oh, girl. You know X. He'll be fine. He's just laying low, staying out of the press."

"The blogs have been brutal." Zara had been watching the melee online for weeks. She couldn't help but feel bad for X because he wasn't that guy anymore. Sure, he'd spent years rebelling against his parents and the public's perception of the squeaky-clean preppy boy he played on television. The Xavier of today had carved out his own slice of the field, helped many young stars achieve success. He didn't deserve the negative attention.

"Where is he?" Zara asked, her voice almost a whisper. "I mean does he know I'm here?"

"I . . ." Skye tilted her head and scrunched up her nose. "Jax wanted to tell him. I'm not sure he has yet, because X didn't mention it to me."

"That's weird."

"I know, but I just work here." She winked. "Did they show you the cloud room?"

"Yes. I'm not sure I'll use it, but it's a good idea."

"It is. There are more private spaces to relax. I'll give you the secret hiding-spots tour tomorrow. Also, if you need any supplies, put together a list and I'll make sure you'll get it."

"You're not my assistant. You get paid to fix shit, not order staplers."

"Hey, you're my girl. I'm here for you."

"I am so grateful for everything that Jax and you have done for me, from the real estate help to the travel arrangements. I can't thank you enough for making such an incredibly difficult time better."

Skye leaned against the desk, a wide grin on her face. "I'm so happy you're here. I know things are different, but it will be great to have my friend near me." She set her phone on the desk. "Let me tell you, I wanted to choke Larry when you told me what went down. We thought he was cool."

Skye attended New York University for graduate school and had spent a lot of time in New Haven with Zara. As a result, she'd gotten to know Larry pretty well over the years.

Zara rested her forehead against the cool desk. "I did, too. To think, I almost gave him some."

Her friend cracked up. "You didn't. Not Larry. He's . . ." She visibly cringed. "No."

Nodding, she said, "Yeah. It's been a long time."

"Lawd, you need help."

Sitting up straight, Zara sliced a hand through the air. "Absolutely not, Skye. No hookups." The last time her friend had set her up, she'd gone out with an agent at Pure Talent L.A. who couldn't stop texting another woman during dinner. He was attractive and everything, but Zara preferred her men to be available, not pining away for someone else.

"You can't hold that one time against me. Darin wasn't the one, but that doesn't mean I can't play matchmaker."

"Neither was Dominic nor Hunter nor Jamaal nor—"

"Okay, okay! Obviously, I don't have that gift."

"Anyway, enough talk of potential baes." Zara leaned back in her chair and stared at the ceiling. "I have to hit the ground running. I don't want to let Jax down."

"You won't." Skye squeezed her hand. The loud buzz of the phone against the desk broke the sentimental moment. Skye picked up her phone. "This is Skye." She met Zara's gaze. "Okay, she'll be there."

"Jax?"

Her friend nodded, stood up, and smoothed a hand down her stomach. "I'll walk you up."

Sighing, Zara stood. "How do I look?"

"I told you . . . fine and fabulous." She squeezed

her shoulders. "Remember, be Zara. He already loves you."

"I know no other way to be." Zara grabbed her purse. "Let's go."

Xavier stared at the clock on the wall. *How the hell is this my life?*

"And I heard that Naomi got a Personal Protection Order against you. Is that true?" Hill Prince asked.

At seventeen, Hill had amassed a respectable fortune, starring in several blockbuster movies before he got out of middle school. He was one of the lucky ones, with parents who really had his best interests at heart. Xavier had spent a lot of time with Hill, choosing to be not just an agent, but more of a mentor, a sounding board. He'd given the young man permission to contact him for anything, at any time, no matter what it was. It was his way of giving back, ensuring that the popular actor had support from someone other than his parents.

"I also read that Ethan Porter had been cheating with Naomi throughout your entire relationship," Hill continued. "Did you hear that?"

And he's a little asshole.

"Did you get a refund on the engagement ring, X?"

"Yes," he replied. Soon as the store reopened after the holiday, he'd sent his assistant to return the ring.

"And then, a friend of a friend said she saw them

vacationing in Fiji, all hugged up and shit. Man, that sucks."

It's official. This was the longest meeting he'd ever had. Never mind they'd only been in the conference room for twenty minutes, it just felt like he'd lost two years of his life.

"Listen, Hill, I'm going to have to cut this meeting short." Xavier gathered the newly signed contract for a 2022 superhero movie role and slid the paperwork into a folder. "Stop by Jennifer's desk. She'll have a copy for you. You'll also receive it digitally."

"Sounds good." Hill gave him some dap. "Thanks, X. I appreciate the work you've done on this. Hopefully, this will lead to an expanded role within the comic universe."

"Definitely," Xavier agreed. "I'm thinking even bigger than movies, too. We'll talk soon. Dinner next week. I might have another opportunity for you."

Hill nodded rapidly. "I'll be around. Peace."

Back in his office, Xavier loosened his tie and jumped right into work, returning calls, sending e-mails, and gathering intel from his contacts in L.A. It had been a couple months since the incident, and it dogged him every day, everywhere. It seemed every conversation he'd had since the holiday consisted of veiled attempts to know more about Naomi and Ethan, Ethan and Naomi, Ethan-Naomi-Xavier.

Work kept his mind from veering to all the ways his life sucked at the moment. He'd gone from being able to eat without paparazzi snapping pics to being stalked outside of his condo and the Pure

Talent building. *Shit*, he couldn't even grab a coffee at the kiosk without the whispers and pitiful looks from employees. Scandal sold, and he was right smack in the middle of it.

"X?" A knock on the door snapped him out of his pity party. When he looked up to find Andrew Weathers at his door, he waved him in.

"What's up, man?"

Drew took a seat on the couch near the window. "Nothing. I figured I'd come check you out before I get on a plane."

Pure Talent had offices in Los Angeles, Atlanta, New York, and Miami. Drew was one of the best, working out of the L.A. office. When Xavier started at the agency, he'd started as an assistant to several agents. His father figured it would be the best way to learn the job. Drew was experienced enough to teach him the ropes, and young enough to relate to him as a colleague and not an elder.

"I might have to head out that way in a few weeks." Xavier finished a memo he'd been working on and saved the file. "Bishop is working on something for me."

"I heard," Drew said. "Good idea. Wish I had thought of it myself."

Recently Xavier approached the business development team to evaluate several new ways to keep Pure Talent relevant in the ever-changing climate and generate revenue for the company. Over the past few years, commissions had decreased and marketing budgets had increased.

Pure Talent had remained profitable, because it

was considered a midsize corporate agency with a boutique feel. The company had come a long way from its print and commercial beginnings. Clients were developed, treated like a valued member of the team. Agents took chances on up-and-coming artists and maintained good relationships with powerhouse clients. But it was time to diversify.

Xavier's background in finance helped him identify sound investments, and he had proposed expanding their social media presence by investing in several tech companies that had proven lucrative for the company. The latest investment? A popular digital media company, with nearly 3 million sub-scribers.

"I have ideas, man." Xavier leaned forward, resting his elbows on his knees. "I just need my father to buy in."

"The numbers don't lie, X. This is huge. And I think packaging it with a new audio division would make this even better."

"Audio, huh?" He'd been watching the popularity of podcasts rise significantly over a short period of time and thought Drew was onto something. "Let's talk about it."

Drew nodded. "I'm ready when you are. But aren't you trying to take Pure Talent into sports?"

"I am. But I have two hands." Xavier grinned. "Besides, I don't need to spearhead Pure Talent Audio. You can do that."

"I'm actually looking to decrease my client roster." Drew handled several of the agency's most talented actors and actresses. "I'm ready for a change."

"Sounds like this is right up your alley, then." He grabbed two bottles of water from his small refrigerator and handed one to Drew. "I'll have Jennifer get with Gwen to carve out time in our schedules."

"So tell me about Naomi."

Xavier grumbled, but gave his friend a rundown of the latest, all the way up to the most recent headline: XAVIER STARKS HEADS TO REHAB AFTER THE DEVASTATING END TO HIS RELATIONSHIP.

"Where do they even get this shit?" Xavier chuckled. "And who the hell are these supposed insiders?"

Drew shook his head. "Probably one of your exes."

"You might be right." Xavier had never denied being a player. He'd dated many women, coast to coast and even abroad. "Dad has been quiet lately."

Frowning, Drew untwisted the cap of his bottle. "Didn't he just return from vacation?"

Xavier's parents went on an extended vacation to Liberia to visit Ana's family, and then spent two weeks at a tropical island resort. He'd received a simple text letting him know they were back two days ago.

"Today is his first day back in the office." He hadn't been summoned to his father's office yet, but expected to get the call at any minute. "I hope he'll be assured that this mess is all behind me, when I give him the rundown on what I've accomplished to prepare for this expansion."

Xavier's client list already included heavyweight boxer Lane Wilson, so he'd already been certified with the Combative Sports League. A few weeks ago, he'd taken the sports agency exams for the National Football and Basketball leagues.

Drew stood. "Nothing like being proactive. He'll be impressed." He finished off his water and tossed the empty bottle into a small recycle bin in the corner. "I better get going, I have to make a few stops before I head to the airport."

"All right."

They spent a few minutes talking about the Lakers and agreed to go to a game when Xavier went to L.A. Not long after Drew exited his office, Xavier received the call he'd been waiting for. His father had requested his presence "in five."

He cleared his afternoon and headed up to the top floor. But when he arrived at his father's office, Jax wasn't alone. No, he had company. A beautiful, poised guest, one who'd haunted his dreams several times over the past several weeks. *Zara.*

Chapter 5

Xavier couldn't say he was surprised. *No, "surprise" isn't the word.* Waylaid? Ambushed? Discarded? Because he knew why Zara was there. Because Jax Starks rarely did anything without a plan of action. Because his father had offered the lovely Zara Reid *his* job.

Stepping into the office, he took the empty seat next to Zara. As annoyed as he was at the turn of events, he couldn't help but admire her. And that was surprising, considering he'd known her practically his entire life, had seen her with pigtails and braces, had let her cry on his shoulder when she'd been snubbed by stupid Henry Farmer. *Who names their son that, anyway?*

When he'd moved to Atlanta, distance and time had prevented them from keeping in touch much. They'd seen each other occasionally at various events for mutual friends, and she attended the holiday party every year. He'd followed her career and knew that she'd left Huntington Sports last month. He also knew that having her at Pure Talent was a win for the company. She already had an established client list and an impeccable reputation in the industry. Even he couldn't deny it was an excellent idea.

If only I can stop staring at her. He let his gaze travel from her pumps to her dark hair, pulled back into a long ponytail. She'd always been pretty, but the woman sitting next to him was flawless. *Stunning, really.*

Their interaction at the holiday party felt different from their normal routine of fist bumps, winks, and side hugs. It was almost intimate, and he'd found himself wanting to explore it, explore *her.*

Once she'd left the room that night, he'd chalked his amped emotions up to too much cognac and post-fistfight energy. Still, he'd needed something that night, and Zara had given him understanding. She'd taken care of him. And she'd even made him laugh.

"Son?" Jax arched a brow. "Did you hear me?"

Xavier blinked. He'd been so engrossed in his thoughts of Zara that he failed to realize his father had been talking, which wouldn't do. What he should've been focused on was Pure Talent Sports. What he shouldn't have been focused on was Zara or her brown eyes—or her lovely body. *I wonder . . .* Instead of imagining his former next-door neighbor naked, he needed to embrace another emotion—anger. As beautiful as Zara was, that job was his.

His gaze flitted from his father to her, then back

to his dad. "Did I miss the part where you told me Zara will be tackling the sports expansion now?"

Jax leaned back in his chair and raised a brow. "I would like to think you'd be a little more welcoming to Zara."

The unbothered look in his father's eyes irritated him. He could have—and wanted to—throw back a sarcastic remark, but remained quiet. Instead, he glanced at Zara, who had shifted in her seat to face him.

"Hi, Zara. I never did thank you for your top-notch medical skills." He held up his hand. "See, good as new."

"Hi, X," she said, a genuine grin on her glossed lips. "I asked about you this morning."

"You did?" If what he suspected was true, and Zara had joined the Pure Talent family, he didn't blame *her*. She couldn't have known that the expansion was his idea, that he'd worked countless hours gathering metrics and making important connections with teams, established players, and possible draft picks. "Well, I'm here."

Her smile wavered and she cleared her throat. "How are you?"

The answer to that question wasn't something he wanted to say at this moment, especially since Zara seemed uncomfortable. So he simply said, "Fine." He eyed his father, before turning back to her. "When do you start?"

"Today." She pulled at her ear and crossed one toned leg over the other. "This morning."

Narrowed eyes landed on his father, who watched

the scene as if he didn't do anything wrong. "Today, huh?" He bit the inside of his cheek and counted to ten. Slowly. "Dad, why didn't you tell me you lured Zara to Pure Talent?"

"Xavier, I've never checked in with you any other time when I've made a decision. Why would I do it now?"

The response stung. His father had been the perfect role model for him. Growing up, most kids in their neighborhood had barely seen their fathers, but his dad had made time with him a necessity. As far as Xavier could remember, his dad had attended every event, because it was important to both of his parents not to just *talk* about being a family.

Yet, Jax didn't get his shrewd reputation in business because he stuttered or avoided conflict. The man was a powerhouse, a self-made man who'd left home at the age of sixteen to make a better life for himself. Pure Talent was the corporation it was because Jax Starks led the company, poured love into its vision. The work, the time, the mission—all of those things were a part of his father. It was the reason why Xavier worked so hard to be able to step into a role that his father filled with ease.

"Um, maybe I should step out?" Zara said, breaking the silence. "I'll give you a few moments."

"Thanks, Zara. If you could step outside for a few minutes, I'd appreciate it."

Xavier watched Zara leave the office, noting the sway of her hips and how good her legs looked in those high heels. When he turned back to his

father, he noticed the small smirk on his face, but
didn't say a word.

"I know you're not in the habit of explaining
yourself to anyone, me included," Xavier said, "but
I need to know. Why is Zara here? Pure Talent
Sports was supposed to be mine."

Jax opened a folder that had been sitting atop of
the desk, pulled out the document, and slid it across
the table. "See this?"

Xavier picked up the document. *Shit.*

"Imagine my surprise when I arrived back from
a relaxing vacation with your mother to find that
the incident that I had hoped would blow over has
gotten significantly worse. And not only do I have
to tend to my company's image, because one of my
best agents lost his cool, I also have to negotiate a
financial settlement to Ethan *Damn* Porter."

A lawsuit. Xavier was officially done. The day
couldn't get any worse. He swallowed roughly. "I'll
fix this," he mumbled.

"No, you won't." Jax leaned forward, resting his
arms on the desk. "I will handle this."

"Is this why you hired Zara?"

"I brought Zara in because I believe in this venture and I feel she would be an asset to the team."

"Really?"

"This is not a punishment, Xavier. The fact is
you're too hot right now. Your name is all over the
tabloids, the blogs, YouTube, and social media. And
this is too big for missteps."

"So that's it? I'm just out of it?"

"I'm not taking you off of anything at this point,

but I am concerned about the negative publicity. Ethan is one of the most popular sports figures in the country. If we're going to do this, we need a balance."

Xavier closed his eyes. "Fine."

Jax stood up and walked around to the front of the desk. A strong hand squeezed Xavier's shoulder. "You already convinced me this is the next logical step for Pure Talent. I told you, I'm ready to take a step back from the day-to-day operations. That time with your mother was heaven. I want more of that. But I have to know that the company is in good hands. And the company is *more* than Pure Talent Sports."

"Dad, I—"

"You have great ideas, and I've seen how hard you've been working. But I'm not convinced you should take the lead on this project."

"And I feel like I'm the perfect person to do the job."

Jax eyed him. "Okay, then." He walked to the door and opened it. A moment later, Zara reentered the office. His father motioned her to have a seat.

"Jax, maybe this isn't a good idea. I feel like I'm stepping on X's toes, and, honestly, I'm conflicted."

His father held up a hand. "You're not stepping on my son's toes, Zara. I apologize if it came across that way. Over the next several months, I want to focus on getting the sports department up and running. I'm interested in how you'll make Pure Talent Sports different from the rest. I haven't decided who will head the new division. I need time to make that decision, and I expect both of you to make it a hard one."

They spent the next hour talking about sports and life. And when he walked out of the office, Xavier smiled. *I'm still in the game.*

Zara dropped her purse on her desk and sank down in the chair. Peering up at the ceiling, she went over every detail of the meeting in Jax's office: Xavier being blindsided, the tension in the room, the pain she saw beneath his eyes when she returned to the office after giving them time to talk. It felt like a powder keg ready to blow.

"So X brought the idea of creating a sports division to Pure Talent," she muttered to herself. And, technically, she was the one standing in his way. Did she want to insert herself into a battle between father and son?

When she'd taken the job, she'd done so on a whim, fueled by emotion. Which was something she'd always been careful not to do. She had no knowledge of the reasons why Jax made the offer. She had no idea of the particulars, just that he was looking to expand into sports and thought she would be a good fit at the agency. Initially she had every intention of politely declining, until Larry and Jeff stabbed her in the back.

Zara couldn't deny the appeal of working for Jax. Everything she would have negotiated into her employment package had already been included. He'd even thrown in perks she hadn't thought of, including a signing bonus and moving expenses. All in all, he'd made an offer she would've been a fool to refuse. Still, she'd had reservations about her hasty decision all the way up to . . . well, even now.

With a heavy sigh, she picked up the phone and dialed Larissa.

"Hey, sissy," Larissa said. In the background, she heard the sound of a drill and wondered what her big sis was doing to Zara's new condo. But her questions could wait for later.

"Maybe I made a mistake?"

The buzzing stopped. "What? Why?"

"I just think there's more at play here than I expected."

"How so?"

Zara switched the phone to her other ear and pulled out her tablet to check her e-mails. "Because X didn't even know I was coming, and, apparently, I'm being considered to actually run the sports division."

"Shut up. Really? That's awesome!"

"Except X wanted the job. And now it's awkward."

"Two things. I told you to call him weeks ago, but you're so hardheaded."

Zara rolled her eyes. "You told me to call him and schedule sex." The conversation started with her confessing that she felt attracted to X at the holiday party for the first time, and ended with her sister suggesting she use her friend to scratch the itch.

"And two!" her sister shouted. "It can't be more awkward than imagining him taking you on a rowing machine at the company gym."

Shit. I should've never told her about that dream. "I call foul. You were never supposed to repeat that."

Her sister laughed. "Hey, it's funny. I crack up about it all the time."

"There will be no X—"

The rest of the sentence—"doing me on any workout equipment"—died on her lips when she looked up and noticed the object of that particular fantasy standing in her doorway poised to knock. *Now I can die.*

"'No X' what?" He stepped into the office.

Zara's mouth fell open and she blinked. Hard.

"Are you okay, Zara?" he asked, concern in his eyes.

"I have to go," she told Rissa before ending the call. Taking a few seconds to center herself, she exhaled before she stood. "X!" *Way too loud, Zara.* She cleared her throat. "Hi. I didn't expect you."

He motioned for her to take her seat again, and she did happily. It was either that or fall over if she tried to walk toward him. "I wanted to talk to you." He sat down in one of the chairs across from her. "I'm sorry about today. Not a good way to start your time here."

"No, don't apologize. I'm sure it must have been hard on you, too."

He shrugged. "I won't lie. It was definitely unexpected."

Zara crossed her legs and noticed the way he followed the motion. "For me, too."

"What happened at Huntington?"

She gave him an abridged version of events, glossing over the smaller details, like how she'd quit on the spot and cussed Larry out before she left. "Your father had offered me the job before the big betrayal, so I took it."

"Well, it's Huntington's loss."

"I worked so hard for that agency," Zara admitted. "And when Larry betrayed me like that, I knew there was nothing left for me there."

"I get it. I would've done the same thing."

Even as children, Zara and X tended to react the same way in most situations. Except she'd given up her penchant for fights somewhere around that infamous homecoming-dance incident in high school and subsequent three-day suspension that landed her without her car for a month.

"It's always worse when it's someone you trusted," she said softly.

"I never did like that clown."

She giggled. "You sure didn't. I never understood why, though."

X smirked, giving her a glimpse of the dimple that drove many women and girls wild. "He always seemed like a snake, like he didn't have your best interests at heart."

"You never told me that."

"It's not like I could have changed your mind about him. You're pretty stubborn."

"I guess you're right," she conceded. "I like to

form my own opinions about the people I let in my life. Usually, I have pretty good instincts."

"Yeah, we all make mistakes."

The room descended into silence, and for the first time since she'd seen him today, it wasn't an uncomfortable silence. Maybe that whole attraction thing was a fluke? "So, tell me, why sports? Why now?"

"Why not?"

"I mean, you've built an impressive career in youth. I've seen the trades. You're tearing it up."

"Thanks. And I'm not unhappy with my job. I just want more."

"Is this about you? Or proving yourself to your father?"

"You know something about that."

"I do." They'd discussed their fathers many times. Her love of sports was directly influenced by her father. She couldn't play the game anymore, but she felt alive every time she stepped into a sports arena. Her father had never been impressed with her desire to jump into the industry as an agent, though. In fact, he'd given her hell for her career choice. But she'd moved forward, anyway, without his blessing. "But Jax has always been supportive of you, even when he didn't agree with your choices."

"True. But he's getting older. He keeps talking about retiring. I want to prove to him that I'll be okay if he does. Aside from the latest debacle, I'm not the same person I was. Yes, I've made mistakes, but I have goals for the company, ideas that I'd like to see to fruition."

Zara smiled. "I think that's great."

"And now you're here." He stared at her. Actually, "stared" wasn't the right word for what he was currently doing to her. His eyes bored into hers, like he was digging for gold, like he was looking for a treasure buried within her. And judging by the way her body tingled and her heart pounded in her ears, she liked the attention.

"Ooh." A burst of air escaped from her dry lips. "I'm starving." She jumped up, walking over to the window to put distance between them. "Skye mentioned something about lunch. I should call her."

Seconds later, she felt him next to her and tried not to look at him. She failed. While he stared out at the skyline, she studied him, noted the changes in him from the fearless boy she'd sent secret messages to outside of her bedroom window. He was X, but he was more. More intense. *Sexy*. She shook that thought from her mind.

"I'm glad you're here," he whispered. "For some reason, you've always made things better."

She squeezed her throat. "Really?"

He gave her a sidelong glance and leaned into her. "Really." It wasn't an abnormal gesture, because he'd done it so many times in the past, but the contact felt like a live wire against her skin. "I missed you."

"I guess it'll be fun to hang out again."

"Dominate the spades table."

She tilted her head back and laughed as she

remembered the heated card games they played in Xavier's playroom. "Definitely that."

"You never did tell me about that conversation you were having on the phone. 'No X' what?"

Heat flushed up her neck to her cheeks. "Nothing," she grumbled. *That damn Rissa.* "You know Rissa is crazy."

He arched a brow. "You know you can tell me."

No, I can't. "X, let it go."

"Okay, okay. You'll tell me one day."

Not likely. "Anyway, I'm going to call Skye. What are you doing for lunch? Want to join us?"

He glanced at his watch. "Wish I could, but I have a meeting in about fifteen minutes. But we should have dinner this week. Where are you staying?"

"I'm walking distance."

"Good." He turned and walked toward the door. "Let's set something up."

"Sounds good," she said, following him.

"Just so you know"—a sneaky grin formed on his perfect mouth—"as happy as I am that you're here, I have no plans to hand you that job."

She raised a brow. "Is that a challenge?"

"Oh, you know it is. And since I know you like to live in denial, I figured it's best that I give you a heads-up. I'm not taking it easy because you're my friend. I play to win."

"Here's the thing, though. I know I'm not like you. Yes, I do live in denial sometimes. I run away from personal problems. But not when I'm at work. Not when I'm negotiating contracts, talking clients off the ledge, and generally wearing a superhero cape at all times for them. This"—she motioned to the room about them—"is where I shine, where I meet things head-on. I'm not scared of a little competition. And I'm not running. So you better get ready because I'm already two steps ahead of you. Bring it." She winked, then pivoted on her heels and went back to her desk.

But when she turned around to face him again, he was standing right behind her. She gasped and nearly toppled over. A warm arm wrapped around her waist to steady her.

"Oh, Zara. You just don't know what you've done," he murmured. His gaze dropped to her lips.

They stood like that for a moment, before she braced her hands against his hard chest. *Damn, he's like a rock.* "I told you I'm not afraid," she managed to get out. "And you can let me go now." The warmth of his body disappeared and she flattened a hand over her stomach to calm the intense flutters. "Bye, X."

"Bye, Zara. Game on."

Soon as the door closed, she let out a long sigh. The game was definitely on. But she just wasn't sure which one they were playing. Or if she even had a chance to win.

Chapter 6

"I told that girl not to mess with him. We both did, right, Zara?" Skye popped a piece of an artisan pretzel into her mouth.

Zara set up her swing and gripped the golf club in her hands. "You did," she mumbled. "We all warned her." With her feet apart and knees bent slightly, Zara bent forward and addressed the ball. A few seconds later, the ball was soaring toward the target. She did a fist pump when she checked the scoreboard and saw that she was now in the lead.

"See!" Skye handed Zara a beer when she stepped back up to the table. "She didn't listen and look what happened?"

"What happened?" Xavier asked.

Zara shrugged. "How the hell should I know? I'm just here to win." She winked and held her beer up to Xavier and let him take the top off. Grinning, she mouthed "thank you" and took a sip.

"Nothing happened!" Duke stood, raising his hands in the air. "And why do y'all have to bring up old shit every time we're together?"

"'Old'? You just took her out last month," Skye said.

Tempest Shaw had been valedictorian of their high school class and a good girl. Recently she'd contacted Zara because she'd run into Duke at some mysterious event. Since then, she'd been acting weird.

"Still, last month is in the past," Duke said. "And since when are you Tempest's number one protector?"

"I think you broke her," Skye mused. "How does one go from focused to . . . ?" She shook her head and shrugged. "I don't even know."

Duke shook his head and stood. "Enough talk about me. Whatever happened between me and Tempest is none of your business."

Skye leaned forward. "You know you just admitted that something did happen between you two."

"Yeah . . . no. That's not what I did." Duke threw a piece of cheese at Skye and she ducked.

The hunk of Colby Jack hit Xavier on the shoulder. "What the hell, bruh?"

"Tell your girl to move on, Zara," Duke said. "Better yet, tell her to get her own shit together with Garrett."

Skye jumped on Duke's back and pretended to choke him. "You get on my nerves."

Zara threw her head back and laughed. "Oh, I missed this." Although Duke lived in Michigan most of their childhood, the young family had spent a lot of time in California. "You two are crazy."

She watched Duke carry her friend over to the faux grass patch and take his turn as Skye remained on his back.

"Look at them fools." Xavier pulled a beer from the open cooler the wait staff had brought to the table.

"Maybe they should have just been together."

Duke bent down, letting Skye go. "Oh, hell no!" he shouted.

"I'd kill him," Skye agreed.

They'd spent the last hour playing golf, drinking beer, and eating. It had been one month since she'd joined the Pure Talent family and she'd enjoyed it *and* her time in Atlanta. The short orientation period at the company consisted of the required classes on sexual harassment, the computer software that agents used, and compliance. She'd attended meetings with legal, finance, public relations, and business development. With Jax's blessing, she'd scheduled personal meetings with each of her current clients to explain to them how her move would affect them. It had been a hectic few weeks of traveling to multiple states, eating out, and signing new agency contracts. When she wasn't working on procuring new talent, she'd spent time formulating her plan for the sports division. Tonight was her first night back in town, after a few days in Detroit.

"How was your trip?" Xavier asked.

"Good," Zara answered. "I'm tired as hell."

"Dad told me he wanted to meet with us Monday?"

Zara nodded. "He sent an e-mail. I wonder what he wants to talk about?"

"Probably my promotion."

She laughed. "Ha-ha. You wish."

He stood and walked over to the play area. Dressed in dark jeans and a tight-fitting sweater, he looked like a poster boy for smart casual attire. The baseball cap he wore topped off his look, and she assumed he'd worn it to prevent people from immediately recognizing him. Of course, his attempt to be incognito hadn't worked because he'd already been pointed out by a few women in the place. He looked damn good, and despite the rousing pep talk she'd given herself before they arrived, she hadn't been able to keep her eyes off of him the entire time they'd been there.

"Stop staring, Z-Ra."

Zara blinked. *Busted.* "Oh no," she mumbled.

Skye squeezed her arm. "It's okay. He's my cousin, but he's hot."

"I don't know what's wrong with me," Zara hissed. She'd shared her woes with her bestie on her first day of work, after he'd touched her and single-handedly set off every nerve ending in her body with the contact. After her best friend laughed at her, she'd commiserated with her about men and their cute, yet annoying, ways. "I can't stop looking at him."

"Girl, nothing's wrong with you."

"Shhh! You're so loud. He's right there." She

pointed at Duke and X, who were talking off to the side.

Skye craned her neck around to peer at the two of them. "He's not paying you any attention."

"Thanks."

"What? You act like you don't want him to, anyway."

"You know that's generic shit talk. Not that I want a relationship with him—because I don't. But it wouldn't be the worst thing in the world if he was just as affected by me."

"What if he is? I can ask him."

"No!" Zara smacked a hand over her mouth. "Girl, no. You're never supposed to say anything about this to anyone. *Ever.*"

Skye giggled. "I love seeing you all hot and bothered."

Yes, she was hot. Her body temperature seemed to shoot up to broil when he was near. And she was definitely bothered, because it annoyed her that he had that effect on her.

"Listen, you're a woman, he's a man." Skye shrugged. "You're both single, attractive people."

"I said the same thing about you and Duke years ago, and you said no."

Skye rolled her eyes. "Correction. I said, 'Hell to da naw.' Besides, he might as well be my brother, and that's against God's plan."

"Whatever."

"It's gonna be okay, sis. Attraction is fluid. He's fine today, but he'll be ugly tomorrow."

Zara burst out laughing. "You're so stupid."

"We should eat donuts," Skye suggested. Before Zara could agree, her friend had waved their waitress over and placed an order for the popular injectable donut holes, stuffed with chocolate or Bavarian cream.

"I ate enough while I was away." Zara patted her belly.

"But not with us. And not these donuts."

Several minutes later, Zara bit into a chocolate-stuffed donut hole and groaned. "Oh, my God, this is delicious."

Xavier slid into his seat and snagged a donut. "Be careful. They're addictive."

She paused, donut midair. "'Addictive'?" She gulped.

He reached out with a napkin and dabbed her bottom lip. And she nearly melted into a puddle. *Get it together, Zara. He's just a man. A hot, sexy as hell, too-damn-fine-for-his-own-good man.* She licked her lips.

"Very." His gaze dropped to her mouth.

"What y'all got going on over here?" Duke frowned, motioning between them and, effectively, dousing the heat that had been traveling up her legs straight to her core. "Looks a little dangerous to me."

Xavier pulled back. "Nothing. I was just helping her out."

"Yeah, that's not what that was. That was foreplay."

Zara's mouth fell open. "What?"

Skye returned to the table from her bathroom

break. "Close your mouth, sis," she whispered in her ear. "And stop instigating, Duke."

"What's up?" Garrett walked into the bay and greeted Xavier and Duke with dap. "Hey, Zara." He gave her a hug, then looked at her best friend. "Skye."

"Garrett." Skye walked away, picking up a club. Duke followed her.

Zara shot Garrett a sad look. "It's . . . Skye," she offered. "She needs time."

"It's been almost ten years," Garrett said. "And *she* broke up with me."

"Because you left."

"I didn't have a choice." Garrett sighed heavily. "You know how hard that was for me, but I had to take care of my sister."

She squeezed his arm. "I know. She knows, too. She's just hurting."

Xavier slid a beer over to Garrett. "It's Skye, bruh. She's always going to be her."

Zara met and held X's gaze. "That's what I said."

He tipped his head to her. Turning to Garrett, he motioned toward the donuts. "Eat some of this food."

Zara slid off of her chair and joined Skye and Duke. She rubbed her friend's back. "Are you okay?"

"I'm fine. It's a big city. I don't normally see him."

"Blame X," Duke said. "He's the one who invited him."

Skye bumped her shoulder into Duke. "I'm not blaming X. Garrett is his friend. He can join us for Topgolf and drinks. It's a free country."

Her friend did a great job of handling PR for every type of situation. She was a master at the poker face, except when Garrett was near. The angst on Skye's face was clear and it made Zara sad, because she truly believed the two belonged together. Despite the earlier jokes about Skye and Duke.

"I think we need a shot," Zara said.

"Hell yeah." Duke grabbed Skye's hand, pulling her back to the table. "Let's go to the bar and take one."

Zara reached in from behind X and grabbed another donut, this time one filled with Bavarian cream. She bit into the confection and closed her eyes at the sweet puff of deliciousness. "Oh yes!" She moaned. "This one is even better. Hm." She devoured the rest and opened her eyes to find everyone at the table looking at her. With wide eyes, she picked up a mound of napkins and hastily wiped her mouth. "What? Do I have something on my face?"

"No." X swallowed visibly, a slow smile forming on his mouth. "You . . ." He exhaled. "I told you they're addictive."

"Yeah, maybe you want to be alone with one—in the dark, at your house," Duke grumbled.

Skye giggled. "Right?"

Her friends burst out in a fit of laughter at her expense, all of them except X. There was no hint of amusement on his face, but his eyes . . . The lingering stare under hooded lids flooded her with warmth. *Damn.* She pulled at her collar. "We're going to the bar," she announced.

Skye's smile faltered and she shot a quick glance at Garrett, who was still chuckling. "Yes! Let's go."

"Carry on," Duke chimed in.

Zara and Duke steered Skye away from the bay and Garrett—and X. And, hopefully, away from the simmering attraction that seemed to overtake her mind and body.

Xavier watched Zara, Duke, and Skye disappear out the door and shook himself out of the haze he'd been in since watching her eat that damn donut. He glanced at the plate of treats and wondered how a woman eating a piece of dough covered in cinnamon and sugar could be so damn sexy. What's worse? He wanted to know how it tasted on her lips.

"Damn, X," Garrett said, pulling him from his thoughts. "It's that bad, huh?"

X tore his gaze away from the door. "What?"

"Zara. And the way you've been watching her all night."

Frowning, he said, "I don't know what you're talking about." Except . . . he did. He knew exactly what Garrett was talking about, because Zara had taken up residence in his thoughts, taunting him with her smooth skin, tight body, and bedroom eyes.

"Keep telling yourself that."

"Stop diverting attention from the way you've been a sorry-ass muthafucka for Skye."

Garrett grumbled several curses under his breath

and finished his beer. "What's going on with your cousin is neither here nor there."

"Right." He opened another beer. "Anyway, we're not doing this."

"Doing what?"

"Talking about feelings and shit. That's not us."

Garrett laughed. "Man, you're dumb as hell."

"Remember that client I told you about?" Xavier asked, changing the subject.

"Yeah. The one you're thinking about dropping?"

"That's her." Xavier had spent the morning trying to mitigate a brewing scandal with one of his oldest clients, Carrie Justice. "She needs special attention. And I just don't have the time." He sighed. "Studios are calling, threatening to shut her down. I'm working on saving a few projects, but I can't have her bad behavior displayed on every single news show right before her next movie releases."

Garrett owned Steele Crisis Management and had stepped in to handle many of Pure Talent's clients. His practice had grown significantly since he'd moved back to Atlanta last year, and he'd recently had to hire an associate.

"What about Skye?" his friend asked. "She doesn't want to take care of it?"

Xavier shook his head. "Nah, she's pretty busy at work."

"Got it. Well, whatever you need. Have Jennifer call my assistant on Monday and put something on my calendar. I have to go to Miami next week, but I'll make it work."

"Thanks, bruh. Appreciate it." A camera flash

nearly blinded him and he reared back and blinked rapidly. A balding paparazzi stood in front of him just snapping away. "Fuck! Get that camera out of here." He stood and started toward the guy.

"X, I heard Naomi and Ethan are marrying in July. What do you think about that?" The camera-man snapped another picture. "Are you attending the wedding?"

Garrett stepped forward. "Man, get the hell out of here with that camera."

"I heard there was a lawsuit," the guy continued.

Xavier clenched his fists, cracking his knuckles. "No comment."

The last thing he needed was another public display of anger. He didn't need to become fodder for another month of misleading blog posts and imaginary Twitter beefs.

"X, what about Ethan?" the guy asked. "Is it true that he's going to be a new client at Pure Talent?"

"What?" he roared.

"He said 'no comment.'" Garrett stood in front of him, blocking him from the camera. "I think it's best you leave."

Xavier scanned the room, noting the building crowd, the increasing amount of phones aimed his way.

"Are you planning to make a play for Naomi at the wedding?" The man just didn't quit. "The rumor is, you and Naomi are still seeing each other. Tell us why you've chosen to be the other man now."

He'd had enough. Xavier reached out and snatched the camera from the man, lifting it in the air with every intention of smashing it on the ground.

From behind him, a hand gripped his arm and squeezed. "X, no." Zara's voice filtered through the rage that had been building inside him for the past few minutes. "Don't."

He looked down and straight into Zara's eyes. Sighing, he lowered his arm and handed the camera back to the man. "Get out of here," he ordered, his voice low and his eyes still locked on Zara's.

The man shuffled away. Skye and Garrett followed him, most likely to negotiate with him for the photographs. The crowd slowly dispersed.

"Let's get out of here," Zara said. She slipped her hand in his and squeezed. The tension in his body dissipated.

"Thank you," he said.

A hint of a smile crept across her face. "No thanks needed."

"Seriously. Thank you." He pulled her into a hug. *Shit.* She felt good—soft and hard in the right places. She smelled like something distinctively Zara, vanilla with hints of jasmine and blood oranges. They stood like that for a few moments, while he warred with himself. He wanted to hold on more tightly, but he knew it was borderline inappropriate to try and turn their connection into something more. Especially since they'd always been good friends and now worked together. More importantly, they were up for the same job.

Clearing his throat, he pulled away. "Ready?" he

asked, noting the way she averted her gaze and picked imaginary lint from her sweater.

"Yes, let's hit it."

Xavier wrapped her jacket around her shoulders, and glanced to his right, where Duke was watching them with interest. He gave his friend a look that said "don't say shit" and followed Zara out of the bay.

Chapter 7

Zara glanced at her ringing phone and smiled. "Hey, Rick."

"Sis!" Rick said. "I've been trying to reach you for a minute. Have you fallen down the Atlanta wormhole?"

She laughed. "No, not at all." She leaned back in her chair and switched her phone to her other ear. Rick had been in her life for five years, and was an important part of her family. She loved him like a brother, and she thought he and Larissa were perfect for each other. "I'm sorry, brother. I've been working long hours."

"I know, I know. Check your text messages, sis."

Zara frowned and hit the SPEAKER icon on her phone. "You sent me a text?" When she opened her messages, she realized the text had come through an hour ago. "I'm sorry. I didn't even notice it." She clicked on his name and squealed. The ring—the perfect cushion-cut halo ring, with a gorgeous yellow diamond—glimmered inside the black box he held in his hand. He'd got it right on the first try.

"Rick! You did this by yourself? It's stunning."

"I had a little help, from Rissa. I've been with that woman for five years and I just listened. And I know her."

Zara held a hand against her heart. "Aw, I love it. And all I have to say is *finally*! When are you going to pop the question?"

"Next Saturday. I'd love it if you could be here. And so would she."

Zara fought back tears. "I wouldn't miss it. Let me move some things around."

"You better."

They spent a few minutes talking about his plans. "Rick, you've definitely made my day. I'm so happy and I can't wait."

"Me neither. See you next week."

"You will. Love you."

"Love you, too."

Zara hung up the phone and stared at the wall. Sighing, she opened up her calendar to check her schedule. She fired off an e-mail to Patrice to move her meetings out. She'd fly in on next Thursday and use the free time to see her mom and sister, under the guise of being homesick.

"Hey." X stepped into her office.

She grinned up at him. "Hi."

Only he didn't smile back. Instead, he eyed her skeptically. "What's going on?"

Running her hands through her hair, she tilted her head to the side and assessed him. He looked tense, irritated. "Nothing. Are you okay?"

"I'm good," he said with a curt nod. "You're here late."

"So are you," she retorted.

"What are you smiling about?"

"Typically, I smile when someone enters the room. Especially if it's a friend I haven't seen in a while."

After their Topgolf experience, after he'd wiped donut sugar from her mouth, after the situation with the paparazzi, and after that full-on frontal hug, she hadn't heard a peep from X. Jax had canceled their meeting and X had seemingly disappeared. It had been a little more than a week, but it wasn't abnormal not to see him. Their jobs involved a lot of travel, so she wasn't upset he hadn't called. *Not really.*

"You were smiling before I knocked." The ice in his tone caught her off guard.

She laughed. "I was talking to Rick."

His jaw ticked. "Who is Rick?"

"Larissa's boyfriend. He's proposing next weekend and he called to tell me."

"Oh, Rick. I remember him." X rubbed the back of his neck and moved closer. "Proposal, huh?"

"Yes. And I'm elated."

He sat down opposite her, visibly relaxing into the seat. The khaki pants, navy blue button-down, and sports coat he wore definitely worked for her. And, of course, he smelled like heaven in a bottle.

"That's exciting." He fiddled with the paperweight that Alma had given her.

"I was just getting my flight to L.A."

"Nice."

She pulled up the airline website and started the search for a ticket. "What's been up?"

"Just finished a teleconference and figured I'd head out to grab something to eat."

Focused on the flights, she pondered different scenarios for her time on the West Coast. If she arrived early, she could squeeze in a meeting with a client or two while in town. If she booked a later flight, she could work half a day here. She rubbed her forehead and bit down on her bottom lip.

"Zara?"

She glanced at him. "Yes?"

"Do you want to grab some food?"

"Um, sure." She decided to get the early flight. She missed her family. It only took a few minutes for her to purchase her ticket and reserve a rental car. Once she finished, she closed her laptop and turned to X. "Okay, all set."

"What do you want to eat?"

"Huh?"

"Dinner?"

"Oh." She laughed. "I'm sorry, food. I'm actually not done here. I need to finish something before I leave."

"Something for my father?"

"No, not at all." Zara had received intel that one of the hottest basketball players in the game was agent-less. It would be a coup if she could get him on her roster. That meant she had to study him, learn everything about him, so she could convince him that she was the woman that would change his life. There was no way she would tell X that, though. She couldn't risk him beating her to the punch.

He pulled out his cell phone. "Okay, then we'll order in."

Half an hour later, Zara bit into a short-rib taco and groaned. "This shit is so good." She licked *queso* from her thumb and took another bite.

Xavier laughed. "You crack me up."

She frowned. "Why?"

"I just . . . I don't meet a lot of women who experience food the way you do."

Zara picked up her lemonade and took a large gulp. "Maybe you need to rethink the company you keep." She dipped a chip into the guacamole and tasted it. *Yummy.* "Where do you find these places?"

"You'll get used to it." He plopped a chili-cheese fry into his mouth. "Atlanta has a lot to offer food-wise."

"I know." She did a little dance while she finished her taco. "I love food."

He sucked in a shaky breath. "I see."

A wave of uncertainty washed over her and she nibbled on her bottom lip. They were seated on the sofa in her office. She'd kicked her shoes off right before she sat down, and she suddenly felt bared to him in an unexpected and uncomfortable way. Was he judging her? Did he find her greediness unattractive? *And why do I care what he thinks?* She sat still for a moment. *Fuck it.* She picked up her second taco and bit into it with a shrug.

"Hey, I'm hungry," she said after she swallowed the bite and noticed he'd been watching her again.

"You're amazing," he said.

She straightened. "Why do you say that?"

"Everything about you is unexpected."

"Please, I'm the same me I've always been."

"You're definitely still you, but you're different."

She swallowed. "Explain." The air changed around them, sparked with electricity and a tension that felt all too familiar.

"It could be the fact that we haven't spent time together in years, but you're . . ." He moistened his lower lip and let out a nervous laugh. "I don't know. Maybe it's my reaction to you that's different."

"Your reaction?"

With his gaze fixed on her lips, he murmured, "Or it could be your mouth?"

"My *mouth*?" Her fingertips brushed against her lips.

X leaned in and she sucked in a deep breath. *Oh, God.* His nose touched hers and she shivered. *Is he going to . . . ?*

"I think it's your mouth," he whispered, his breath mingling with hers, pulling her to him, lulling her with some sort of X-spell.

"Um, that's . . ." She felt the meat in her taco fall to the plate on her lap. Jerking back, she jumped up, tipping the plate onto the floor. "Oh no!" She grabbed a stackful of napkins and dropped to her knees to clean up the mess. "Oh, shit."

"Zara." His hand on hers stopped her frantic scrubbing. "It's okay. I'll call the janitor for this floor. I'm sure he's still in the building."

She stopped her crazed movements and sat back on her legs. "I . . ." She dropped her head. "Great." His chuckle made her stomach quiver.

"You're good." He placed a call to the janitor service. A moment later, he hung up the phone and peered over at her. "They're on the way."

"You know you're wrong, right?" she told him. "I really wanted that taco."

He barked out a laugh and stood. Holding out his hand, he waited until she placed her palm in his; then he pulled her to her feet. "Let's go get you another one. And have a drink."

"In public," she added, grabbing her purse and stuffing her laptop into her bag. "Ready when you are."

In retrospect, Xavier could have gone about this differently. He wasn't the type for big overtures. He didn't get as far as he had by being anything other than forthright. That's why it was surprising that he'd essentially inserted himself into Zara's weekend in L.A. First, by moving up his planned meeting with Andrew and Bishop by two weeks. Second, by finagling a ticket onto the same plane that he knew she'd be on. And, thanks to Skye, he knew she'd be late, which gave him the opportunity to board before her.

One of the flight attendants stopped at his row and greeted him with a warm smile. "Good morning, Mr. Starks. What can I get you to drink?"

"Hi"—he peered at her name tag—"Kayla. Coffee is fine."

"Cream and sugar?"

"No, thanks."

She handed him a hot towel and an amenity kit, before she jetted off to the next customer. Glancing at his watch, he peered at the door. Zara wasn't just a *little* behind, she was late as hell. The doors of the plane would close in five minutes. He considered texting Skye, but decided against it. She'd be there.

Instead, he unlocked his phone and read a text from Hill. He smiled at the excitement in his client's message that he'd landed the role and a lucrative video game deal as well. He'd be voicing his character on every game related to the series. He responded with a Gif and a congrats.

"X?"

He looked up and smiled. "Zara."

"Wh-why? What are you doing here?" She scanned the area, a frown on her beautiful face. "How did you . . . ?" She fumbled with her carry-on, nearly dropping it on his head, before he stood and took it from her, sliding it into the overheard compartment easily.

"Window seat or aisle?" he asked, chuckling at the confused look in her eyes. She eyed him silently, multiple emotions playing over her features. "How about you take the window?" he offered, motioning for her to take her seat. She plopped down into the chair, grumbling nonsensical words and sliding her briefcase under the seat. He sat next to her and leaned against her, shoulder to shoulder. "Good morning, sunshine."

She ignored him, muttering something about ruined plans and lack of lip gloss this early in the morning. He hid his smile as the flight attendant returned with his coffee and took Zara's drink order, which consisted of two mimosas and a bottle of water.

They sat in silence until Kayla returned with her drinks. She finished the first mimosa in record time, before the attendant even left, and handed her the empty glass.

With raised eyebrows, he asked, "Thirsty?"

"Oh, God," she grumbled, before turning to him, fire in her eyes. "How are you here?"

"I'm flying to L.A."

"No." She shook her head rapidly. "No, you're not flying to L.A. Skye is supposed to be on this flight. Not you."

He shrugged, enjoying the interaction. "Something came up."

"But you can't do this." She pointed a perfectly manicured finger at him. And he resisted the urge to suck it into his mouth.

"Can't do what? Fly on a public airplane?"

"No, fly on *my* airplane. I mean, my flight."

He laughed. "You're silly."

She folded her arms across her breasts. "You're a stalker."

"A 'stalker'?"

"Yes."

He leaned forward, closer than he'd planned. And she jerked back. "How am I a *stalker*? I have business in L.A."

"Right. All of a sudden, you have business in L.A." Her lips pressed into a thin line and he wanted to reach out and rub his thumb across them. "Very convenient."

"Is there a problem here?" he asked, unable to hide his amusement. "You, of all people, should know that travel is an important part of my job. Do you have a problem with me doing my job?"

"Of course not." She shot him an incredulous stare. "I just . . . I didn't expect you. And it's early. I'm not a morning person."

"Yet you get up and go to the gym every morning at five."

"Shut up," she hissed, pulling out her phone. He caught a glimpse of the text she'd typed to Skye: I'm going to kill you.

"Don't be too hard on her," he said with a chuckle.

"Shut up," she repeated.

An hour into the air, she turned to him. "Why are you really here?"

He closed the magazine he'd been pretending to read and looked at her. She was stunning, her cheeks flushed and eyes wild and suspicious.

"Are you buzzed?" He arched a brow.

"No," she said. A little too quickly.

"Sure?"

She'd had three mimosas in under an hour, and while there wasn't much alcohol in the drink, it was early in the morning. And he knew Zara didn't eat breakfast. She'd barely touched the egg sandwich the flight attendant brought to her, and had only eaten two pieces of honeydew.

"Very," she replied.

"Good. What was your question?"

"X, we had a moment in the office last week."

He hadn't expected her to bring up their impromptu dinner last week, because nothing happened after they left her office. He'd taken her to Henry's Midtown Tavern for her tacos, and they'd talked about everything other than the heated moment, before they went their separate ways. The next morning, he'd hopped on a flight to New York for a premiere.

"We did," he said, allowing his gaze to roam over her face. For an early-morning flight, she was magnificent. Her hair was pulled back into a ponytail and she'd put on little makeup, which was exactly the way he liked her.

"You almost kissed me."

He nodded. "I did."

"And then we didn't see each other for a week. We didn't even talk to each other. And now you're here."

"I am."

"Well?" she prodded. "Why?"

"Because I felt like it would be an opportunity for us to talk without interruptions—and in public."

She bit her lip, a smile peeking out. Then she giggled. "You . . . you get on my last nerve."

"And you're beautiful."

Rolling her eyes, she waved a dismissive hand at him. "Stop playin'."

"I'm serious. Look, Zara, what's happening between us is weird, right?"

"*Good* weird? Or *bad* weird?" She tapped a finger against the tray.

"*I don't know* weird. It's *not-normal-behavior-for-us* weird."

"Exactly. Which is why it might be best if we don't address it."

"Oh, because you don't like to face your personal problems?"

With narrowed eyes on him, she said, "How about because we work together? And it's bad business to sleep where you work, especially since we're up for the same job. Why confuse things?"

He rested his head against the seat and peered up at the ceiling. *Why am I doing this?* The answer to his question was obvious. *Because I want to.* He wanted *her.* He'd spent a crazy amount of time obsessing over her, thinking about what she was doing, contemplating if she dated anyone. That night at the office, he'd heard her talking to a man over speakerphone and he remembered how he'd felt when he heard her tell that man she loved him. Then he recalled the relief that washed over him when she'd told him it was Rick. It occurred to him that he wasn't ready to see her with another man. Which was ridiculous. *Right?* Because she wasn't his. Not even close. *But she could be.*

"I can't stop myself," he admitted softly.

She gasped. "I don't know what to say."

He shot her a sidelong glance. "Zara." They stared at each other for a moment. "I can't turn back the clock and pretend that I don't feel things for you I've never thought possible."

Her mouth fell open. "What are we supposed to do with this?"

Shrugging, he said, "I don't know. So I figured I'd move up my meetings and take the chance to talk to my friend about it." He threaded his fingers into hers. "Because you *are* my friend. You've always been my friend, no matter how far apart we've been. We should be able to talk about this and be okay with whatever comes of the conversation."

"You're right. I just . . . I've never been in this situation. Friends are friends, romance is romance. Usually that's separate for me. But us? X, we work together, we grew up together, and now there's this thing that won't go away. And if I'm being honest, I can't afford to risk everything for something that might be fleeting."

The comment stung, but he knew she'd spoken truth. Every step they made would have lasting consequences, whether it be at work or with friends or between them.

"And then the work part. I've been burned, most recently by someone I trusted. Even though I probably shouldn't have," she added under her breath.

"I would never hurt you like that. Yes, we're competitive. Yes, we want the same job. No, I wouldn't stab you in the back, take your ideas and pass them off as mine. I'm going to get the job because I deserve it."

"Oh?" She snorted, pulling back and studying him with a wicked gleam in her eyes. "You deserve it, huh?"

"Absolutely."

And this interaction—the easy way they were with each other; the fact that they understood each other without a question; the fact that space and time hadn't changed who they were, or how they complemented one another. It was everything he didn't know he craved in life. He'd dated many women, but no one had demanded he be unapologetically him. Most wanted something, whether it was status or fame or money. Zara wasn't one of those women, and he loved that about her. She didn't eat salad to impress him; she never ran out of the room to burp; she always admitted when she was wrong.

"Confession time," she said. "This feels good to me. I love how we are with each other."

"Me too."

"I don't want to lose focus, though. Moving across the country, taking this job, has been a big adjustment for me. Don't get me wrong! I love it at

Pure Talent. But I can't afford to take my eyes off the prize."

"That's fair."

"I trusted Larry and he hurt me. And he wasn't you. We didn't have the history that you and I do. There are so many ways this can blow up in our faces, and one of the best things about being in Atlanta is seeing you more than once a year."

"I get it," he said. "I do."

"So, can we just agree to table whatever this is for now?"

He smirked. "I'll try."

"Thank you," she mouthed. "Now tell me what business you have in L.A."

Xavier told Zara about his plans for Pure Talent Audio and she'd listened intently, added some of her own ideas and encouraged him to think bigger. For the rest of the flight, they chatted about her desire to work more with sports properties, representing the owners of sports and entertainment facility owners to guide and manage the development of their facilities. She also expressed interest in getting involved with Pure Talent's philanthropic efforts.

The more she talked, the more he was sure he wouldn't be able to do as she asked. Because he wanted Zara Reid. He wanted her more than he'd ever wanted anything or anyone else.

Chapter 8

Zara let the top down on the luxury convertible rental she'd splurged on and merged onto the I-405 North toward her Brentwood home. The mild seventy-degree weather was just what the doctor ordered. She couldn't wait to sleep in her bed and cook dinner in her kitchen. Soon as their flight landed, she'd hightailed it to the shuttle, while X headed to the driver he'd hired. She'd offered to drive him, but he'd let her off the hook by telling her that he'd planned to meet Bishop and Drew at the Pure Talent L.A. office. After an awkward silence and a stiff hug, they'd gone their separate ways.

The enlightening conversation they'd had on the plane still sat with her. In her head, she'd turned over every word, every movement, every look, multiple times as she waited for her car. And even now—when she should have been enjoying home—she was thinking about him, wondering where he was and what he was doing.

Several minutes and a few frustrated moments of road rage later, Zara pulled into her driveway. The

Spanish-style home had been her first present to herself, once she received access to her trust fund. When she'd bought the house, she'd spent time and money redecorating it, installing new hardwood floors and knocking down a few walls to create the open concept. It felt good to be back home, in her little slice of heaven.

She jumped out of the car and walked around the yard, assessing the landscaping and pulling a few weeds she'd found. The gardener she'd hired had done a good job of maintaining the lawn and trees. While she was there, she planned to get out in the dirt and do some work herself.

Inside, she quickly opened the windows and let the fresh air in. On the kitchen table, there was a note from her housekeeper to Larissa, reminding her she'd be out of town for the week. Speaking of her sister . . . she picked up the phone and texted her that she was in town.

Zara opened the refrigerator. The only thing inside were two bottles of water and a bottle of white wine. She found a notepad and jotted down a grocery list, before she retreated to the master bedroom to shower.

"Zara?" Larissa shouted, entering the bedroom thirty minutes later.

She emerged from the bathroom, clad in a robe, and right into her sister's waiting arms. "Rissa!" They embraced. "You're here."

"You texted, I came."

"I'm glad." Zara walked into her closet and searched for an outfit to wear. She'd purposefully left a lot of her clothing at her house, because she did a lot of work in L.A. and had hoped to spend a significant amount of time there. "I need to go to the grocery store. I want to cook dinner here tonight for you and Mom."

"That sounds good to me. We can make an evening of it."

Settling on a pair of loose-fitting khakis, a white T-shirt, and a black blazer, she laid her clothes out on the bed and walked back into the bathroom.

Rissa followed her. "You are a sight for sore eyes, sissy."

She eyed her sister through the mirror. "I know. It's only been a couple of months, but it feels like a year. I missed your face."

Zara applied a light foundation and pulled her hair out of the ponytail. She quickly put on her eye makeup and styled her hair. Soon they were on the go, making a trip to the mall and the grocery store, before returning to Zara's house.

"I love this kitchen," Rissa said, rinsing a strainer full of lettuce under the faucet.

Zara cut up the strawberries for the salad. "Me too. Thanks for taking care of my house for me."

"It's no trouble. So, what's been going on in Atlanta?"

She paused a bit before continuing her task. After she cut up another strawberry, she glanced up at Larissa, who'd started making the homemade salad dressing. "I almost kissed X."

Her sister's loud gasp made her smile. "*What?* And you're just *now* telling me. We've been together for hours." Rissa walked over, stood right next to her, and stared until Zara stopped cutting and met her waiting gaze.

"Stop staring at me." She dumped the strawberries in the bowl of romaine lettuce and fresh spinach. "Nothing happened. But there have been a few moments between us."

"I knew it!" Rissa grinned. "You want him."

Rolling her eyes, Zara pulled out a frying pan and the pound of bacon she'd purchased. "He's hot. Who doesn't want him?"

"That's besides the point. I'm not talking about anyone but you."

Zara told her sister about the office incident. "Then he shows up on the plane this morning on purpose, just so he could talk to me."

"Wait a minute, he's here? In L.A.?"

"Yes." She laid five pieces of bacon in the pan. "He flew in for business. He even got Skye involved." Her best friend had called her right before she'd showered earlier and asked how the flight was. Zara couldn't even bring herself to be outraged at Skye, because she knew where her heart was. "But we had a good talk and decided not to pursue anything."

"Are you kidding me, Zara? Why? If both of you are feeling each other, why not explore it?"

"Because! It's too much for me right now. I can't do that to myself." She flipped the bacon. "And what if it doesn't work out. Then we'll be at war at work. There will be no fun group nights, because we can't stand each other, like Skye and Garrett."

"First of all, you're not Skye and he's not Garrett. Two, you need some. I hate to see you working all day, every day, and not enjoying life."

"I love my job. I really do. I was nervous at first, but I think it's a good fit."

"You're missing the point."

"No, I got it. You're happy with Rick and that's great! I'm happy for you. But the way my life is set up right now, I can't." Zara sighed. She'd already given reasons, which she thought were valid, to X earlier, and she didn't want to do it again. "I shouldn't have to convince you that I know what's best for *my* life. Why can't you just trust me to live the way I see fit?"

"I don't want you to end up alone."

"I'm not alone. I have friends, I have my job, I have you and Mom. I'm good." She looked at her sister. "Don't worry about me. You just focus on your happy."

"Fine. I won't tell you how to live your life. But can I just say that the woman I see in front of me right now is a boss. You have done your thing in a male-dominated field. I would never underestimate you. I just want you to have more than that. I want you to know what it feels like to love someone with everything in you and have that love returned with as much passion as you can stand. I want you to experience waking up in the morning with some-one who makes you feel safe and warm, even on the coldest days." A tear fell down her sister's face and

Zara swiped it away. "I know that the deterioration of Mom and Dad's marriage did a number on you. Hell, it shook me up, too. I worry that you're afraid to step out there because of that."

Zara closed her eyes tightly. "No. That's not what's happening here," she lied. Because her parent's relationship *did* influence how she viewed men and love and commitment.

Watching her mother after the divorce had left an indelible mark on her. And she recognized that her hesitance to start a relationship had something to do with the example she'd had in them. She'd spent a lot of time and money in therapy to learn that about herself. Which was why she wasn't in a rush to jump into a relationship. She wasn't ready. And she definitely wasn't willing to try her hand at love with X and risk going out in a blaze of glory if it didn't work.

"Rissa, I'm good," she repeated. "I promise."

"Okay, sissy, if you say so." They went back to their food duties and then Rissa broke the silence. "Did you at least cop a feel?"

"Shut up, you nut." Zara tossed a hand towel at her sister.

Hours later, the doorbell rang. Excited to finally see her mother, Zara hurried to the door and flung it open. "Mom!" She embraced her mother. "I missed you so much."

Regine pulled back and wiped tears Zara hadn't realized were there. "Zara, baby!" She held her cheeks in her soft hands. "You look beautiful."

Regine Houston-Reid had a promising career as

a pastry chef, before she met and married Zara's father. The two had a whirlwind relationship, followed by back-to-back babies, leading Regine to make the unfortunate decision of putting her career on hold to raise her family. While some women balked at her leaving everything behind during the height of the women's movement, Regine loved being a wife and mother. That is, until Zara's father decided he didn't love being a husband.

Zara had watched her beautiful mother hold her head high through a tough, public divorce. Regine had never once walked out of the house without her makeup or her hair done. The woman before her was a classic beauty, with brown skin and long, wavy hair. And at fifty-eight, she didn't look a day over forty—which often garnered comments that she could have been Rissa and Zara's sister.

"So do you, Mom." Zara hugged her mother again, before she pulled her into the house. "Dinner is almost ready. Have a seat."

Regine sat near the window and pulled out her phone. "Baby, do you have a bottle of water?"

"I got it, Mom." Rissa walked into the kitchen from the pantry and grabbed her mother something to drink. "How was your day?"

"Long. I spent the entire day with a friend of mine. She's in town on business." Regine took a sip of water. "You'll never guess who I ran into at her hotel."

"Who?" Zara brought the finished salad over to the table and set it down.

"Xavier." Regine eyed Zara over her frames. "Did you know he was in town?"

"She sure did," Rissa offered before she could answer her mother.

Glaring at her sister, Zara said, "He's in town on business."

"And they caught the same flight together," Rissa added.

If she doesn't shut the hell up . . .

"Anyway," Regine continued, "I invited him to dinner Saturday. I thought it would be fun to get together. It's been so long, and since I missed the holiday party last year, I want to be able to catch up with him."

Rissa grinned. "It will be nice to see X. I haven't seen him in a while." Her sister gave her a mischievous wink, and for the first time, Zara didn't want X and Rissa in the same room together. There was no telling what would happen, or what her sister would say.

"He's so handsome," Regine said. "That looks delicious." She sniffed the platter Zara had placed on the table seconds ago. "I told him I wouldn't mind if he asked Zara out."

Zara stopped in her tracks. *"What?"*

"Oh, this is good." Rissa took a seat next to her mother.

Regine scooped a heap of pasta on her plate. "I'm not even sure how you haven't noticed how fine that man is, sweetie. I tell you, those Starks men are blessed in the looks department." Her mother popped a mushroom in her mouth. "It's a shame that Naomi girl left Xavier for that dog-face Ethan Porter."

Rissa laughed. "Mom, you're on a roll. I love it!"

Speechless, Zara joined her mother and sister at the table and proceeded to fix her own plate.

"Zara, don't you think he's a nice-looking man?" Regine tasted the chicken. "Um, I taught you well, girl. Delectable."

She swallowed hard. "Mom, I don't think—"

"Yes," Rissa cut in, unbothered by Zara's best murderous glare. "She does think he's hot."

"He's all right," Zara lied. But when both women stared at her in disbelief, she amended her statement. "Okay, he's pretty nice to look at."

"So, what's the problem?" Regine asked.

"That's what I'm wondering," Rissa grumbled.

Regine glanced at Rissa, then at Zara. "Am I missing something?"

"Yes."

That damn Rissa. "No, Mom. You're not missing anything. X and I are friends."

"Friends who almost kissed." Rissa sipped from her glass of wine. "I'm sorry, but I can't take it anymore. Mom, you need to tell your daughter to get her shi—I mean her stuff together. On the plane this morning, X told her that he was attracted to her."

Zara gripped her fork tightly and tried not to think about throwing it at her sister as she told their mother an abbreviated version of everything that had happened until that point. By the time Rissa finished her story, Zara was livid.

"Zara, what's the problem?" Regine squeezed her hand. "From what I'm hearing, you like him."

Closing her eyes, Zara took a calming breath. "I love X. We're friends. That's all we can be right now. What Rissa left out is that we're up for the same job at the agency, and it would be reckless to start a relationship with him."

"Oh," Regine said. "That's responsible, sweetie. You definitely need to keep your eyes on the prize."

Zara nodded. "Exactly."

Regine had always understood Zara's desire to win, to succeed. And had never questioned her on work. "I just hope you know that work won't curl them toes at night," her mother added under her breath.

Rissa choked on her water, sliding to the floor. "I'm dead, Mom. You killed me."

Zara pressed her lips together. "We're not having this conversation tonight. Can everyone just accept that I know what I'm doing?"

"I'm just sayin'"—Regine twirled her fork around her plate—"I worry about you."

Oh no! Zara set her fork down on her plate. "Why, Mom? Because I don't have a man? Because I'm not married with a kid on the way? Because I'm committed to my career track right now? Rissa isn't married with kids and she's older than me."

"Not that much older," Rissa said.

"So, what's the big deal if I'm not willing to risk everything for some dick," Zara said, not even caring that she'd used the word in front of her mother.

"Sweetie, believe me, I get it. I'm proud of the

woman you are. No, I don't think you need to give up your job for a relationship. I don't want you to make the same mistakes I did. At the same time, I can look at you and tell that you're lonely." Zara opened her mouth to speak, but Regine rushed on. "And there's no rule that says you can't have it all. That's all I'm saying."

"That's what I told her," Rissa said.

"Leave your sister alone, babe." Regine assessed Zara. "Just give it some thought. You're young. You can have fun without changing your life or your career. And you're deluding yourself if you think anything between you and X will be meaningless 'dick.'" Regine finished her wine. "I love you, but I'm still your mother. Don't talk to me like I'm one of your friends."

"I'm sorry, Mama." Zara sighed. "I guess you have a point."

"Thank the Lord," Rissa said with a satisfied grin.

"But that doesn't mean that X is the man I should be having fun with." Zara refilled her mother's glass. "I do miss dating, so I'll make an effort."

"That's all I want you to do, sweetie. Enjoy life while you still can, because tomorrow isn't promised. I think we all know that too well." Regine's chin trembled and Zara knew she'd been thinking of Zeke. Losing a brother had been hard, but she couldn't imagine how her mother felt losing a child. She stood and wrapped her arms around her mother. Rissa joined her and they squeezed her until she shouted, "Let me go! You're messing up my hair."

The women spent the rest of the evening on the patio off the kitchen. Dinner had turned out good, the wine was flowing, and the conversation never stalled. Zara had enjoyed every minute of mother-daughters time.

"Check this out." X pointed on the upward trend on the spreadsheet. "I think we're on the right track with this, Drew." He'd spent the morning at the Pure Talent office, poring over the proposal for Pure Talent Audio. The L.A. location had touch-down space for agents working on the West Coast. Xavier had set up shop in an empty office facing Wilshire Boulevard. "It's time to get on my dad's calendar."

Drew closed his laptop. "I'll call Megan and set something up." He leaned back in his chair. "Are you sure you don't want in on this?"

Xavier shook his head. "No. I trust you to handle it. I'm already busy with the sports expansion."

"That's right. How's that going?"

"My father called me this morning, raving about a preliminary proposal Zara had sent him late last night." And it got under his skin that she'd snuck that in while he was busy fantasizing about her ass. Literally.

"She's good, man."

"Yes, she is. But I'm not worried. When he sees what I have planned, that job is as good as mine." Xavier shifted his laptop and showed Drew what he would present to his father when he met with him on Monday.

"X?" Zara knocked on the door. Xavier snapped his laptop closed, nearly crushing Drew's thumb in the process. She arched a brow. "Damn, did I interrupt something?" She stepped farther into the office, looking like a goddess in pink and white. And those shoes . . . *Shit*. The high-heeled strappy sandals nearly did him in.

"No," he said, shifting in his seat. "We were just talking."

Zara waved at Drew. "Hey, Drew."

His mentor stood and embraced Zara. "How are you?"

"I'm good, thanks." She took the empty seat next to Drew. "I thought I'd stop by and check out the office, since my sister had to go to work to handle something."

X observed her, cataloging everything about her, from her messy bun to her rolled-up sleeves, from her lightweight pants to her painted toes. She laughed at something Drew said, and placed her small hand on his friend's arm. The arm he now wanted to rip from Drew's body. He shook his head, chiding himself for the possessive thought. Because he'd promised her that he would table the discussion. Because time away from her scent and her smile yesterday helped him see that she was right. They did need to focus on Pure Talent Sports. Not on each other.

But then she turned that smile on him and asked, "Did you eat lunch?"

And all he could do was shake his head and say, "No. Wanna grab something to eat?"

Drew eyed him with narrowed eyes and a knowing smirk. "I'm going to have to catch you two later." He stood and picked up his laptop. "I'll check in with Megan, X, and let you know the meeting date."

Xavier nodded. "Sounds good." Once he was no longer staring into her eyes, the haze he'd been under a few minutes earlier had cleared. He leaned forward. "Mind if we don't get lunch today? I have some work I need to get done here."

"Oh." He looked up in time to see her smile falter, and immediately felt like an ass. "Okay. I definitely understand."

"If I want to get this job, I have to get on the ball. Dad called me and gushed about the e-mail you sent him."

Zara's eyes widened. "Yeah, I finished up late last night, and figured I'd send it. Before you could steal it." She laughed. "Just kidding."

A small part of him wondered if she really was joking. "Do you really think I would do that to you?" If she did, they had bigger problems than the building attraction between them.

Turning away, she muttered, "It was a joke."

"Zara, look at me." It took a few seconds, but her eyes met his.

"Tell me something." He weighed his words for a moment, before he continued. "Were you and Larry together?"

"*No.*" She scrunched her nose. "Why would you ask me that?"

"Just curious. He seems to have really done a number on you."

"No. We weren't together. I told you, I thought he was a friend, and he wasn't."

"You wanted it to be more?"

"I thought about it," she admitted. "But we never took it to the next level."

"Do you trust me?"

She hesitated. A little too long for his taste. "Yes, I do. But that doesn't mean I'm ready to tell you all my secrets. This is still game on, so you don't get to know all of my moves."

His heart pounded in his chest as he thought about her moves, over him, underneath him. "You're killing me."

She blinked. "What?"

"I promised you that I wouldn't try to explore this thing between us. I'm trying to stick to my word, but you're so damn tempting."

She touched her parted lips with her fingers. "I thought we were just talking."

Those innocent, wide eyes staring back at him had ensured that conversation was the furthest thing on his mind. He ached to touch her, to run his fingers through her hair and down her cheek, to kiss the delicate column of her neck. And damn it, he knew she wanted him to do it. It was in the way her eyes darkened and how she instinctually leaned in when he spoke.

"Come here."

Her eyebrows squished together in a frown and she shook her head slowly. "No," she said breathily.

He got up and walked over to the door, closing and locking it before he returned to his seat. "Zara, come here," he asked again.

"Why?" Her voice was a whisper, like it had taken an effort just to get the word out.

"Please?" A moment later, she stood finally and walked around the desk until she was in front of him. He patted the desk. "Sit here."

"What do you want, X?"

He reached out and tugged at the drawstring on her pants, enjoying her sharp intake of breath. "I have to know . . ." He leaned forward, rubbing his nose against her stomach and nipping the bared skin there.

"Know what?" Her nails dug into his shoulders. "X, you're . . . You can't do this."

With hands planted on the desk, caging her in, he stood slowly. He searched her eyes for a sign, for any hint of "no" or "stop." His fingers dug into the desk. "Zara?" he whispered, dipping his head down and brushing his lips against her neck. "Do you trust me?"

"No." She shuddered. "I mean, yes."

"I have to know."

"Know what?" She grunted.

"If you're as wet for me as I think you are." Her gasp echoed in the silent office. "And if you taste as sweet as I think you do."

"Oh, God," she whispered.

He bit her neck softly, then trailed a line of wet kisses up to her jaw, then her chin, and finally her mouth. He fused his lips to hers, kissing her with everything he had. And as he nipped on her, sucked on her, reveled in her moans and the feel of her against his body, he realized he could never stop.

Chapter 9

His lips, his tongue, his hard body against hers, his strong hands roaming her body, his low, soft moans . . . *Oh yes.* He felt good. Every part of him felt like heaven.

There was no frantic removing of clothes, no skin-on-skin action, papers were still piled neatly on the desk. She wasn't naked. Not even close. But she felt like he'd stripped her bare. Every nip, every lick, every stroke of his tongue against hers, took her higher. So high she could probably burst open from the pleasure But . . .

It isn't right.

And she should stop him.

Oh God.

"Zara." He sank his teeth into her shoulder.

She yelped, digging her fingers into his scalp, reveling in his soft hiss against her ear. "Don't stop. Please."

She wasn't against begging at that point. Unfortunately, she didn't have to, because he wrapped an arm around her waist and lifted her onto the desk.

He pulled back, his hooded eyes meeting hers. A ghost of a smile formed on his lips. "Zara, I need you to be sure." His voice was a low rumble.

This was the moment of truth: stop and die a slow, horny death, or go and come. And the way her body reacted to him, she knew that orgasm would be glorious. "I'm sure." She fisted his shirt, pulled him to her, and sucked on his bottom lip before kissing him fully.

Slow and deliberate quickly turned into fast and frantic. He tugged her sweater over her head. With one flick of his hand, her bra was hanging off of her shoulders, and his mouth was on her breasts, kissing, biting, and licking.

Zara unbuttoned his shirt and pushed it off, trailing her fingers over each hard ridge of muscle on his stomach and around to his back. She felt him, hard and pulsing against her, and unbuttoned his pants, pushing them off of his waist. Her pants followed, flying past her head and landing somewhere behind her.

"I can't stop," he murmured against her stomach.

She shuddered as his words washed through her, touched a part of her that hadn't been touched in a while. *It's been so long.*

His tongue dipped into her belly button, his lips brushed over the waistband of her panties. Lower, lower, and then . . .

"Oh, my."

"Shhh. Quiet, sunshine."

He slipped one finger inside her heat, right before

his tongue swirled around her clit. She couldn't breathe, she couldn't think, she couldn't . . .

"Oh, damn."

He sucked her tiny bud into his mouth.

"Oh, shit, I'm coming."

Her orgasm shot through her like a bolt of lightning, sharp, fast, and electric.

Zara collapsed against the desk, groaning as he kissed his way back up to her mouth, dipping his tongue inside and kissing her with a passion she knew she'd always crave.

"Condom," she managed to say.

He broke the kiss, standing to his full height. He pulled one from his wallet, flashing the gold wrapper in the air then tearing it open with his teeth, before he sheathed himself. With his hands on her hips, he sank inside her.

A low groan pierced the air and she wasn't sure if it was him or her. It didn't even matter, because he'd filled her so completely, she wanted to weep. Soon he started moving slower, deeper, faster, slower. Another orgasm started in her stomach and spread to every inch of her body as he pounded into her, moving in and out.

"So good."

Again she didn't know who'd spoken. And she didn't care, because she was so close, so ready to fall over the edge, that when he drove into her one last time she . . . His mouth on hers stole the scream she wanted to let out. Seconds later, he followed her over, letting out a long, low growl.

Her body buzzed with the need for more, and

she almost let herself give in to the pull. But the knock on the door stopped her from diving in headfirst.

"Shit." Mortified, she pushed him off of her.

Good thing he had great reflexes, because he caught her before she slid on the floor. Frantic movements followed, him tugging on his pants, her trying to find her pants and her . . . *Oh, there's my bra.* She swiped it up and struggled trying to put it on. It took a moment, but she located her shirt under a chair.

"Okay," she said, slipping it on.

He grinned. "Your hair." He reached out and tucked an errant piece of hair behind her ear.

"Is there a mirror in here?" She grabbed her purse and fumbled around inside for a comb. She quickly ran it through her hair. When she finished, she looked at him. "Do I look okay?" *And not freshly fucked?*

He smirked. "You're glowing."

"Don't let it go to your head." She took a seat and he opened the door.

"Drew told me you were . . ."

Zara turned and smiled weakly at Bishop Lang.

"What's up, Zara?"

She gave an even weaker wave. "Hey."

Bishop looked at X, then at Zara, then back at X. A wide grin formed on his face. "Am I interrupting something?"

"No," X said. "We were discussing a client."

"Okay, I can come back."

"No need." Zara jumped up and walked over to

the door. "I'm going to go." *Don't look at him, Zara.* She kept her eyes on Bishop. "How's Paityn and married life?"

Bishop smiled. "She's good. Running around getting ready for tomorrow."

Her sister's bestie, Paityn Young—Duke's older sister—moved to L.A. from Michigan several months ago. And Rissa had been instrumental in getting Bishop and Paityn together.

Zara smiled, thinking of the upcoming proposal. "I'm so excited for Rissa. I talked to Rick today and he's taken care of everything. He won't even let me help."

"That's good."

Finally Zara shot X a quick glance. "I'm going to go."

He nodded, but didn't speak.

"I'll see you both tomorrow."

An hour later, Zara walked into Tallula's Restaurant and scanned the dining room. Skye and Rissa were seated in a corner booth. Turned out her friend hadn't totally abandoned her. Soon after she'd done a brisk jog of shame through the office, she'd received a text from Skye that stated simply: **I'm here. Meet me at Tallula's in an hour.**

Steeling herself, she strolled over to her sister and friend and slid into the booth. "Hey."

"What's up, Z-Ra?" Skye sipped her drink.

"I ordered your favorite drink," Rissa said, sliding

the Bourbon Street Lemonade toward her. "I almost had to drink it myself. What took you so long?"

"I lost my underwear," Zara blurted out.

Skye snorted, nearly choking on her drink. "What?"

Rissa stared at her, mouth hanging open.

Skye wiped her mouth with a napkin. "Warn a sista before you spring something like that on her."

"What exactly do you mean by that?" Rissa asked. "How does one lose her underwear?"

The waitress brought back a platter of nachos *sencillos con pollo* and a plate of guacamole, salsa and chips. They quickly placed their orders and waited until the young lady disappeared.

Skye leaned in. "Okay, girlfriend, spill it."

Zara took a big gulp of her drink. "I left my panties in X's office." She swallowed. "After we had sex on the desk." She placed her hands over her cheeks. Panic welled up in her gut as she waited for her girls to react.

It took a moment, but Rissa reacted first by pulling a fifty-dollar bill out of her purse and smacking it in Skye's waiting hand. "Shit, now I need to go to the ATM."

Skye stretched the bill in front of her and pretended to inspect it, before stuffing it into her bag. "That's what I'm talking about. I have spending money."

Zara gaped at her sister and Skye. "You're betting on me now?"

"Hell yeah." Skye bit into a nacho.

"Sissy, you know how we do."

"This is unbelievable," Zara grumbled. "Here I am confiding in you bitches and this is what I get? I'm in a crisis!" She leaned forward. "I got busy at my office."

"Technically, it's not *your* office. Your office is in Atlanta."

She glared at Skye, who had the sense to avert her gaze and eat another nacho. "Anyway, I need help. I'm a hot-ass mess right now."

"I know you're flipping out right now," Rissa said, "but I have questions. And I need answers."

Dread filled her gut in anticipation of her sister's questions, but she motioned for her to go ahead.

"One, how did you get from 'me and X are friends, and nothing more' to sexing him on a desk? Two, how the hell did you not learn anything from me and keep an extra pair of panties in your purse, not because you might want a little afternoon nookie, but simply because it's just smart? And three, since you broke the no-sex-at-the-office rule, was it at least good?"

"And four and five," Skye added, "where is X, and what the hell are you going to do now?"

Zara massaged her forehead with her hand. "I don't know how it happened or what I'm going to do about it. One minute we were talking, the next minute he was stripping my clothes off—and I was letting him. I took my spare pair of underwear out of my purse when I switched this morning. I'm assuming X is still at the office, probably poking another notch in his belt. And, yes, that shit was good."

It was so good that Zara's body still hummed with pleasure an hour later. She already wanted seconds, even though she doubted she would ever initiate a repeat, because . . .

This should have never happened in the first place.

She finished her drink, slamming it on the table. "And I don't appreciate how you just mocked me, Rissa. I don't sound like that." Her sister made it a point to change up her voice into some high-pitched whisper whenever she repeated something she'd told her.

Skye barked out a laugh. "You definitely do, sis. When you're stressed, that's how you sound."

"I told you." Rissa shrugged. "I lived in the same house with you for years. I know how you talk."

"Okay. Let's dissect this." Skye scooped a chip into the guac and handed it to Zara. "Eat this while I talk." Zara took the chip and stuffed it into her mouth. "So the attraction that's been obvious to everyone else has spiraled out of control and you finally threw caution to the wind and let yourself give in to it. Which is good, by the way. You needed to get some. Maybe now you'll get your chill back. But the way I see it, you only have two options. Tell X 'thank you' and keep it moving, or tell X 'thank you' and meet him in the bedroom for a repeat. Or the office, if that's where you're comfortable."

"I still want to hear about how good it was." Rissa forked a piece of chicken from the nacho plate and bit into it. "And is this a secret? Because I have to tell Mom."

Zara's eyes widened. "You can't say anything to Mom. Are you crazy?"

"Hey, I bet her twenty dollars you'd do it eventually. She owes me."

She closed her eyes and muttered a curse. The fact that her mother bet on Zara's willpower didn't sit right with her. "I don't even want to know why you and Mom decided talking about my sex life was a good idea. But you better not tell her shit, Rissa. I mean it."

"Fine. I won't say anything." She shot her a sinister smile. "For now."

"Forever." The waitress brought their food out. If tacos were a drug, Zara would definitely have a problem. She picked up one of the fish tacos she'd ordered. Memories of the last time she'd eaten a taco flooded her mind and she set it back on her plate. "I don't know what I'm going to do."

Skye paused, fork midair. "What do you want to do?"

The responsible—and right—thing to do was very different from what she actually wanted to do. Because if X walked into the restaurant at that very moment, she'd be hard-pressed not to go with him and let him have his way with her again.

"She wants to do it again," Rissa said matter-of-factly. "It's all in her eyes." Her sister twirled her fork in an imaginary circle around her eyes.

Skye squinted her eyes at her. "I think you're right, Rissa. I can see it, too."

"Okay, it was hot," Zara admitted. "I wouldn't mind a repeat. But I just don't think it's wise."

Skye frowned. "Why? You're both adults. It shouldn't be this hard."

"It's hard because it's *him*. And I just don't think it's smart to start something I'm unsure I can finish." Mind made up, Zara picked up her taco. "It's settled. No matter how good it was, I'm just going to tell X that we can't do it again."

"Okay." Skye glanced at Rissa.

"Good. You made a decision." Rissa smirked. "Now that you've figured it out, can we talk about what I should wear to my surprise proposal tomorrow?"

Zara cracked up. "I should have known your ass knew all along. Do me a favor and make sure Rick knows I didn't say a word."

"Nobody had to say anything. I know him." Rissa's chin trembled in a surprise display of emotion. "And I can't wait to be his wife."

Zara and Skye awed and gushed. They finished their lunch without bringing up X and her missing underwear. Though, in the back of her mind, she knew she was fooling herself. The chances of her and X *never* having sex again were slim to none, even if she planned to try and stay far away.

The Roberts family had spared no expense on the "simple" family dinner. Xavier arrived on time and had been promptly escorted to the backyard, where soft jazz played over speakers. People mingled near the infinity pool, and a long table had been set up to allow guests a view of the city below.

Over to his right, Bishop and Paityn stood near the full bar, chatting with Rissa and Rick.

Urick was the middle son of wealthy business developer Spencer Roberts. Jax and Spencer had golfed together many times, so when the older man spotted Xavier, he greeted him with a hug. "Xavier, welcome. What are you drinking tonight?"

Xavier told a server that he'd like a cognac neat and smiled at Mr. Roberts. They made small talk about housing prices and potential investments. And he tried to pay attention, but his mind wasn't focused on Brentwood real estate or secondary markets. Instead, his eyes were riveted to the woman across the lawn.

Zara had arrived twenty minutes after him, exquisite in wide-leg pants and a sheer blouse with a plunging neckline reminiscent of a 1950s movie star. But that smile almost took him out at the knees. Even though it was directed at one of Rick's brothers.

"How's your father, Xavier?" Spencer asked. "Is he still contemplating retirement?"

"That's what he said," he told the older man. "But I hope he sticks around for a long time to come."

"I'll have to look him up next time I'm in Atlanta. Maybe I can get him out on the green."

"He would definitely make time for that." His father spent a lot of time golfing, either with his mother or with clients. The man loved to be out on the course and didn't care who joined him.

"Excuse me, son. One of my partners has just arrived."

Xavier set his empty glass on a tray. Skye waved at him and he walked over to her. Kissing her on the cheek, he said, "Cousin."

She grinned. "Hi, X. You look handsome tonight."

"And you're beautiful, as always." He scanned the faces of the guests.

"She went inside with Rissa," Skye offered. "In case you were looking for Zara."

He side-eyed his cousin. "What makes you think I'm looking for her?"

"Because you've been watching her since we got here. And doing a very bad job of hiding your perusal." She laughed.

He twisted his watch. "Glad you're enjoying yourself at my expense."

Skye wrapped an arm around his. "Oh, come on. Chill out. I think it's adorable how you can't keep your eyes off of her."

"Shut up," he grumbled. "She left something at the office. I wanted to give it to her."

"Oh." Skye covered her mouth. "I guess you should find her and give whatever it is to her."

He observed his cousin, noted the not-so-sly smirk that peeked out from behind her hand. Narrowing his eyes on her, he asked, "What do you know?"

Bishop had been in the middle of a story when X had spotted the black lace under the chair his friend had been sitting in. Not wanting Bishop to see them, he interrupted him and suggested they head out for lunch. Then he'd "conveniently" forgot something in the office and went back to grab the garment, stuffing it in his pocket. He thought about keeping them, but decided her panties would be a good way to get her attention, since he figured she'd ignore him tonight.

Skye shrugged. "Nothing."

He'd been around her long enough to know when she was lying. "Skye."

She retreated back a step, not even bothering to hide her grin now. "What? Don't you think you better deliver the package?"

She knows. "You owe me."

Her brows pulled down into a frown. "For what?"

"For taking your side in the breakup, even though you were wrong as hell. And we won't even talk about the crime you committed that I covered for."

Skye pouted. "I hate you." She fumed, crossing her arms and glaring at him. "And I wasn't wrong."

"You were. But since you're my cousin, I backed you up. Against one of my best friends. You. Owe. Me."

She grumbled a curse. "Shut up and give her the panties, fool. And give her some space. She'll make the next move when she's ready."

"What else?"

"She's feeling you. But you already know that."

Victory. Satisfied, he pinched her cheek. "Thank you."

A sharp nail pressed into his nose. "And if you even think about telling her I said anything, you'll be on my shit list. And we both know that's not a great place to be."

He grabbed her finger. "I wouldn't."

She massaged her temples. "I'm such a traitor."

Zara reappeared seconds later, this time she was with Rissa and their mother. "Bye, Skye." He walked over to them. "Good evening, ladies."

"Xavier Starks." Rissa hugged him. "You look good." She glanced at Zara and a wide, knowing grin spread across her face.

And she knows, too.

"I told you!" Regine winked at her daughters and then hugged him. "Hi, son."

He planted a kiss on the older woman's cheek. "Hi, Ma."

Growing up in the neighborhood, everybody called everyone's mother "Ma." It was their thing and indicative of the type of community they built. Although they'd lived in a diverse area, the black families formed a close-knit bond and made it a point to be there for each other. Support. Whether attending a wedding, a baby shower, or a funeral.

He looked at Zara. "Hi."

"X," she breathed. "How are you?"

"Good."

Rissa's eyes darted back and forth between them, still grinning from ear to ear. "How long are you in town, X?"

"Until tomorrow evening."

"Thanks for taking time out of your schedule to come. I know you're busy with work."

"I appreciate the invitation."

"I plan to visit Atlanta in a few weeks," Regine said. "Maybe we can all have dinner together? I haven't seen Jax and Ana in years."

"Great. I'll make sure I tell my parents."

"I was telling X how sorry I was to hear about the drama at the holiday party," Ma told her daughters. When he'd run into her at the hotel the other day, Regine had told him how lucky he was that he didn't marry Naomi. "I hear all these stories on those celebrity gossip shows, and I have to wonder where they get their information."

"You got me," he said. "I have no idea."

Regine leaned forward, like she had a secret to tell them. "That woman didn't deserve you," she whisper-yelled. "The little trollop."

Xavier barked out a laugh. "You sound like my mother."

Zara giggled. "Mom! That's not nice."

Regine rolled her eyes. "I'm too old for nice. The only thing I have at this age is the truth."

They all dissolved into laughter. Xavier remembered evenings on the patio, eating pound cake and drinking lemonade with Regine. The woman had a natural sense of humor, even back then.

Dinner was announced a short while later, and they made their way over to the table.

"Why don't you two sit here?" Rissa pointed to two chairs next to where her mother had just sat and nudged Zara toward X, causing her to nearly trip and fall. He gripped her waist to steady her.

"You're ridiculous, Rissa." Zara straightened, slipped from his hold, and took her seat.

He sat next to her and leaned in. "I have something for you."

Her eyes flashed to his. "If you pull those out here, X, I swear—"

"No worries, sunshine," he whispered, resisting the urge to rub his nose over the soft spot under her ear. Her smell wrapped around him like a tight hug. "We'll talk later."

The conversation died down mostly, once the food arrived. Although Zara was seated next to him, they didn't talk much. She mostly made small talk with her mother and the older woman across the table. He'd talked to Skye, who was sitting next to him.

Talk piped up when the wait staff brought out assorted desserts and coffee later. When all the guests had been served their choice of dessert, Rick stood and thanked everyone for attending. The young councilman turned to Rissa and thanked her for loving him, and dropped down to one knee and presented a ring. Every woman around the table cried, some discreetly wiping wet eyes and some outright sobbing. And X was on Kleenex duty, handing out tissues to Skye, Zara, and Regine.

Rissa's loud "yes" sparked a round of applause as everyone around the table stood and cheered them on.

Zara turned to him, a wobbly smile on her lips.

"I'm a mess." She giggled and dabbed at her eyes. "My makeup is probably running."

In that moment, she was anything but a mess. She was radiant. She was everything. "You're beautiful." He brushed his thumb over her cheek, and she didn't push him away.

"We should talk," she said.

"Tell me when."

"Zara!" Rissa barreled over to them and pulled Zara into a hug, effectively pulling them both out of the moment. "I got my selfie!"

Regine joined them, forming a group hug. And before he knew it, Zara was being pulled away from him toward Rick and the Roberts family. She glanced back at him, her gaze locking with his for a second before Rick embraced her.

He watched Zara celebrate the upcoming nuptials with her family and wondered if he would always be *that* guy with her, inserting himself into her world just to see her, to smell her, to touch her. He'd never been so laser-focused on a woman before. And he damn sure never put in effort for female company. Now he was standing in line for someone, angling for affection that he didn't know he wanted or needed. *Get your shit together, X.* This wasn't him. But when she eyed him from across the room and smiled, he knew he would willingly jump through hoops for her. And that was the part that scared him the most.

Chapter 10

"Thanks for coming so quickly, Zara." Jax stepped aside so that she could enter his office. "Have a seat."

"I hope everything is okay, Jax." The minute she'd arrived at the office that afternoon, Patrice had informed her that Jax had requested a meeting. Since she'd been out of town for an extended weekend, she hoped she didn't miss anything important. "Did something happen while I was out of town?"

"Nothing like that," he assured her. He took the empty seat next to her. "Before we start, I wanted to congratulate you and your family. I heard the good news about Larissa's engagement."

She relaxed a bit in her seat. But not too much, because despite her history with Jax, she couldn't let her guard completely down. "Thank you."

"Urick Roberts is one of L.A.'s brightest stars. I look forward to seeing his impressive political career soar."

"I think so, too. He's sharp and he loves my sister."

"Just so you know, don't hesitate to take the time

you need to help prepare for the wedding. If you need to work from L.A., I have no problem with that."

"Thanks, Jax. I don't foresee spending a lot of time at home, but it helps to know that I can be there if I need to." One of the things Zara appreciated about Jax was his commitment to flexibility and work-life balance. She guessed it was one of the reasons there was little turnover in the company. Most agents had remained loyal to the man and Pure Talent.

"Xavier told me he had a great time with your family."

Jax went on about good times in the neighborhood for a few minutes, while Zara wondered what else X had told his father about his time in L.A. The idea that Xavier told Jax anything about L.A. stuck in her gut like a heavy paperweight. Back home, they hadn't spoken about their liaison, but she'd already decided to let him know that, as good as it was, there would be no repeat performance, no encore. In the office or anywhere else. Yet, even though she'd made her decision, she'd wavered on it several times since then. Because she'd never been loved like that before, never felt simultaneously wound up and set free. The strong, physical connection between them had taken her by surprise. And her body begged her for more.

"Ana has already reached out to Regine about her visit to Atlanta, so beware"—he chuckled—"there will be a dinner party."

She sagged slightly into the chair, grateful this wasn't going to turn into a conversation about inappropriate workplace relationships. "Sure. When my mother ran into X, I knew it would be only a matter of time before plans were made for one of your famous dinner parties."

"Anyway, I called you here today because I've had a chance to review your proposal. I love where you're going with it. Your proposal aligns with my own thoughts."

"I'm glad to hear that."

"As you know, this industry is highly competitive. Agents have notoriously had no qualms with poaching clients or even snatching lucrative deals from agencies. Intel is very important to our bottom line."

"True." Larry's poaching of her ideas was commonplace everywhere. During her career, she'd had several potential clients lured out from under her by dirty men who thought she wouldn't put up a fight because she was a woman.

"During his last day in L.A., Xavier stumbled across information that could place us in a better position to break into the sports market."

Zara tensed. *Oh, Lord.* While they were away, X had asked her if she trusted him. In spite of herself and her past, she admitted that she did. And she didn't want to assume that he'd stabbed her in the back or betrayed her confidence in any way. Still, she couldn't deny the doubt that had slowly crept in with every minute that ticked by.

"What type of information?" she asked.

"Information that could change things for us going forward. As a result, I'd like to shift some of your focus in the upcoming months leading to the Pure Talent Sports official launch."

Clearing her throat, she asked, "Shift my focus? What exactly does that entail?"

"Philip Whitney has cultivated a market share that can't be denied with his agency."

Zara was very familiar with the Whitney Agency, having interned for Philip during law school. The man had recently been featured in several publications, because his firm represented more HBCU players than any other firm. The small agency focused almost exclusively on football clients, but it did rep a few boxers and a handful of basketball players.

"Phil and his sons have worked extremely hard on their company and their reputation." Jax picked up a folder that had been lying on the desk. "According to a credible source, he's thinking of selling."

Zara's eyes widened. She knew Phil to be extremely devoted to his firm. She never imagined he would sell, especially considering his sons were partners and it was the quintessential family business.

"That's surprising. I never thought Mr. Whitney would consider selling."

Jax handed her the folder, and she opened it. Inside was a document illustrating the financial outlook of the Whitney Agency, the sharp decrease in commissions over the last several years obvious in the blue lines of the graph.

"With their bottom line shrinking the way it has,

and Philip nearing retirement, it's smart business to consider all his options. What I'm proposing, though, is a consolidation of sorts. Pure Talent absorbs Whitney and his sons, and all of their clients."

With the wheels now turning in her head, she thought of the possibility of merging the two companies. The Whitney Agency had been reeling from a changing market, but had mostly maintained their roster. It made sense to merge with a bigger company, one that had a similar mission, and one with bigger pockets and contacts that would ultimately benefit their current clients.

"Ah!" Jax pointed at her, a gleam in his eyes. "You see how huge this can be."

Zara met his waiting gaze. "I definitely do. And I agree this could be a game changer."

The older man grinned. "This is exactly why I want you on this team. Not only do you have a personal history with Phil and his sons, but you understand how important this is for us. If we launch with an established roster of clients, that bodes well for us long-term."

"A small boutique sports agency within a larger agency with an established boutique feel."

He winked. "You got it."

Excited, Zara stood and paced the room. "I can see this thing. The selling point should be that we don't want to dismantle what they've already started. We want their clients, but we want their people, too. Mark and Dorian Whitney are excellent sports attorneys and they've worked tirelessly for their firm. There's no reason why they can't be great here, too.

When you said X stumbled on information, I didn't realize how valuable this piece of intel was."

"Well, then it's settled. I want you and Xavier to work together to draft a proposal for Phil."

Hold on. What? She stopped and turned slowly. "You want us to work together?"

"I've already scheduled the meeting, third week of June, after the NBA Finals, and before free agency starts in July."

"Jax, I'm not sure. This is all X. I would hate to step on his toes by jumping in on this."

He tilted his head and assessed her. "Zara, when I brought you in, I had definite plans for your role in this company. My son has given a lot to this company. His ideas have been integral to this expansion, but he doesn't have the experience that you do. I have no doubt that he'll master this, like he has everything else I've given him, but he's not there yet. Even if he was, Xavier as the head of the sports division is not where I see him landing."

Frowning, Zara turned over Jax's words in her head. "Why put us in competition with each other for this position?"

"Because it's a means to an end. Right now, my son is putting pieces together to launch an audio division. But he's not intent on leading it, he's working to help some of my best people take the lead. That says more to me than leading *one* division of this company."

The writing on the wall was clear and bold. Jax was preparing Xavier to lead the company, not just the sports division. He'd brought her in to do that. Nodding, she simply said, "Okay."

"Good. Now we're on the same page."

Yes, we are. And she and X weren't even on the same chapter of the page Jax had written with his words. Which made her final decision the good one, and the office dalliance the bad one. Any romantic relationship between her and X—whether it was as friends with benefits or as friends to lovers forever— had been doomed with that one comment. Ignoring that simple fact would do her no good.

Emerging from Jax's office half an hour later, Zara burst into the stairwell. She descended the steps to the lobby and straight to the café. She placed an order for a large mocha smoothie. While she waited, she opened her e-mail app and noticed an unread message from Larry. She deleted it. The next unread message, from Christian, read: I'm here. Meet you at the hotel?

She smiled and fired off a response: Be there in twenty.

Later, Zara and Christian were seated at a table at the Ritz-Carlton Atlanta's restaurant, AG. She took a sip of the pineapple mojito she'd ordered. "I'm glad you're here."

Christian Knight had famously walked away from a successful career as one of the best closers in the league a year ago to run a nonprofit mentoring program for the youth of Detroit. Zara had tried to talk him out of retiring at such a young age, but the pitcher wouldn't budge. And looking at him now, she knew it was the right decision for him. He and his wife, AJ, were happy and his business was thriving.

Christian eyed her curiously. "Rum at lunch? That's not like you."

Sighing, she said, "A lot of things aren't like me lately."

"Is it the job? Atlanta?"

She shook her head. "I love my job. Jax and his team have made me feel welcome. In fact, I just got out of a meeting with him that would have made me ecstatic a few weeks ago."

"But?"

"But it feels hard."

He frowned. "The work?"

"No. X."

"Ah." He leaned back in his seat. "So this is about Xavier, not the job."

She snorted. "You have no idea."

"Well, tell me. I guess turnabout is fair play."

When Christian met AJ, it was under less than perfect circumstances, considering his current wife had written an article implicating his ex-wife in an illegal prostitution ring. But the two had found common ground, and subsequently love. But if Zara hadn't been the one to knock some sense into him when his trust issues had threatened to ruin his burgeoning relationship, the pair might have let everything slip away. Which would have been unfortunate, since they were so good for each other. And her friend was happier than she'd ever seen him.

"You don't have to tell me anything I don't already know," she said. "Things are different between me and X"—she closed her eyes—"and against my better judgment, I let my guard down and he kind of just slithered inside."

He laughed. "'Slithered'? Like a snake?"

"No. He's not a snake. He's a good guy. But you know me and good guys."

Zara's last relationship ended spectacularly when her boyfriend of three years was arrested for possession of an illegal substance. And she'd had no clue that he was a drug addict, even though the clues had been there all along. That was the last time she dated a professional athlete. Then prior to Keith, there was Reggie, the man who made a living fleecing older women out of their fortunes.

"Hell, I thought Larry and I could give it a go, despite his glaring asshole-ish ways," she added with a chuckle. "What can I say? I'm a jerk magnet."

Christian laughed. "I don't know about that. We all take chances on people who aren't worth it. And we learn life lessons from those experiences. From what you're saying, though, Xavier isn't a jerk. So if he's good to you, why not see where it could lead?"

"Because we work together. And work and relationships complicate things. Common sense tells me that it's better if we leave this flirtation where it is. Which is exactly what I was going to do." Except she wanted him, she wanted another night—or two.

"I won't pretend to know what you should do, because I would probably make the same decision in your shoes. At the end of the day, you have to be happy with your choice, though. And there's something about him that's preventing you from being okay with your decision to not pursue this." He shrugged. "To me, that's enough of a reason to rethink things."

"It won't work. Especially now." With X on track to take Jax's place as the head of Pure Talent eventually, how would that look for her? Could she really work with and for someone she had a sexual relationship with?

"Thanks, man." She opened her briefcase and pulled out a leather binder. "Now, enough about me. Check out these zeroes. As your agent, I have to tell you the truth. You'd be a fool to turn this down."

They spent the rest of their lunch meeting discussing the current deal on the table and future prospects for her friend. And as they chatted about endorsements, licensing, and life after baseball, she knew that doing anything more with X could jeopardize everything she wanted and needed to do for her clients.

"Cancel Christmas." Xavier smacked the five of spades on the table, cutting the ace of hearts that Duke had just played.

Zara had decided to host game night at her place—cards, Taboo, and food. Rick had unexpected personal business in town, and Larissa had decided to join him.

"I see you, partner." Zara grinned when X took the next book, too.

Although they'd talked often about "the Whitney Project," as she'd termed it, they hadn't seen each other in person since L.A., due to their schedules. She'd stupidly thought a little distance would keep her desire in check, but X had a sexy phone voice and he still looked good on video chat. And now that he was sitting across from her, she couldn't stop staring. Again.

Skye groaned. "I hate playing against y'all. There is such a thing as sore winners."

"That's right." Xavier dropped the ace of spades. "Don't cry, cousin. I know you don't have any more spades."

"Shut up, man." Duke took the next book and then played the king of clubs. "It's not over yet."

"That's what you thought." X cut that card with another spade. "You just paid for our flight."

Zara laughed at X's dramatics when he stood and smacked the big joker down. The next card swished over the table toward her. This time, it was the little joker. "It's over now."

The rest of the hand went fast, with X talking shit and Duke fuming. By the end, Zara and X had eleven books to their two.

"Get y'all asses up." X gave Zara a high five. "Next."

Skye pushed her chair back and stalked off, mumbling curses along the way. Duke shook his head and walked away. After X and Zara won against Rissa and Rick, the group decided it was time to eat.

The menu consisted of grilled burgers, bacon-wrapped asparagus, and summer salad. After the group went through three bottles of wine, Zara stood and went into the kitchen to grab more, as well as the dessert. She pulled the strawberry icebox cake from the fridge and smelled it. Using a spoon, she scooped some of it and sampled the sweet treat. She licked the remaining whipped cream from her spoon.

"Looks good."

Yelping, she dropped the spoon on the floor. "Oh, my God, X!" She picked up the utensil and dropped it in the sink. "I hate when you do that." As kids, he'd made sport of scaring her. She hated it then, and she hated it now.

He inched closer. "I'm sorry." He reached out, and she flinched. "Easy. You have some"—he brushed his thumb over her chin—"whipped cream." He licked the cream off of his thumb. "Figured you didn't want to walk out with that on your face."

Zara let out a shaky breath. "Thanks."

"We never did get a chance to talk." He stepped closer. Too close. "I figured it was time we do that."

The edge of the counter bit her back. "Ouch." She hadn't realized she'd retreated backward. "Not here, X. There's a roomful of people out there. This conversation is better left for alone . . . time. I mean, private." Once the words left her mouth, she thought better of being alone with X. "Um, actually, I don't think we even need time alone for me to say what I need to say."

He squinted suspicious eyes at her. "And what would that be?"

"It's simple." She brushed past him and pulled some plates from the cabinet. "We had a nice time in L.A., but considering our work situation, that can't happen again."

"Ah, the brush-off."

"No." She touched his arm, his incredibly muscular bicep, to be exact. "Don't say it like that. We're adults, and we're friends. I just think it's better that we keep that same energy."

"Really. That's unfortunate."

"I'm not saying this right. I—"

"No, you're very clear. But since this is a friendship, I think I should have a say in how we move forward."

"Why?"

"Because it's only fair if I say what I need to say."

"Fine." She grabbed forks from the drawer and napkins. "Go ahead."

"Zara, look at me." His voice was low, raspy. In other words, sexy as hell.

"I'm not doing that. No." The last time he sounded like that and asked her to do something, she ended up naked on his desk.

"Zara, come on."

She let out a heavy sigh and turned to him. "Yes."

His gaze raked over her, the heat in them flooding her body with a warmth that she'd missed over the past week. "You're beautiful, smart, kind, perceptive. Soft."

Soft. She frowned and tried not to take offense at the term. "Wh—"

He pinched her lips closed. "Hold up. Let me finish. Not 'soft' in a *run-over-you* type of way. But a *skin-so-soft* way, in an 'I can't wait to run my hands over your body' type of way. Because I do want to touch you again." He leaned down, brushed his nose against hers. Every word stoked a fire in her and made her want him even more.

"X, I . . ." *Oh, God, his hands*. On her shoulders, stroking her skin.

"But you have to be okay with that," he whispered, resting his forehead against hers. "So, if you want to put a halt to this, I'll do as you ask. No moves until you're ready, set . . ."

"Go," she breathed.

Their lips touched in an intense kiss. Nipping, sucking, licking—she wanted more of everything, more of him. Her hands were everywhere, brushing against the stubble on his face, over his shoulders, down his arms, around his back. She couldn't stop touching him, couldn't stop . . . *Shit, he can kiss*. She slipped her hands underneath his shirt and—

The sound of laughter from the other room broke their trance and she jumped back. "Oh no!" She shook her head. "This can't happen again. *Never again*. I have to go."

"Zara, wait."

She picked up the cake and the saucers and walked out of the room. Zara hurried into the living room, where the others were chatting about something she couldn't care less about at the moment. She felt X behind her, watching her.

"Dessert is here," she announced. Rissa and Skye exchanged glances with each other. "And it's good."

"And wine," he added.

"Um, sister," Rissa said, gesturing to her hair. "You might need to . . ."

"What the hell is going on with y'all?" Duke asked.

"Nothing," Zara said. "Why?"

"Well, your hair didn't get the memo." Skye sipped her water. "Mirror time, girlfriend."

No. Zara rushed to the mirror. Mortified at the haphazard bun on her head and the glazed look in her eyes, she tried to smooth her hair down. X watched her through the mirror and she glared at him.

Shrugging, X set the wine bottles down. "Taboo, anyone?"

There were so many things wrong with this picture. The second worse part was he knew that she wanted him, because . . . *hello?* She'd given him the "go" that he needed to seduce her. And the worst part? Despite knowing all the reasons it wasn't a good idea, Zara wanted him to succeed. In fact, she was looking forward to the seduction.

Chapter 11

"Come on, now." Zara stood. "That's a foul!"

Xavier laughed when Zara shouted a colorful curse at the referee before she took her seat again. "You crack me up."

She grinned at him and winked. "I can't with these players."

They'd spent the last several weeks working long hours, trying to get the proposal done for the Whitney Project. When Jax stopped by with premium seats for the Eastern Conference Semifinals game that night, they'd decided to go.

After game night at her place, Xavier had purposed within himself not to pressure her or even act like he was pressed to be with her. He'd expected her to relax around him, but it almost felt like she was disappointed that he hadn't broached the subject of them again. She would never tell him that, though. Instead, she'd put on a front, almost being overly friendly to him.

"Come on, Porter!" she yelled.

Xavier grimaced at the mention of Ethan Porter. The blogs were still abuzz with stories about his "secret" affair with Naomi, and there was still speculation that he would crash the wedding. X had no intention of going anywhere near that event. He didn't even know where it was, and wanted it to stay that way.

She nudged him with her shoulder. "He sucks."

He barked out a laugh. "I won't argue with that logic."

"Yes!" Zara clapped her hands. "And one!"

The loud buzzer sounded and the crowd went crazy. Atlanta was now headed to the conference finals. Standing, he held out a hand and waited for Zara to take it. "Ready?"

"Sure." She slipped her hand into his and stood.

"Hungry?"

She nodded. "I could eat."

They made their way through the crowd into the main space. Throughout the night, Zara had been greeted by several people, mostly men who'd flirted with her shamelessly. The thing that bothered him the most was that she didn't seem to care. She'd even flirted back in some cases, much to his irritation.

Now she was talking to a player's wife, setting up a meeting for Monday.

"Hi, X."

He recognized the voice immediately, but hesitated on acknowledging it because he didn't want to see *her.*

"X?"

Sighing, he turned slowly. "Naomi."

She smiled, her dimples on full display. In the past, one glimpse of her dressed to the nines would have made him happy. Although he hadn't been in love with her, her actions had still hurt him because he'd been committed to her. He'd changed his life around to be with her. And she'd squandered everything, spit on what they'd shared, by dumping him the way she had.

"It's been so long," she said. "I didn't expect to see you at a game."

Even before Naomi and Ethan had made a fool of him and contributed to his humiliation playing out on every media outlet for the world to see, he'd rarely attended basketball games in the city. Sure, he loved the sport, but he was devoted to the Lakers. The only reason he'd been in the arena tonight was Zara. Getting the chance to spend time with her was worth the potential celebrity sighting.

"I don't plan to make that same mistake again." She could take that however she wanted. He didn't care. "What's up?"

He scanned the area, looking for cameras and incognito photographers itching to snap a pic of two ex-lovers talking. The last thing he needed was more publicity, speculation that he and Naomi were headed for a reunion. *Hell no.*

"I saw you in the crowd and wanted to see you, to check on you."

He frowned. "Why do you think you need to 'check' on me? I'm fine."

"You definitely are fine." She twirled her hair in her finger, a motion that had often endeared her to her fans. Unfortunately for her, he wasn't one of them.

"What is this, Naomi? Did you conveniently forget that you played me in front of the whole world? Are things not as great as you'd have everyone believe they are with Ethan?"

"No." She clenched her hands into fists. "I wanted to talk to you because we were friends. I miss you. I'm sorry about everything."

He snorted. "Yeah, I'm definitely buying that."

"Seriously. We spent a long time together. I guess I didn't realize how much it would feel like a death, now that we're not talking."

"A 'death'? Wow."

"Don't misunderstand me." She gripped his wrist. "It's been long enough. I think we should have a conversation."

He gently wrenched his wrist from her grasp. "You said everything that needed to be said when you announced your engagement to another man on Page Six, without respecting me enough to give me a heads-up. You said what you needed to say when you walked into my father's house and invited us to your wedding. There's nothing to talk about. There's nothing between us. You're a client of the agency, and I'll treat you accordingly. We're not friends, we're not anything."

"Are you ready, X?" Zara asked.

When did she get here? He glanced down at her and smiled. "Yes." He turned to Naomi. "Congratulations. Be happy."

* * *

With his hand on Zara's back, he ushered her
out of the arena and into the warm Atlanta air. The
car ride back to the office was quiet, but it wasn't
uncomfortable. Once their Uber parked in front of
the Pure Talent building, he hopped out and
jogged around to her door, opening it for her and
helping her out.

"Do you still want to get something to eat?" she
asked.

"We can."

They chose a small diner near her place for
dinner. Zara ordered breakfast and he ordered
dinner. She shared one of her pancakes and he
gave her half of his French fries.

She dipped a fry into his ketchup. "How was
that?"

He glanced up at her. "What?"

"Seeing Naomi at the game. It must have been
hard."

"Not as hard as I thought it would be."

She bit into the fry and chewed slowly, watching
him as if she was trying to figure him out.

"Why are you staring at me like that?"

Shrugging, she took a sip of her water. "I just
don't believe you."

He barked out a laugh. "Wow."

"Hey, I call it like it is."

"Why don't you believe me?" He rested his
elbows on the table. "And when have you ever
known me to lie to you?"

"I don't think you're lying, X. I just know how it feels to see someone after they've hurt you. And I don't believe that you're as unaffected as you think you are."

For a moment, he'd thought about what she'd said. His relationship with Naomi didn't end in an ordinary way. There were no arguments, no misunderstandings. There was no hashing out of issues—just a news announcement and speculation from various news outlets. As far as he'd known, they were good. So good that he'd purchased a ring, and he'd had every intent to present it to her and to propose. But what had pissed him off more than any of that, more than the fact that she'd left him for another man, and even more than the fodder he'd become in the news? How the hell did he not *know* they weren't on the same page?

"You're right," he conceded. "It bothers me that I could be so clueless. I marched forward with an expensive-ass ring, ready to commit to her for the rest of my life. And she was lying to me every day for months, telling me that she was on set when she was with him. I was blindsided because I wasn't paying attention. That's what bothers me the most about this." Not losing her, not the public fallout, but the way he'd buried his head in the sand and forged ahead with his agenda. *My plans.*

She placed her hand on top of his. "It's not your fault that you had faith in your relationship."

"Is that what that was?"

"In a sense." She shot him a wry smile.

"I hate liars. And I hate being made a fool of."

"But you weren't wrong to trust her. Yes, you were focused, but we all are. We all give up something for our jobs. It takes a special person to be okay with what we do. The traveling, the social events, the time away from home dealing with everyone else's problems."

The pained look in her eyes told him she'd dealt with something similar, a relationship that burned to the ground because her man couldn't handle her job. He wanted to ask her about it, but decided to table that conversation.

"It's the nature of our business," she continued, "so don't blame yourself for trusting that you and Naomi were on the same page."

He flipped his hand over and entwined his fingers with hers. "You're so beautiful."

She giggled and dropped her head. "You just ruined a very sincere moment."

"How? I'm being sincere."

"Conversation over. I'm hungry." She sighed, picked up her fork, and stuffed a piece of pancake in her mouth.

A little while later, they stepped out onto the sidewalk and set off toward her condo. They walked at a slow pace, enjoying the night air and people watching. To their right, a group of ladies snapped selfies in front of one of the bars. In front of them, a couple strolled leisurely, wrapped in each other's arms, only focused on one another.

"I wonder what their story is," she mused beside

him, her hands wrapped around the cup of coffee she'd ordered before they left the diner.

He watched the couple that was now kissing like they weren't in public, like they didn't care who noticed their display. "What do you think it is?"

"New."

He glanced at her, noted the way she stared ahead.

"They met not too long ago and decided to go on a date. This is their"—she hummed—"third date. And she's decided to let him take her home." She peered at X. "What do you think?"

He tore his gaze from her and looked at the couple. They'd started moving again, the man with his hand wrapped around the woman's waist. "Maybe it's their first anniversary. He decided to take her out to celebrate. Now they're going home to their apartment for Netflix and chill."

She turned to him, a playful gleam in her brown eyes. "Okay, I can see that."

"Or she could be his side chick and they're on borrowed time before he has to go home to his wife," he added.

"Aha! That must be it. Except they're making out like they don't have a care in the world. That's not husband-with-mistress behavior."

They both laughed.

"I don't know. Nowadays people don't really care about getting caught," he said.

She sighed and took a sip from her cup. "It's

kind of sad when you think about it. Hard to trust anyone."

"Right. But then I see my mom and dad together . . ."

"They're so happy. I don't think I've ever seen them unhappy. I remember shipping their relationship when I was a kid. I wanted to have something lasting like that." Their gazes met again, held for a moment, before she averted her eyes. "Little did I know it takes a strong man to love a woman the way your father loves your mother."

"Especially in this industry." They continued silently for several minutes before he asked, "Do you like it here in Atlanta?"

Her face lit up. "I do. And no one is more surprised than I am about it. You know me, I'm an L.A. girl, through and through. Even when I went to Yale, I never thought it would be permanent."

"But you can see yourself settling down here?"

"Actually, I can." She tossed her empty cup into a nearby trashcan. "It's weird, though. When I first took the job, I was sick about leaving home. Even though we didn't see each other every day, or even every week, I couldn't imagine not living minutes away from my mom and Rissa. But it's not that bad. I still see them at least once a month."

"That's the best part of this job."

"Right? Sometimes I get tired of trudging through airports, sitting in the crowded seats, and sleeping in hotels, but I love being mobile. I can work from anywhere, and I love that Jax encourages it."

"Yeah, he's good like that."

"The transition has been smooth. Which I appreciate."

"I like having you here." When they made it to her apartment building, he walked her up the stairs to her door. "Well, I'll see you tomorrow."

"Thanks for walking me home, X. I had fun tonight." He nodded and turned to leave. But her hand around his wrist stopped him. "Wait."

"Yes?"

"Want to come in for coffee?" she asked, shifting from one foot to another. "I m-mean, I can never have enough."

"Are you sure that's a good idea?" He searched her eyes. He could tell she was struggling with something. Zara wasn't a nervous person. She'd never been someone who had a hard time articulating her thoughts. He loved that about her. But as he watched her stutter over her words, he realized that he also loved the fact that *he* made her nervous.

She closed her eyes. "Okay, so it might not be the best idea. But I also don't want us to fall into this awkward phase where I'm unsure what to say to you, and you're working overtime to be this nice guy." She smacked a hand over her mouth. "I didn't mean that."

He gripped her hand and pulled it from her mouth. "I know what you meant."

Her shoulders slumped and she blew out a frustrated breath. "I'm glad someone does," she muttered.

"Listen, Zara, I know that you're against taking

this any further. And I'm not in the habit of forcing anyone to do anything they don't want to do." He stepped closer. "I don't want you to have any regrets."

"Why don't *you* have any regrets? I mean, you're ready to jump right in with no reservations. And all I can focus on are the many ways this can go wrong."

"Zara, if we constantly focus on what's wrong in a situation, we'll never be able to see what's right."

"True, and under different circumstances, I could imagine—"

"More?"

Their gazes held for a moment.

"Remember when we'd play hide-and-seek in your backyard and you'd always find me?" she asked.

The change of subject was jarring, but he went with it. "Sometimes I thought you hid where you knew I'd find you."

"Because I did. I always wanted you to find me, because I knew I'd be safe with you."

He smirked. "I remember you saving me a few times, too."

"When you got into your father's liquor cabinet!" She laughed. "That was *so* funny."

"And you covered for me, lied your ass off—badly. But you didn't want me to get in trouble."

"I would do it again in a heartbeat."

"I know."

"That never changed, even once we stopped playing childhood games and started going to parties. When I was uncomfortable, I called you."

"Because you knew I'd never let anything happen to you."

She gripped the bottom of his shirt, nibbled on her bottom lip. "Being here in Atlanta would have been so much harder if you weren't here, because you're that safe place for me. Over the last several years, I can pinpoint times in my life that wouldn't have been so bleak if you'd been there, if the distance hadn't been so wide."

Xavier remembered the day he'd heard about Zeke. He'd wanted to go to her right then, but things got in the way, stupid obligations that didn't matter in the long run. He wondered what else she'd gone through. She'd opened herself up to him in a way he suspected was new for her. In that moment, he realized he wanted to fix everything wrong in her life.

"I'm here now," he whispered.

"Exactly. I'd like to keep it that way."

The slight tremble in her chin told him she was on the verge of crying, which wasn't something he wanted to see. So he tried to think of something that would lighten the mood. Anything to make her laugh.

"It's okay, Zara." He brushed a finger over the worry lines that had set into her forehead. "It's okay to tell me you want me."

She blinked and reared back, nearly tripping to the ground. Lucky for her, he was quick and reached out in time to prevent her fall.

"Oh, my God. You get on my nerves." She smacked his shoulder. Then she burst out in a fit of laughter. And it was like music to his ears. "Thank you, though. I needed a laugh break from all that seriousness."

He chuckled. "Glad I could help."

"I do," she blurted out.

His eyes flashed to hers. "You do what?"

"I want you." She stepped into him.

He cradled her face in his hands, peered into her wide eyes. "Are you sure? I need you to be sure, Zara."

Her mouth was a whisper away from his, so close he could smell the hazelnut on her breath. She brushed her lips over his. "I can't promise I won't run away from this tomorrow. But tonight . . . I'm so sure."

"Open the door, Zara. Now." Because if she didn't do something soon, he'd pin her against the door.

She jumped into action, fumbling around in her purse for her keys. It took several seconds, but she pulled them out, nearly clipping his nose with her key chain. "Ooh, I'm sorry." She pushed the key into the lock and opened the door.

Then his restraint snapped. He pulled her to him, devouring her mouth and pouring everything he had into the kiss. They only broke apart to breathe before he claimed her lips again. Her soft moans and the way her fingers felt against the back of his neck drove him into a frenzy, wild with a need he'd never felt before.

"Zara," he whispered, pulling back. "If you want to stop—"

She placed a finger over his mouth. "I don't. Now shut up and give me what I want." She smirked. "Unless you want me to die of horny frustration."

He chuckled, tugging her to him. "I definitely don't want that." He placed a lingering kiss to that beautiful mouth of hers. Slowly he unbuttoned her blouse, placing soft kisses over her collarbone, between her breasts, down her stomach as he bared her.

"X," she moaned. "Please."

Her soft pleas nearly took him out. She was killing him, but he loved every minute of it. Finally he pushed her shirt off. In L.A., they'd had quick and dirty. Now he wanted to take his time, unpeel every layer she had, savor the time he had with her.

He kept his gaze on her as he unbuttoned her pants and dropped to his knees. He wanted to taste every inch of her, memorize how she felt under his tongue. "Step out of these," he commanded softly.

She did as she was told, kicking her pants off.

Xavier rubbed his nose over her core, inhaling her sweet scent before he kissed her over the thin lace fabric there.

"Oh," she groaned. "Yes."

Standing to his full height, he dipped his finger into her bra, unhooking it and letting it fall open. He took a nipple in his mouth, sucking greedily.

"Please," she begged, sinking her nails into his shoulders.

"Please what, sunshine?" He kissed his way up to her mouth, pressing his lips against hers. "Tell me."

She let out a frustrated curse and tugged his shirt

off. "Don't make me wait." She unbuttoned his pants, pushed them off of his hips, and slipped her tiny hand inside his boxers and stroked him. "I want you."

Gently he removed her hand and wrapped his arm around her waist, lifting her and carrying her over to the sofa. He lowered her down onto the soft cushion. He nipped the inside of her knee, and his tongue grazed the spot he'd bit. She shivered under his palms as he ran his hands from the soles of her feet, up her legs. His fingers trailed a line up her inner thigh, and she arched her back when they grazed her sensitive nub. He massaged her with his thumb, and pushed two fingers inside her. It didn't take long for her to climax, coming long and hard under his ministrations.

The sight of her beneath him, coming *for* him, took his breath away. He couldn't hear anything but her, and he couldn't see anyone but her. Hell, he couldn't even think straight beyond the ache in his gut for her, the desire to claim her as his. *Forever.*

Leaning in, he touched his tongue to her, enjoying the purr that escaped her kiss-swollen lips. Humming against her, he coaxed her, wound her up with his mouth until she shattered again, screaming his name over and over again.

When she opened her eyes, he smiled at her. "So beautiful. Come here."

He gripped her thighs and pulled her to him, pressing against her and sliding into her heat. Someone groaned, and he hoped it was her, but he was pretty sure it was him. Because she felt so good, so warm, so much like home, that he wanted to sit there for hours, just like that, connected to her intimately. But soon the urge to move, to claim, took over. He watched her as he began to move, in and out, out and in. She met him thrust for thrust, giving and taking in equal measure. Soon the need to release overwhelmed him, demanded that he finish. With eyes locked on hers, he quickened his pace, felt his control unravel.

"Come for me, Zara," he whispered, taking her bottom lip into his mouth. He grazed it with his teeth and kissed her deeply.

Zara let out a hoarse cry as she fell over, trembling wildly beneath him. And he followed her shortly after, groaning as his orgasm pulsed through him, wringing him dry.

With her legs still wrapped around him, he turned with her in his arms and sat on the floor, resting his back against the couch. He felt the rumble of her laughter before he heard it. Pulling back, he asked, "What are you giggling about?"

"Would you believe I'm hungry again?"

He laughed and smacked her butt. "Well, then, let's get you something to eat. Because I'm not done with you tonight."

Chapter 12

"Ooh wee, there's going to be smoke in the city tonight."

Xavier adjusted the graph on the financial report he'd been working on, then peered up at Skye. "What happened?"

She stepped farther in the office, closing his door. "That's what I'm here to find out."

With his attention focused on his work, he grumbled, "I'm trying to get this done and sent to Drew before lunch, Skye. Say what you need to say."

"How was the game last night?" She perched herself up on the edge of his desk and picked up his stress ball.

He paused, fingers over the keyboard and glanced at her. "Why?"

It had taken willpower he didn't know he possessed to leave Zara that morning. She looked so peaceful, like a beautiful naked angel sent down just for him. The first time he'd tried to leave, around five o'clock in the morning, she'd coaxed him back to bed with wet kisses and an oral treat. Finally, after another round of morning sex in the shower, he'd left.

"I heard you saw Naomi," his cousin said.

"I did." An e-mail popped up from Drew. He read it and typed off a quick response. "Zara told you?" However, he didn't know how Zara could find time to tell Skye anything. The last time he'd seen her, she was trying to find something to wear because she had an early meeting with a client. The only other way Skye could know he'd seen Naomi was . . .

Oh, shit. He lifted his gaze. "Who leaked it?"

Skye arched a brow. "Who didn't?"

He let out a low curse and pushed his chair away from his desk. "Hit me with it."

She pulled out her phone. "It's mostly the usual. 'X and Naomi secret tryst at the arena,' 'Naomi sneaks out to see her ex in the middle of the play-off game,' 'The lovers make plans to run away together.'"

He groaned. "This is stupid."

"But that's not all."

"Skye, just tell me."

"Apparently, there's a love triangle."

He frowned. "That's not new. That's been the angle all along."

"No, not you, Naomi, and Ethan."

He closed his eyes as the pieces clicked together in his head. "Zara?"

"Exactly."

Rubbing frustrated hands over his head, he groaned. "She's going to flip out."

"Yeah, she is. Have you checked your Twitter

account? People are invested in this, man. I mean, your mentions are blowing up. You might be trending now."

"Shit."

"By the way, did you give her panties back?"

He glared at her. "You need to handle this." He stood and paced the room. Chances were highly likely that there would not be a third night with her after this. She was going to run for the hills, for sure. "Put out a statement, or something. I don't care what you do, just make it go away."

"Already on it."

"Does my father know about this?"

"Of course, he does. He actually checks his Twitter account. I keep telling you that you need to tweet. People are jumping on this because you're being too mysterious. Put your shit out there, and folks won't care about you anymore. It's fun to speculate."

"I told you I don't tweet. And I'm not going to start to satisfy the masses."

"You and Zara"—she shook her head—"peas in a pod. She won't even get a Twitter account. No IG, no Snapchat. Shit, her Facebook account has one post this year."

He shrugged. "What does that have to do with anything?"

"This is a business. Social media can improve your business, expose you to new clients and deals. It's important."

"How did this conversation become an *ABC Afterschool Special* on the benefits of Twitter? My assistant handles my business accounts. That's for business. What you're trying to get me to do is personal. I lived most of my childhood in the spotlight, and I'm not interested in diving back in for any reason."

"Too late, X. You're in, whether you like it or not."

"I'm done, Skye. Just take care of it. I have a conference call to prepare for."

"Oh!" She let out a humorless chuckle. "Do this, Skye. Handle this, Skye. You know what, I'm sick of you and everybody else. What would you do if I wasn't here to fix your messes?"

He shot her an incredulous stare. "What the . . . ? Skye, what are you going through right now?"

"Hmpf." She muttered something under her breath about all the shit she had to do. "Fine. I told you I'm on it. But just so you know, my world doesn't revolve around you and your drama."

"Wait." He squeezed her shoulders. "I'm not sure what's going on with you, but I appreciate you in my life. And I'm grateful for everything you do for me, all the times you've saved my ass." Tears welled in her eyes, and he was taken aback at the display of emotion. "What's wrong?"

"I had my performance review with Carmen this morning."

"I take it you didn't like what she had to say."

"That's an understatement. This isn't how I envisioned my life at this age. I should be running the damn Publicity Department, not reporting to a person who doesn't know shit about the business. I'm tired of running around, putting out fires all day. At thirty-three, I was supposed to have my own firm. I was supposed to be married with one-point-five kids. I was supposed to be . . ." She trailed off, but she didn't have to finish her thought for him to know what she wanted to say.

Garrett and Skye had spent years together. They were so close, so in tune with each other, a wedding was a foregone conclusion. Until it wasn't. And when that relationship ended, Skye had jumped headfirst into another relationship, which ended with her humiliated on her wedding day.

He pulled her into a hug. "Skye, you're doing exactly what you're supposed to do right now. That doesn't mean you won't segue into the things that you want to do eventually. If you want to do more, set up a meeting with Dad and talk to him about it."

"I can't do that, X." Her shoulders dropped. "I'm not going to pull the family card here."

Xavier understood that. He'd never assumed he would get anywhere in the company because he was Jax Starks's son. Every job he had, every client he signed, had been because of his own tenacity. He wasn't naïve enough to believe having the Starks name hadn't offered him some benefits, but he liked that Jax gave him the autonomy he needed to carve out his own path within the agency.

"I get it," he said. "Why don't you let me put the bug in Dad's ear? He knows Carmen is full of shit, and as far as I'm concerned, you're running circles around her."

"Let me think about it." She sniffed. "I have to go."

"You're the closest thing to a sister I have, Skye. I want you to be okay."

"I'm fine, X. Just having a moment. I'll start kicking ass in an hour."

He laughed. "All right. Take your moment."

Skye grinned. "Thanks, cousin."

"You're—"

"Xavier Jackson Starks." His door slid open and Zara barged into his office, straight to his desk. She smacked a piece of paper on his desk, a print-out of the Page Six story naming her as the foil to the supposed reunion between him and Naomi. "Fix this shit."

"That's my cue." Skye threw up the deuces and hurried out of the office.

Traitor. Xavier picked up the paper and pretended to read it for a few minutes while he formulated a response.

She snatched the paper from him. "You're not reading this. Stop playing, X." She waved the paper in his face. "See this? This is reason number four thousand five hundred sixty-seven why we can't do this."

He looked at the office door, noticed Jennifer standing in the doorway with an amused grin on her face. *That damn Skye left without shutting the damn door.* He walked over to the door and told Jennifer to hold his calls before he closed it.

"Zara, calm down." He approached her slowly. "It's not that bad."

"'Not that bad'?" she shouted. "Are you crazy? It's bad. It's *really* bad."

The urge to touch her, to tuck an errant strand of hair behind her ear, hit him like a brick. He shoved his hands in his pockets. "They're reaching. Everyone knows we're friends. It's no secret that we've known each other for years."

"Except we're not *just* friends anymore."

"We are."

With raised eyebrows, she said, "Really? Hmpf."

What the hell is that? "Hmpf." Skye had made the same sound earlier, and it irritated him then, too. "As far as everyone knows, yes."

"This is a nightmare. I'm a damn professional, X. I don't have torrid affairs with high-profile men, and I damn sure don't relish being referred to as 'the other woman.'" She pushed the paper into his chest. "We need to plan. We need a solution."

She stalked away from him and he couldn't help but smile at her antics. He also couldn't help the way his body responded to her. The olive-green skirt and white blouse hugged her curves like a second skin.

"X, we have to do something."

"Zara, relax. Skye is on it."

She slumped against the wall and let out a shaky breath. "Okay. Fine. I'll let Skye handle it. But what is your dad going to think?"

"Nothing," he answered. "He won't care."

"Are you sure about that?"

"Positive." He inched closer to her, finally allowing himself to reach out and run his thumb over the gold charm on her necklace. "You look good." He leaned in, ran his tongue over her earlobe, before nipping it with his teeth.

"X. Oh, God." She melted into him, wrapped her arms around his neck and kissed him.

Far too soon, before he could lower her onto the couch or even pin her against the wall, she pushed him away and walked to the window on the other side of the office.

He sighed. "What is it, Zara?"

"This can't happen again, X."

He resisted the urge to roll his eyes. Swallowing, he said, "Okay. If that's what you want."

"I think it's best that we cool it." She tugged at her shirt. "I can't be at the center of a media scandal. I can't be *that* woman. I've already received three calls this morning from clients. *Three!*"

"Don't tell me they're threatening to fire you because of this."

"No," she said. "They're blazing on me."

He blinked. "What?"

"You know what that means. One of my clients laughed so hard, I had to hang up on him. I'll never be able to live this down."

"So you're not worried about your reputation?" He didn't know whether to be offended or amused.

"Oh, I absolutely am."

He stepped forward. She retreated backward. "Zara."

"Look, I'm the weakest link. I already can't stand the heat. Instead of working today, I'm looking at my colleagues, wondering what they think of me. And, damn it, I need to be on my game. Not dodging photographers or surfing the Net for articles and videos about me and you—and me and you and Naomi."

"I think you're overreacting."

"Probably. That's what I do. That's why I'm so successful—I overreact. I have contingency plans in place at all times. I make sure to keep my life private. This?" She motioned back and forth between them. "I can't do it. I need my peace."

He let out a heavy sigh, resignation setting in. Zara was stubborn as the day was long. He couldn't spend twenty-three hours of his day trying to convince her that she was wrong. "Fine, whatever. You want this to stop? Okay. You want me to let go of the idea of us? I got it. You can go, Zara." He sat down at the desk. "Now."

The room descended into a tense silence. But she didn't leave, she didn't even move. "X, I—"

"What is it?"

"I told you that I couldn't promise you I wouldn't run. This is me." She shrugged. "I'm running."

"Okay. You don't have to keep telling me that. Run your ass out of my office."

She laughed. "Really?"

He chuckled, unable to stay angry with her. "Seriously, Zara. Let's not do this. We're grown as hell. I told you that I'll never do anything you don't want me to do. I meant it."

She bit down on her bottom lip. "It's that easy for you?"

"Damn, woman, you're killing me." He got up

and walked around his desk to where she was standing. "I never said it was *easy,* because it's not."

"Good. I'm not forgettable."

He smirked. "You're definitely not."

"It's just not a good idea."

"Okay."

"Okay." She hesitated a beat. "Bye."

"Bye. I'll talk to you later."

Their gazes locked on one another, and like magnets, they drew in closer. His heart shifted, his fingers itched to touch her.

"X, I—"

"Fuck it," he grumbled before pulling her to him and kissing her. *Hard.* The last thing he registered were her whispered pleas for him not to stop. Then he was lost.

"Oh, shit." Zara tried to untangle her blouse, which had been thrown across the office. "This happened again." She pushed an arm through her sleeve, followed by her other arm, and attempted to button her shirt. But her fingers were shaking uncontrollably. She'd done it again. She'd sexed Xavier in the office. She'd broken all her rules more than once. And she'd loved every single minute of it. "This wasn't supposed to happen again."

He slid his pants on and zipped them. "Um-hm. That's what you said."

She twisted her skirt around and tugged it down over her hips. "Why did I do this?"

"Because you wanted to?" He buttoned his shirt easily, making her even more furious at him.

"How can you be so calm? I'm sure Jennifer heard us."

"You are pretty loud."

She smacked his arm. "I'm not."

"You definitely are."

Zara fixed her watch and picked up her necklace. *How the hell did this come off?* "I have a meeting in an hour. See what you did!" Good thing her meeting was a video conference. There was no way she'd be able to shower and still be on time.

"Me?" He smirked. "I think that was a joint effort."

She felt him come up behind her. "Help." She swept her hair up, allowing him to put her necklace back on. His lips brushed against her neck, then her shoulder, reigniting the churning in her gut that never really seemed to stop when he was near. "I have to go."

"Should we talk about this, or are you back to running?"

She sighed, turning to him. He wrapped his arms around her waist, resting his hands on her ass. Which is right where she wanted them. "Maybe I'm not running anymore."

"What?" He let out a faux gasp. "I can't believe it."

"Okay, I think we need to set some ground rules, since we've established that I can't seem to walk away from this."

He kissed her neck. "I'm good with rules." He brushed his lips over her jawline to her ear. "As long as they don't involve going back and forth about all the reasons we shouldn't be doing this."

Smoothing her hands over his broad shoulders, she kissed his chin. "No sex at work." He opened his mouth to respond and she covered it with her hand. "I'm serious, X. I have to maintain professionalism at all times."

He nodded slowly, and she removed her hand.

"And you can't tell anyone," she added.

"So you want us to be a secret?"

"For now. And no promises," she continued.

"'Promises'?"

"Meaning I'm not your automatic 'plus one.' We're not checking in with each other about our whereabouts. You don't get to know what I'm doing every hour of the day."

"That's fair." He grinned. "That goes both ways, ya know."

"I'm good with that. I don't want to label whatever this is between us. That just makes me anxious. I'm not ready to be in a relationship, but I do love the way we are with each other. Let's go with that for now."

"Got it." He swayed back and forth, as if they were dancing to their own beat. "Is that all?"

"We have to be honest with each other. Even if it hurts."

"That's us, anyway." He frowned. "I don't plan on that changing."

"All right." She tried to pull away from him, but he held on tighter.

"I have one rule. We're friends, no matter what."

Relief. She embraced him. "Yes, please. Never forget that."

He gripped her chin in his hand and then kissed her. He was gifted with his lips, his tongue, his . . .

Oh, my.

"You better go before we break rule number one," he murmured against her mouth. "Again."

"Yes," she whispered, her eyes glued to his lips.

"Bye, Zara."

When he said her name, her stomach tightened. "Bye." She rushed out, closing the door behind her and slumping against the wall outside.

"Are you okay, Zara?" Jennifer asked. "Did you need anything?"

She straightened, running a hand through her hair. *Shoot, my hair is probably a mess.* "I'm good."

"I'm sure you are."

Zara froze. "Not a word about this, Jenn." She walked away, not missing the soft giggles coming from his assistant. She didn't stop until she made it to her office. Inside, she fixed her hair and makeup before she took a seat at her desk, just in time to catch the call from Rissa.

"Hey, Rissa."

"I found my dress!" her sister shouted.

Excitement bubbled in her stomach at the news, but she couldn't deny she was sad that she hadn't been with her sister when she said "yes" to the dress. "Really? That's good."

"I mean, I saw the dress," Rissa amended. "Online. At this bridal shop near Detroit."

"So you haven't tried it on?"

"Not yet. But I've already contacted its designer, Allina Smith. I love her stuff."

Zara grinned. She was familiar with the bridal designer and knew Rissa would be beautiful in an Allina Smith original. "Oh, Rissa, she's pretty amazing. Send me a pic."

"No, I want you to be surprised when I try it on."

Zara's heart swelled and tears threatened to fall. "I can't wait to see you in it."

"Sissy, I know it's the one. I just have a feeling. So, can you get away and meet me in the D next month? I'm thinking either the first or second weekend in June?"

She opened her calendar. Christian was throwing his wife a birthday party in Detroit the second weekend, which she'd wanted to attend. *This works.* And he'd be glad she could attend. "If you can make it the second weekend, I can make that happen," she told her sister.

"Oh, good. I think that might work best for Paityn, too. Let's go with it."

Most of Paityn's family lived in Michigan, and Zara was sure Paityn would come because that would mean time with her many siblings and parents.

"Okay, send me the details and I'll book my flight."

"I will, once I confirm."

Zara's phone pinged, indicating that she'd received a text. "Maybe I'll bring Skye."

"I'll call her myself. Mom is super excited."

"Me too. I can't wait to spend time with y'all." It had been a long time since they'd escaped to a destination together. She looked forward to chilling with her girls.

"While we're there, you can try on bridesmaid dresses."

Zara groaned. "Not this early, Rissa. This appointment should just be about you. And I thought you weren't going to make us wear froufrou dresses."

From previous conversations with her sister, she got the gist that the wedding was going to be small, intimate. Rissa had even wondered aloud if she needed bridesmaids in the traditional sense. Somehow no bridesmaids had morphed into two bridesmaids, but they could wear what they wanted. Now it was bridesmaid dresses. The idea of flouncing down a long aisle, in a too-tight dress, with a bouquet of flowers, which would more than likely make her sneeze, made her queasy. But she'd do anything for her sister.

"I know I said that, but I've been pinning things on my Pinterest page. And I'm thinking of photographs. It would be cool if we were cohesive."

"Fine."

"We're thinking next summer? That gives us plenty of time to plan."

"What happened to a destination wedding?"

"I tried to get Rick to agree, but his parents have their hearts set on a traditional wedding."

"What about you? What do you want?"

"I want Rick," Rissa said simply. "That's it, that's

all. The wedding is cool, but I'm just ready to spend the rest of my life with him."

Once again, tears pricked her eyes. Rissa had been through a lot in her life, and it made Zara feel so happy that her sister was finally getting her happily-ever-after. She wondered what that felt like. To be so happy with someone she couldn't wait to say vows in front of God and everyone else. To be so in love with someone that nothing else mattered but their love and their life together. The thought sobered her as much as it thrilled her. And, for the first time, she looked forward to finding that *one* person who made her feel treasured. Then a tiny voice inside her, the one that spoke things she was afraid to say out loud, mused, *Maybe I already found him.*

Chapter 13

"Patrice, did you receive Jointer's contract revisions?" Zara slipped her shoes off, and rested the phone between her ear and shoulder. Her assistant had taken a much-needed vacation. And while she hated to contact her while she was out, she needed to get this agreement done.

Patrice told her where she could find what she needed on the drive, and also told her where she kept the physical copies. Since arriving at Pure Talent, Zara had made countless new connections and had even signed two new clients. Patrice had been an integral part of the team, streamlining several processes. The younger woman had also expressed interest in becoming an agent one day, and had tagged along with Zara to several meetings.

They talked for a few more minutes about her schedule, and Zara let her know that she would be in L.A. during the Memorial Day weekend. Once she ended the call, she went to her assistant's desk to pull the contract.

"Zara, hi."

Glancing up, Zara smiled. "Hi, Ma."

Ana Starks strolled over to her and pulled her into a tight hug. There had always been something so comforting about Xavier's mother. Her accented voice, calm and soft. Her familiar smell, like amber and orchids. The way she seemed to know things about everyone. She had a way about her, a superpower, that made all of the neighborhood girls want to share things with her. As a teenager, Zara recalled spending many days sitting at Ana's feet while getting her hair braided. She loved listening to stories about life in Liberia, becoming a supermodel, marrying for love, and running a business.

Ana brushed a thumb under her chin, like she'd always done. "I've been meaning to come by and see you, but life has gotten in the way."

"I definitely understand, Ma. It feels like I'm always on the go, mostly running in circles for clients." *And having sex with your son.*

"Oh, I know that circle all too well. I do live with Jax Starks. My son is Xavier Starks. So I get it, but we'll do better."

She'd seen Ana a few times in the building. The older woman had been instrumental in helping Jax build the agency. It was her successful career in modeling that had prompted Jax to go into entertainment law. And over the years, she'd worked in varying capacities for the company. Currently she'd been spearheading many of the Pure Talent Foundation initiatives.

Zara tucked the contract under her arm. "Come in, Ma." She motioned toward her office. "I'm trying to get a contract done. And get home in time to cook a decent dinner."

"Oh, well, I won't keep you long."

She sat down. "What's going on?"

Ana walked around the office, inspecting the art on the walls and the pictures on the shelf. "I spoke with your mother. Hard to believe she's moving to Paris."

"Yeah. We were pretty shocked, too." And since Rissa's engagement, her mother had postponed the move, citing all kinds of reasons for staying a little longer. "I think she's going to stick around for the wedding planning."

"Ah, yes. Rissa is engaged. I'm so happy for her."

"We all are."

"What about you? Are you dating?"

As if she had no control over her body, her knee started bouncing. The question was simple enough, but there was nothing *simple* about what she was doing with X. She scratched the back of her neck. "Um, not really."

"Zara, I know your work is important, and I'm not going to pressure about finding a husband. But I hope you're building fun into your hectic schedule."

"I have fun." That came out too loud and defensive. *Great, Zara.* "I mean . . . I hear what you're saying. I've made a point to go out more."

"Good. I'm glad. If you've learned one thing from me, I hope it's to enjoy life." Ana sat down and crossed her legs. "And you know I'll be checking on you more often."

She smiled. "I'd like that."

"My husband told me you were interested in delving into our philanthropic activities. We can always use you on the team."

"I'd love to be involved."

"Great. Let's set up a lunch meeting soon."

"Definitely."

Ana tilted her head. "Actually, what are your plans tomorrow night?"

"Um . . ." Zara swallowed. "I didn't have concrete plans." Except she'd already agreed to meet X at some restaurant he'd been trying to get her to try. "Why?"

"Why don't you join us for dinner? At the house?"

Although she'd given up trying to stay away from X, she wasn't ready for a family dinner with his parents. "Oh, you don't have to—"

"Yes, I do. It's been too long, and I'd love a chance to talk to you outside of the office. We can have a good dinner, good wine, and amazing conversation."

Damn. "I couldn't impose." She shook her head. "Besides, I have to check with the person that I was supposed to get with, and I . . . um . . . um . . ." Zara wanted to throw up. She wasn't a good liar, had never been able to make up excuses on the fly. Whenever she tried, she always seemed to end up in trouble. And there was no good reason for her not to say yes. If things were different, she wouldn't have hesitated to accept the offer. "Okay."

"Perfect." Ana stood. "I'll set everything up. X and Skye can join us as well."

"Looking forward to it," she said.

Later, Zara poured a glass of wine for both her and X. He'd come over after work. "Your mom asked me to come to dinner tomorrow."

The entire interaction with Ana had taken her by surprise. She'd spent the rest of her workday obsessing about it, wondering if his mother suspected anything. *Why would she, though?* It wasn't like she and X were parading around, humping each other in public. She was so paranoid, they barely touched each other when they were out together.

X eyed her over the rim of his glass. "What did you tell her?"

Shrugging, she spooned roasted potatoes onto two plates. "I told her okay." She opened the drawer and pulled out a serving fork, then transferred chicken breasts from the pan to their plates.

"So, what's the problem?"

It had been two days since they'd decided to keep seeing each other in private, and she'd been wracked with overwhelming doubt since then. It didn't help that she'd been turning over potential conspiracy theories about Ana knowing more than she wanted anyone to know.

Having a physical relationship with anyone without strings wasn't her thing. And jumping into a friends-with-benefits arrangement with X seemed destined to blow up in her face.

She cleared her throat and gave him some of the fresh green beans she'd sautéed. "Nothing. I've been here for months and . . . Forget it. It's just not normal."

X stood and walked over to the table. "Why isn't it? You've eaten with us plenty of times."

"Back in the day." She joined him at the table. "And not since we've been sleeping together."

"Do you want to make up an excuse not to go?"

"I already tried that. You know I'm not good at stuff like that."

He laughed. "Yeah, I wasn't going to suggest *you* offer the excuse."

"Ha-ha. What were you going to do? Lie for me?"

Shrugging, he chewed on a piece of chicken and swallowed. "I would have figured something out, if you're really *that* uncomfortable."

"I'm fine. Look, I was just shocked, that's all. Don't you think it's weird?"

"I'm sure it's no big deal." He shrugged. "She's been asking about you. Makes sense why she would extend the invitation."

"Do you think it has anything to do with the article?" The Page Six article had insinuated there was something going on, but would Ma know about it? Would she care?

"I doubt it. It's probably because she loves you and wants to have dinner."

Zara stared at her food for a moment, then met

his waiting gaze. "Okay, if you say so. It just feels kind of convenient. We're trending, and now she wants me to come to dinner."

"Oh, I see."

She nodded. "See you get it now. It's not just me."

He reached over and pulled her chair closer to his.

Laughing, she climbed onto his lap. "What are you doing?"

"I need you to hear this." He kissed her, once on her lips and once on her neck. "You do have a problem."

"Exactly."

"Your problem is you're thinking too hard and too much about this. It's dinner. That's it."

She brushed her thumb over his stubbled cheek. "Fine. I'll be there with bells on."

"And when it's over, I'll bring you back here." He undid the top button of her blouse. Then the next one, and the one below that, placing kisses to her chest along the way. "I'll strip you bare." He pushed her shirt off. "And I'll make you forget everything you're worried about." He nipped on her bottom lip. "Okay?"

Wrapping her arms around his shoulders, she kissed him fully. "Okay. But you don't have to wait until tomorrow to take my mind off of things." She yelped with delight when he stood abruptly, cradling her in his arms. "X!"

"I'm definitely up for that challenge. *Literally*. As long as you're okay with cold chicken, because it's going to be a while before I'm through with you."

She threw her head back with laughter as he carried her through the condo to her bedroom. "I think I'm okay with that. It was a little dry, anyway."

Xavier's mother had pulled together a feast in less than twenty-four hours. She'd prepared the meal herself, which was a special treat because she rarely cooked anymore. When he'd walked into the house earlier, he'd immediately sampled some of the collard greens simmering on the stove, before she'd kicked him out.

Now seated around the dining-room table, enjoying the food and talking about everything but work, he was glad she'd done it. Having his mom and dad at both ends of the table, Skye across from him, Zara next to him, felt good. It felt right.

"Thank you for this, Ma," Zara said. "Dinner was delicious."

"Oh, sweetie. It was my pleasure." Ana took a sip of her wine. "I enjoy having my kids here."

His parents had chosen to stop at Xavier, but Ana had been a motherly figure to many nieces, nephews, godchildren, and neighborhood kids.

He reached out and squeezed his mother's hand. "Love you."

"I love you, too, babe."

Jax cleared his throat. "Son, I have something to tell you."

X met his father's gaze. "What's up, Dad?"

"I'm unable to attend Naomi's wedding in July." His father finished his drink. "I'll need you to go in my stead, to represent the agency."

What? His body tensed.

"*Jax.*" The warning tone in his mother's voice told X she wasn't happy with the request, either.

"Ana, please." Jax sighed. "Xavier, she is still a client of the agency, and someone from the agency should be there."

"I agree. Which is why her agent should go. Shouldn't Karl go to *his* client's wedding?"

Karl Harris was a top motion picture agent for Pure Talent. He'd represented Naomi since she starred in her first movie.

"And he'll be there. But she hand-delivered an invitation to us."

"No, she delivered that invite to you and Mom," he said through clenched teeth. "Not me."

"A Starks needs to be there. And it would be helpful if you went, showed the world that you're not bothered. The gesture could also go a long way for the settlement negotiations. I'm sure Skye would agree."

He glanced at Skye, who lowered her gaze, giving him the answer to the question before he could ask. He hated the idea that Ethan was suing him and the agency, but he felt that going to that wedding wouldn't help. It would only embolden the gossip and Ethan.

"I show the world that I'm not bothered every day!" Xavier shouted. "I don't think about her. I don't talk about her. I don't care what she's doing!

"In business, we sometimes have to do things we don't want to do. I'm asking you to do this for me."

Xavier counted to ten, taking slow, calming breaths. "No, this isn't going to work. You know I'd do anything for you, but I can't."

"It's not about you. It's about—"

"I know," X growled. "It's about Pure Talent."

"X?" Zara squeezed his knee. "It's okay. I'll go with you. We'll make an appearance, and even congratulate the happy couple. Then we'll leave."

"Great," Jax said. "Zara will attend with you. The wedding is in Fiji, at the Nanuku Auberge Resort. I'll arrange travel."

"I'm not going to that shit." He stood, tipping the chair over. He wasn't in the habit of talking to his father like that, but he had no choice but to make himself perfectly clear. "Why would you even want to put me in that position? To be gawked at, speculated about? To have camera phones in my face? To be the butt of every single joke on social media? And the fact that you even asked pisses me off. So find someone else to make the overture, because it won't be me."

And without another word, he stormed out of the dining room. He needed air. He had to get the hell out of the house.

Twenty minutes later, he'd attempted twenty shots and missed them all. With his eyes on the basket, he dribbled three times before sending the ball sailing in the air again. When it bounced off the rim, he cursed.

"X?"

He gripped the ball in his palm, not taking his eyes from the target. He jumped and released, watching as the ball hit the backboard before passing through the hoop. *Finally.*

"Xavier?" Zara repeated.

Dropping his head, he sighed. He heard her footsteps as she neared him, imagined the determined look in her beautiful eyes. Then he felt her hand on his arm, squeezing, offering him comfort. "Zara, please. Just go."

"It's nice out here. Why do your parents have a trampoline and a tree house?"

Even in his anger, he couldn't be mad at her. "My mother is obsessed with the idea of grandbabies."

"As in your kids?"

He bounced the ball and then chucked it away. "Not necessarily. She has godchildren, nieces, nephews . . . they're all getting married and having kids."

"Gotcha. Can I ask you something?"

"Go ahead."

"Why is this so hard for you?"

He blinked. "Are you really asking me that? Why would I want to go to Naomi's wedding?"

"You wouldn't. I wouldn't. But you're pissed on a level I don't understand. Do you still want her?"

"Hell no. I don't want Naomi. I told you that. I wasn't in love with her, but I didn't want to get played, either. And I definitely don't want to watch her marry the man she cheated on me with."

"I get it. This isn't what you want. But you don't understand what's at play here. At the end of the day, it's one event, one night. You get an all-expense-paid trip to one of the most beautiful destinations in the world. With me." She shrugged. "You can do this."

"That's not the point!" he yelled. He wasn't mad that Naomi was getting married. What upset him was the way his father seemed so content to put him in the line of fire, with the media, with Ethan.

She circled him, stopping when they were face-to-face. "I know you're upset with your dad, but he's just doing what he thinks is right."

He walked away, putting some distance between them. With his hands out at his sides, he said, "I work my ass off for him and his company. But it never seems like it's enough. What the hell is going to that wedding going to prove? *Nothing*. He's made it up in his mind that I should be there, and that's it. He always has some plan. And he doesn't give a damn about how I feel."

"That's not true."

"How would you know?" He regretted the words and his tone as soon as they left his mouth. But he couldn't take it back.

"Wow!" She shook her head. "Are you really going there?"

"I'm just being real. You haven't been here, Zara. Up until a few months ago, you were happily living your life on the other side of the country. I only saw you a few times a year, if that. And I'm not blaming you, but . . ." He paced back and forth slowly. "You haven't been here."

"Remember when I tore my ACL in high school?"

That wasn't something he'd ever forget. He remembered what he'd worn to the game, who he was with, and her bloodcurdling scream.

"I cried for hours," she continued. "And not from the pain, but because my own father didn't even show up. I was in the hospital, I had surgery, and I got a bouquet of flowers and a two-line note from my dad. He didn't even call me."

Xavier remembered that, too. He ended up sleeping in her hospital room that first night—along with Rissa. Just to be there with her, to make sure she knew he cared.

"X, you have a father that has shown up for everything you've done. Every game, every audition, every premiere. He's been there, he's been present. Those are not the actions of a man who doesn't think you're good enough. That doesn't equate to him not caring about you or your feelings."

"Zara, I—"

"No. You want to see a father who doesn't give a damn? That would be my father. The man who *is* a client at the agency I just left, the man who wouldn't let me represent him, the man who doesn't even know I moved to Atlanta. I haven't heard from him, I don't call him. He doesn't take me to lunch or to the golf course. He's not here."

I'm officially an ass. He approached her, reached out to grab her hand. But she moved away. "Zara."

"Be upset. Because it is messed up. But don't let her and Ethan Porter drive a wedge between you and your dad. Go to the wedding, make the appearance, have sex on the beach, then come home and live your life."

He grabbed her hand.

"X, we're in your dad's backyard. Out in the open."

"I don't care." He pulled her to him, and this time she let him. "Sex on the beach, huh? The drink? Or with you?"

She winked at him. "I'm down for whatever." They laughed.

Bending down, he placed a kiss on her temple and held her in his arms. Finally he pulled back. "Down for anything?"

Zara traced the line of his nose. "Yes."

"How about that trampoline over there?" He motioned to the huge screened-in structure behind her.

She turned, and a slow smile spread across her face. "I'll race you." Then she took off running. And he had no choice but to follow her.

Chapter 14

Zara couldn't concentrate, she couldn't think. Because her mind was on X. They'd spent the last week together, eating dinner together, watching television, or just sitting outside on her deck and talking. And they'd explored each other. *Oh yes,* he'd spent hours pleasuring her in ways she didn't know existed. She was far from a prude, but *damn.* X was in a league of his own.

Now she was staring at her computer monitor, a contract in front of her, calls to be returned. And she couldn't bring herself to do anything productive because she'd rather be doing him. And she felt dirty. In a double-cheeseburger-with-extra-cheese-and-sautéed-onions way. In a margarita on the rocks, salt on the rim, double Patrón type of way.

Pull yourself together, Zara. She spent a few minutes giving herself a pep talk about focus, work, being the best. *You got this.*

Shaking her mind free of wayward thoughts, she attempted to write an e-mail to her new client, letting him know that she would be in attendance at his next game and asking if he needed anything from her. But when she read over the e-mail, she noticed she'd written "lick" where she should have written "luck." As in "good luck." And she'd actually addressed the e-mail to Xavier, instead of Zander. She couldn't escape him—his smile, his voice, the touch of his fingers against her skin.

Zara deleted the entire e-mail and decided to wait to send. Rubbing her palms over her legs, she stood and stretched. It was nine o'clock at night and she'd been in the office since eight in the morning. It was way past time to go home.

A soft knock on the door, followed by a soft greeting, made her smile. Because she hadn't seen him all day. And she'd missed his face. "Hey," she said. "I didn't know you were here."

Holding up a paper bag, he said, "Figured you'd be hungry." He entered her office and set the bag down on the table near the couch. "I brought Chinese."

As if on cue, her stomach growled. "Good, because I'm starving."

"Guess I came right on time."

A few minutes later, they were eating. She'd stretched out on the couch with her back against the armrest and legs on top of his lap, a white carton of orange chicken in her hand. And it felt normal, like they were meant to be like this with one another.

He dipped his chopsticks in the shrimp lo mein. "Taste this." He held it out for her and she sampled it. "Like it?"

"Yum." They switched cartons, and she took

another bite of his food. "I'm going to have to start meal prepping again. My skirts are getting tighter."

"You look good to me." He popped a piece of chicken in his mouth. "I know I thank God for those hips every time I look at you."

She nearly choked on a noodle. She took a sip from her bottle of water. "You have to stop doing that to me." Giggling, she shook her head. "Always catching me off guard with your little comments."

He arched a brow. "I meant every word."

She pointed a chopstick at him. "Rule number one still stands."

"Are you reminding me for my benefit or yours?"

She cracked a smile. That no-sex-in-the-office rule was hard, especially when he smelled so good. "Anyway, did you look at the revisions I sent over on the proposal?" They'd finalized the plan for the Whitney Project and planned to take it to Jax in a few days. "I loved your ideas about the rollout. Hopefully, we can win Phil over."

X shrugged. "We'll see. I heard he has reservations about selling to us."

"Why?"

"Because of me."

She lowered her food, resting the carton on her lap. "You? What's the reason?"

"Ethan. Apparently, they're in talks to sign him and are worried that merging with us might dead the deal."

She tilted her head and assessed him. He didn't appear too upset by the development, but she was. The idea that one man could ruin everything frustrated her. Especially since Ethan Porter had been let go by several agents because of his bad attitude and constant need for drama. He'd tried to get in with Huntington last year, had even approached her and Larry to represent him, but Jeffrey ultimately didn't want to take him on because of his behavior. The small forward had been in the press for one scandal after another since he'd joined the league.

"They're probably thinking of the potential endorsements," she said. "Scandal sells, as you know, and he's hot right now. Despite his behavior."

He reached over and pulled a shrimp out of her carton. "Exactly. I don't blame them. It's business."

"Well, we just have to convince them that our way would be best for their bottom line." She took another bite of food. "It will work out."

"In the meantime, Pure Talent Audio is moving forward. So that's good."

"I heard." The office rumor mill had been buzzing about the new division. Many of the agents were excited about the possibilities. "Have you considered partnering with a production studio? Maybe launch an audio network?"

"Even better. We're piloting an in-house studio that will be accessible to our clients."

Her mouth fell open. "That's pretty awesome. Where?"

"Near the Pure Talent L.A. office. Bishop was able to secure the space. We're working with interior designers now so that we can get to work on construction."

Zara listened intently as X gave her a quick rundown of the strategic plan. As he explained what they hoped to do with the studio, she chimed in on a few ideas. The more he talked, the more she appreciated and admired him. She loved the way his mind worked. And the best part? She never had a hard time understanding him, because they were so much alike.

"You're the bomb," she said, flipping through the PowerPoint presentation he'd pulled up on his phone. "This is huge, X. I'm surprised you don't want to run it."

"I don't need to. Besides, it was a group effort. I couldn't have done it without Drew and Bishop."

"And so modest," she teased.

"Not really. I like spreading the wealth, empowering others to take the reins."

"Signs of a leader. I think you're more like your father than you realize."

"I'll take that as a compliment."

Even when X was running around, breaking every rule he could, the respect he had for his father was always evident. "It is." She paused, thinking of how she could say this without giving too much away. "If you could do anything in this company, besides sports, what would it be?"

He tilted his head to the ceiling, a slight frown on his face. Finally he looked at her. "I don't know if it's just *one* thing. I love having my hand in different things, helping others develop ideas. I like having the flexibility to present ideas to colleagues and let them run with it. And I also enjoy representing clients."

As he talked, her conversation with Jax replayed

THE WAY YOU TEMPT ME   201

in her mind. The older man's reasons for bringing her to the agency made perfect sense. X's ideas, his willingness to think "big picture" for the agency, to step aside and let others lead, were all perfect qualities for someone who would eventually step in as head of the company. The only problem was, he'd yet to think that far ahead.

"So you'd never give up your youth clients?"

"No. If I can help someone avoid making the same mistakes I did, I'm definitely going to do it."

Every time he revealed a piece of himself, her heart cracked open a little more. Because what she felt for him in that moment was more than lust, more than the need to be with him physically. And she could make every excuse for how he made her feel, but she already knew she wouldn't be okay when this ended. If she wasn't careful, she'd be in love soon.

"Okay." Her voice came out breathy and shaky. She gripped her throat.

"Are you trying to deter me from the matter at hand?" he asked, a wicked gleam on those full lips of his. She wanted to kiss him. No, she wanted to take his clothes off and lick him all over.

"Oh, please." She let out a weak laugh. A strained whimper was more like it. Because she was in deep shit if every conversation between them about work ended with her imagining him naked and on top of her—or beneath her.

"You just want sports all to yourself." He winked and placed a quick kiss on her lips.

"I already won the job. I'm just biding my time for the big reveal."

"Keep telling yourself that." He set a fortune cookie on her lap and cracked one open. "Hm . . ."

She eyed him, tempted to ask what it read. He knew she hated those things and had refused to eat them. And she made it a point never to read the stupid sayings inside ever since they were teenagers when she'd let a fortune propel her to ask Jacob Pierce to a dance, only to have him laugh in her face in front of her entire class. Xavier had tried to get her to read several since then, telling her that she needed not to blame the cookies for Jacob's ignorance. Little did X know, she'd relented one other time, when she'd been struggling with a big decision and the message in the cookie said: *I can't give you any answers. I'm just a cookie.*

Unable to resist, she asked, "What does it say?"

"Open yours."

Grumbling a curse, she popped hers open. Rolling her eyes, she showed the paper to him. The *blank* paper. "See, this is why I hate these things." He laughed. "Useless. I guess I have no fortune."

Still chuckling, he said, "That's not true. I can read your fortune based on my message."

Curious, she asked, "What did yours say?"

He held it up and pretended to read, "You will get lucky tonight."

Laughing, she snatched it from him and read it aloud. " '*Your relationships will improve with time in bed.*'" She laughed, tossing it back to him and watching the tiny piece of paper float in the air before it landed on his arm. "You're silly." She wiped happy tears from her cheeks. "It doesn't say that."

"Actually, I think it does." He pulled her onto his lap, and placed wet kisses down her neck to her shoulder. "Which means we only have one thing left to decide."

She caressed his face and kissed him soundly. "And what would that be?"

"Your place or mine."

"This feels so good." Zara relaxed against Xavier's chest, the hot bathwater sloshing around them. "Thanks for this."

They'd decided on his place after dinner and had barely made it in the door before he stripped her naked and made love to her on the floor of his living room.

He rubbed his hands over her stomach, traced her belly button with his fingers. "I can definitely get used to this." He brushed his lips over her ear, down her neck. "*You* feel good. I want you," he grumbled against her ear, before he nipped the sensitive skin. She gasped. "Right now."

Xavier pressed his erection against her core and she purred. A second later, he was inside her, guiding her movements as they made slow, sweet love. There were no words, no frantic touches. Everything about it was perfect: the way they fit together, the way they moved together, and the way they came together, with eyes closed and lips fused together.

As unexpected as this thing between them was,

he found himself wanting to dive right in. He wanted to know everything about her, even the parts she'd been afraid to tell anyone else. He wanted to consume her thoughts. He needed her to ache for him. Because now he knew that he wanted to devote his time to her. Now he knew that he would never be able to live without this.

After the last tremble shot through him, he relaxed against the tub and washed her body, spending a little extra time with his fingers against her clit until another orgasm thundered through her.

She entwined her fingers through his, leaning against him. "This is nice." She tilted her head up and he circled her nose with his. She grinned. "Being with you."

He placed a chaste kiss on her lips. "Very."

Zara had requested they keep what was happening between them private, but he wanted to take her out on a proper date—reserve a private booth at some swanky restaurant, feed her good food, make her laugh, and share a decadent dessert with her.

"What are you doing next weekend?" he asked.

"I have to go to Detroit. Rissa is dress shopping and Christian's having a birthday party for his wife."

"That's good."

"Why?"

"Just wondering if you'd let me take you out."

"On a date?"

"Yes."

She was quiet for a moment, and he wondered if this was the point when she told him that could never happen. But she surprised him when she said, "That sounds nice. Where would we go?"

"I can't reveal my secrets," he told her.

"Well, you know Detroit is a nice city. Plenty to do." She looked at him, nibbling on her lip.

He brushed his thumb over it, releasing it from her teeth. "Is that your way of asking me to come to Detroit with you?"

"If you want to come, I wouldn't mind."

With narrowed eyes, he asked, "As your 'plus one'?"

She rolled her eyes. "It's not like you haven't come to parties with me before. I just told you not to *expect* to be my plus one."

"You do realize people will see us together." He rubbed his thumb over her nipple. "And I already can't keep my hands off of you."

"Well, I guess you'll have to refrain until we're alone in my hotel room."

He thought about it for a minute. Could he go to Detroit and pretend she wasn't *with* him when everything about them together screamed that she was?

"I'll have to check my calendar," he told her, chuckling when she pouted. "But I'm sure I can make up a good excuse to be in Detroit the same weekend you are." *Other than just wanting to be near you.*

"Good." She kissed him.

"I like what Christian is doing with the youth." He'd been following the retired baseball player's mentoring program since he'd started it and could appreciate his devotion to the cause.

"He's doing great work. I'm proud of him."

There was a time when no one would have been surprised if Christian and Zara ended up together. The two were thick as thieves, often spotted out at several events. The notoriously private athlete had deliberately avoided the press and shunned questions about his personal life, so the speculation was mostly an errant blog post here or there, even after he married his first wife. But now that he was happily married to AJ, the world had moved on from the popular player's love life.

"It's a good program," he said. "We donated to the scholarship fund."

"You did? Thank you. He works so hard."

"He's always seemed very serious." Although he wouldn't consider Christian a friend, they'd had several interactions over the years. Zara had even brought him to the holiday party one year.

"He is. So intense, always brooding. But I'm glad he has AJ. She loosens him up. I remember when Zeke met him, he . . ." She trailed off as she often did when speaking about her brother. "Anyway, they liked each other a lot. I was actually with Christian when I got the news. About Zeke."

He waited, hoping she'd continue.

"I'm glad he was there. I literally passed out, and he caught me."

Xavier couldn't help but feel jealous that Christian had been there for her, that the other man comforted her. *I should've been with her.*

"It took forty-five days for me to cry after my brother died."

Xavier hated to hear the pain in her voice. He kissed her shoulder. "That's understandable. You were probably numb."

She entwined her fingers with his. "I couldn't believe it. He had so much life ahead of him, so many things to accomplish."

Zeke was not only a talented ballplayer, but he was smart. He'd placed just as much emphasis on his education as he did on the game. Xavier remembered Zeke beating him at HORSE one time—leaving him flat on his back and out of breath—to go inside and study for a final. When he'd entered the NBA Draft, after he graduated with honors, his dream squad had picked him up in the first round. X was proud of Zeke for doing both, being an amazing athlete and a scholar.

"I couldn't look at the car," she admitted, her voice trembling.

News of the three-car accident in Los Angeles reached the nation in a matter of minutes. And Xavier and Skye had watched in horror as the picture of Zeke flashed across the screen. "I'm sorry, baby." He buried his face in her neck and held her tighter against him, hoping to give her some of his strength. "I'm so sorry."

"Thank you."

She was crying, but he didn't want to draw attention to it by even wiping the tears he knew were falling from her eyes. It was hard to know what to say in these instances. "Thoughts and prayers" always seemed to fall short. So he chose to sit there, offering comfort in the way he held her, the way he listened.

"We'd spent a day together the week before the accident." She sniffed. "It was a family day. Mom and Rissa came over and we barbecued, played cards, and just chilled with each other. We laughed so much all day. But I got a call from a client and had to take it. On their way out, I gave him a hug. But I . . ." Her voice broke and so did his heart. "I didn't tell him I loved him."

"He knew you did."

"I wish I had said it. I was distracted when they left my house, and I didn't say it."

"Zara, I knew Zeke. I've been around you all for a long time. He knew."

"Mom said the same thing."

"Because it's true. And he loved you, too."

"I loved him so much. He was the best brother I could have ever had. I miss him."

"I do, too. I know if he was still here, he would be in Atlanta every chance he got. And would threaten to kick my ass if he knew you were here with me like this."

She laughed. "You're so right."

"He didn't play about you and Rissa."

"You'd think he was the oldest, not the youngest. Always telling me what to do. So bossy."

"Like someone else I know," he teased.

She pinched his arm. "Stop. I'm not bossy."

"Whatever you say."

Zara had made sport of telling people what to

do. They'd argued about it a lot as kids because she always had to make up the rules and be in charge of everything—whether it was fort placement or who would be "it" in tag or hide-and-seek.

"But I think he might not be so upset about this. He loved you, told me time and again how he thought you were one of the good ones."

Xavier smiled sadly. "That means a lot to me. I wish we'd been able to spend more time kickin' it."

"Those other guys I messed around with . . . yeah, he didn't like any of them. I remember he went crazy when my ex stole my watch."

Xavier had heard the story from Skye years ago. Keith Borders was a pro-football player for Arizona and had been forced to retire when he was arrested. "Shit, I definitely understand that. I ran into him not too long after that, and Duke had to stop me from knocking him out."

"I didn't know that."

"Yeah, I wasn't happy with him. Especially since you met him at one of my parties." He'd introduced them during his twenty-fifth birthday party. And he hated that he had done that, every day since then.

"You know it's not your fault. I've introduced you to crazy women before."

"Yes, you have! I'll never forget Freaky Farrah."

She laughed. "I still feel bad about that."

"You should."

When they'd first moved to Atlanta, his parents threw a big party during summer break. Zara had brought along her college roommate, Farrah. The anthropology major had expressed interest in him, and back then, he made it a point to get around and had often used his celebrity to ensnare women. This time, it backfired big-time on him. Especially when Farrah brought him bones for presents, popped up at his campus apartment with skulls and other weird shit. When he'd let her down easy, she'd flipped out and camped outside his place for days with a sign begging him to call her. She'd even harassed his friends. Ultimately he ended up getting a PPO against her.

"I still can't go to the Museum of Natural History without thinking of her," he said, enjoying her soft giggles. "There have been parties there and I cringe whenever I see one of those bird fossils."

"Oh, my God! I'm sorry for that."

"Not your fault."

They sat in silence, wrapped in each other. "I've never shared how I felt about Zeke with anyone."

"I'm glad you felt comfortable enough to talk about it with me." He gripped her chin, tilting her gaze up to his. "You know you can always talk to me, Zara." He brushed his lips against hers. "Never doubt that."

"I won't. Thanks, X."

Chapter 15

"Well, if it isn't Ghost." Duke dapped Xavier when he approached the high-top table. The sports bar they frequented was packed, full of men and women watching the NBA Finals.

"Shut the hell up, man," X grumbled, bumping elbows with Garrett, before he sat down. "What's up, bruh?"

"Shit." Garrett tipped his chin, gesturing to the waitress who'd been hovering near the table, watching them. "Get this man a Modelo and a shot of Patrón."

It didn't take long for her to return with his drink. She also slipped him her number on the cocktail napkin, which he promptly balled up and stuffed inside an empty glass.

"What was that?" Duke glanced back at the young woman as she sauntered away. "She was fine as hell."

"Leave it alone." X took his shot and chased it with the beer. Garrett eyed him quietly. "Stop looking at me."

"I'm curious," Garrett said. "Duke is right. You've been absent lately. You even missed the fight."

Xavier hadn't missed the heavyweight championship fight. He'd watched it with Zara at his place. As far as he was concerned, beer, nachos, and Zara in one of his shirts—and nothing else—was better than hanging with a bunch of fellas. Even if it was Garrett's fight party.

"I'm sure y'all got it in without me," X murmured.

"And you missed *Chef Battle.*"

That night, he'd whisked Zara away for a mini staycation and couples massage. "You won." He shrugged. "I was happy for you."

"Where you been, bruh?" Garrett asked.

"Better yet, who you been with?" Duke added, slamming his empty beer bottle on the table. "As in, who you been creepin' with? Because you damn sure aren't missing a fight that we've been waiting on for months for anything other than some ass."

"I caught the fight, man." He gulped his beer. "With Zara," he added under his breath.

"Whoa!" Duke leaned back in his seat, shaking his head rapidly. "I didn't expect that shit."

"Wait, so you've been hanging with Zara?" Garrett said. "Sports agent Zara?"

"Good friend Zara?" Duke motioned for the waitress.

"Yeah." X scratched the back of his neck. "We've been working on something for my father."

"Is that all it was?" Garrett smirked. "Because you've been acting crazy around her since Topgolf."

Duke laughed. "That whole donut thing was hilarious."

"Exactly. Shocked the hell out of me."

Xavier glared at his boys as they ticked off all the weird incidences since Zara had moved to town. Duke even blurted out something about L.A. *I'm going to beat Bishop down.*

"Then there was that game night at her place." Duke howled.

His friends gave each other a fist bump. "That's right," Garrett said. "The messy hair."

X frowned. "Bruh, you weren't even there."

Garrett shrugged. "I heard about it."

"I'm done with this. We're not talking about this shit anymore." X stopped the waitress when she walked past and ordered buffalo wings. "I watched the fight with Zara because we worked late and it made sense." It definitely made sense to work her late and often, before and after the match. It was a win-win situation in his eyes. "And we're friends. Now drop the subject."

He lifted his gaze up to one of the monitors just as Porter sank a three-point shot right at the halftime buzzer. The bar erupted into applause. If Atlanta won tonight, they'd take the lead, two to one. And as far as he could tell, he was the only one in the bar rooting for them to lose.

Garrett stood, clapping with everybody else. "Good shit, good shit."

The waitress appeared a second later, her eyes on X as she leaned in and asked if she could get him anything else. He ordered another round for the table.

"Did you see that bullshit game the other night? Those damn refs. There's no way this series should be tied right now," Duke said.

X waved a dismissive hand in the air, still pissed about his team losing by one point in overtime. "Man, I don't even want to talk about it."

"And Bowman is limping. We might be down a man in the next game."

"We?" X raised a brow. "Since when are you rooting for Golden State?"

"Since Detroit didn't make it past round one."

Garrett snickered. "Are you really surprised by that?"

Duke shook his head. "I'm serious. Wait till next year. The team is still building."

"They been building for about twenty years," X joked.

"Fuck y'all." Duke had been rooting for Detroit since they were kids, and had been disappointed more times than not. But he never wavered or turned in his fan card. That was serious devotion. "Man, whatever."

They talked about the NBA for a few minutes, then started on football. Conversation between them had never been stilted. There was always something to discuss, from video games to sports to food to movies.

"What you got up this weekend?" Duke asked.
"My parents are throwing Asa a graduation party. Took him long enough to get his degree, so they're

celebrating. Figured I'd show up. Wanna roll out with me?"

"To Detroit?" He knew his best friend's huge family would provide a good excuse for him to be in Michigan. Asa was the baby of the Young clan. "What day?"

"Saturday. It's an all-day thing. You know Ma. She can't wait to entertain. Paityn and Bishop will be in town, too."

Perfect. He cleared his throat. "Yeah, I can be there."

Duke flashed a sinister smile his way. "Zara will be in town, too. Apparently, she's dress shopping with Rissa. Maybe y'all can get some of that *work* done in the D."

Garrett choked with laughter.

Xavier didn't miss Duke's emphasis on the word "work," which told him nobody was buying that "just friends" line. And he couldn't blame them, because if the shoe was on someone else's foot, he wouldn't buy that excuse, either.

His phone pinged and he opened the messages app. The first message was a picture of Zara's bare stomach. He swiveled around in his chair, turning his back to them.

You do know hickeys went out with the '90s.

He chuckled, zooming in so he could see the mark she'd circled. Which wasn't a damn hickey. During a particularly intense lovemaking session, when he'd bent her over the glass table at her house, she'd scratched herself.

He texted back: Blasphemy. That's a tiny sex wound. Not a hickey.

Tiny dots jumped around on the screen, letting him know she was typing a response. He glanced back to find his boys watching him curiously—Duke with folded arms, and Garrett with raised eyebrows.

Soon a string of laughing emojis appeared, along with a GIF of a woman sinking to the floor with the word "Dead" flashing on the bottom.

He couldn't help it. He barked out a laugh, but quickly sobered when he once again looked back at his friends. His phone buzzed again and he looked down at the screen:

Okay, I have to pack. See you later?

Do you want to see me later?

A blank stare emoji popped up a second later.

Zara responded with, I'd love to see you now. But I know you're with the fellas.

Xavier thought of a good excuse to leave, but decided against it. Because if he left now, they would forever clown him. It would also be a strong indication that he was officially whipped.

Give me a few hours. I'll come put you to sleep.

Zara's response came a second later: Looking forward to it.

Yeah, I'm whipped. He slowly turned around to face his boys. "Don't say shit," he told them. "Where the hell is that waitress?"

On my way. Countdown to my head between your legs.

Zara almost dropped her phone when the text came through. "Oh, shoot."

Throughout the day, X had sent a series of inappropriate, yet tempting, and downright sinful messages, promising her a night of unfiltered pleasure. And she couldn't wait.

"Are you okay, Z-Ra?" Skye studied her. She felt her forehead. "I'm getting worried about you."

Flushed, Zara fanned herself. "I'm good. You know I hate being late."

She rushed around her room in the Westin Book Cadillac Detroit hotel, trying to get dressed for the party. She'd spent most of the day with the bridal party, starting with the early-morning appointment at Allina Smith's store. They'd sipped mimosas and laughed about past shenanigans. Zara had teared up when Rissa walked out in the beautiful dress she'd fallen in love with and screamed when her sister shouted "yes." Paityn left them to attend her brother's graduation party, but the rest of the group continued on to lunch, then mani-pedis. It was a welcome day of relaxation and good company. She'd enjoyed every minute with her favorite people.

"Christian won't leave without you." Skye picked up a throw pillow, hugging it to her chest. She plopped down on the bed.

Zara eyed her best friend out of the corner of her eye, noting the whimsical look in her eyes. "Are you okay, hun?"

"Yeah. I'm just so emotional lately." She fell back against the mattress. "I just cry at everything, even commercials."

"Aw, I'm sorry, Skye. Rissa says sex will cure that." She slipped on the white one-shoulder jumpsuit she'd chosen for the occasion.

"Rissa is crazy." Skye giggled. "She's been hanging around Paityn too much."

"She does have a point, though." She fiddled with the sleeve. "Can you zip me up?"

Skye stood and walked over to her. "This is gorgeous." She zipped her up. "X is going to eat you up tonight."

"What makes you think I'm seeing X tonight?"

Her friend peered at her in the mirror, a soft smile on her face. "I know he's in town. And he already left the graduation party for parts unknown."

"Duke loves to gossip." Zara shook her head in amusement. "He cracks me up."

"Z-Ra." Skye pinned her with a serious stare. "Spill it."

Zara twisted to see how she looked from the back. "I swear Spanx are woman's best invention."

"You don't need them."

"I do. Your cousin feeds me too much food."

"You're actually admitting that you're eating together?"

"You know we are." In the many weeks since they'd started this *thing* that she was scared to call a "relationship," they'd eaten together most nights—if they were both in town.

"So, what is this?"

With a heavy sigh, Zara lifted her shoulders. "I don't know. It is what it is. We have rules, and one of them is we're not going to label it."

"You made up that shit, didn't you?"

"Yes!" She put on her jewelry, silver bangles and teardrop earrings. Her hair was pinned to the side. "I had my reasons for it at the time."

When she'd made up the rules, she'd been short-sighted, consumed with thoughts of sex, ready to explore the physical attraction they shared. Since then, he'd turned her inside out, made her feel like she was on fire every day.

"And now?" Skye pressed.

"Well, I've officially lost my composure." Hell, she might have lost her mind, too, because when he was in the room, when he was near her, she had a hard time seeing anything but him. "And I love the way he makes me feel."

Beautiful, capable, intelligent, safe. He treated her like a priceless jewel. He made sure she was good all the time, held doors open for her, walked on the street side of the walk. Everything he did, she adored. Even the things she couldn't stand about him suddenly didn't matter. And she found herself wanting to breathe in his air, sunbathe in his light.

"Are you in love?"

"No." *Yes.* Zara loved him . . . in a way that was pure, all-consuming. It frightened her, and most days she didn't know what to do with the overwhelming feelings inside. She didn't plan on telling him, either. At least, not yet. *Maybe not ever.*

"Well, I love the thought of you two together."

"Okay, Skye."

"I'm serious. I've never seen him the way he is with you."

"I think you're confusing our long-term friendship with more."

"No, I'm very clear. And just so you know . . . I know my cousin. There is a label here."

Zara's lips parted and her heart skipped a beat and took off running. "What?"

"Your rule? 'No labels'? Yeah, no. That's not the reality." She squeezed her shoulders. "You better get going. I'll walk out with you. I told Duke I'd be there in an hour."

Zara and Skye walked to the hotel lobby. Although Skye yapped on about something or other, Zara couldn't hear a word she said because her brain was screaming, her heart was racing. The conversation in the room had rocked her world, tilted everything on its axis.

Skye looped an arm through hers, tugging her out of the way of a group of hotel guests. "Thanks," she muttered absently, glancing up just in time to see X walk into the hotel. *Damn.* She'd never seen anything as fly as X dressed up. The heather-gray suit he wore fit perfectly. His white shirt was unbuttoned at the collar.

She felt a sharp elbow to her back and lurched forward, right into X's chest. "Ow!"

He gripped her hips. "Whoa." Pulling back, he tilted his head. "You okay?"

She tossed back a glare to her bestie, who waved, before she answered him with a nod.

"You look good."

"Thanks," she whispered.

He ran a finger down her cheek, and she almost forgot where they were and nearly kissed him. Almost. Then she heard Skye's soft "aw" in the background and retreated back a step. Straightening, she said, "Ready to go?"

The car ride was relatively quiet. They'd talked about little things, his flight in that morning and the graduation party. She'd shared with him some details from her day with her family. She'd wanted to lean into him, smell him, feel his arms around her. But the driver had been a lot starstruck and had already asked too many questions about X, about them. She didn't want to take the chance that they'd end up in some article.

When they arrived at their destination, one of the hosts escorted them aboard the *Ovation*. The luxury boat was beautiful. Guests milled around the main deck, the dining salon, greeting one another with hugs and kisses. Christian had spared no expense. Every detail, no matter how small, was perfect. Round tables framed the room, while several cocktail tables were lined in the center, offering the choice to sit or stand. Each table was covered with charcoal-gray linens, clear charger plates with silver rims. White and Picasso calla lilies spilled from glass vases, and purple lighting illuminated the room.

The host led them up the stairs to the middeck lounge. The lounge area had several plush couches and high-top tables for mingling. An outdoor deck was on one end, and the bar was on the other. The *Ovation*'s top deck also featured a sundeck, which served as the dance floor, and another full-service bar. It was also where she found Christian, standing near the bar with AJ.

When he spotted her, he motioned for her to join them. "Zara." He pulled her into a tight hug and shook X's hand. "What's up, X? I'm glad you could make it."

She embraced AJ. "Happy Birthday, girlfriend."

"Thank you," AJ said. "You look gorgeous."

Zara giggled. "Thanks, girl. So do you. And you're glowing." The birthday girl was stunning in a purple halter-neck bandage dress.

"It's called spa day." They both laughed.

"You remember X, right?" While Christian had been around X several times, she couldn't remember if she'd ever introduced him to AJ.

"No, we haven't had a chance to meet yet. Nice to meet you, X." AJ gave him a quick hug. "Thanks for coming."

"Good to meet you, too," X told her. "Happy Birthday."

"Thank you. I can't believe my baby did all this."

"I know," Zara agreed. "You definitely outdid yourself with this one, Christian." She patted his shoulder. "I'm proud of you."

"I'd do anything for her." AJ beamed when Christian kissed her cheek.

X leaned in. "Can I get you something to drink?"

She glanced at him and scrunched her nose. "Hm, maybe I'll have a glass of white. Riesling?"

He nodded and excused himself.

AJ smirked. "Girl, he is even hotter up close."

"I'm standing right here," Christian mumbled.

"And you're looking as fine as ever." AJ pecked him on the lips. "I see one of my coworkers. Let me go greet them."

AJ hurried off, leaving Zara and Christian standing alone.

"I see you handled that situation with X. I have to admit, I'm surprised you brought him." He squeezed her shoulder. "I'm proud of you," he said, echoing her earlier words to him.

"Don't be. We're friends."

He coughed into his hand, while murmuring "Bullshit."

She pulled his hand away from his face. "Stop! I'm serious."

"Whatever you say. But he doesn't look at you like you're just his 'friend.'"

"Shut up." A loud horn blared and she felt the

boat move, setting off on a cruise on the Detroit River. She felt Christian's eyes on her, watching her. "Stop looking at me like that."

"I think it's cute you brought a date."

"Okay, yeah. We're not having this conversation. And I'm *not* on a date."

He chuckled. "So you say."

Seconds later, X appeared with a snifter filled with an amber liquid and her glass of wine; she wondered if he'd heard any part of her conversation with Christian. "Thanks," she said, taking a sip. And when she looked at Christian again, she didn't miss his smirk.

They chatted about the play-offs for a few minutes, until the dinner announcement was made. It included courses of Caesar salad, lobster mac-n-cheese, mashed potatoes, prime rib, and beer-battered chicken. Dessert was a chocolate-chunk concoction, served with a custom blend of coffee, which made Zara hum with glee.

After Christian toasted his wife, the party really started as people traipsed off to various parts of the yacht. The DJ turned up, beckoning people to the dance floor with the mix of R&B, hip-hop, and slow jams.

Zara and X ended up on the second-floor deck as the party raged on above them. They were getting closer to the dock, signaling the river cruise was nearing its end. The Ambassador Bridge loomed to her left, and the Renaissance Center stretched out above all the other buildings. The city had seen a resurgence of life in the last several years and she couldn't be happier. Each time she'd visited the D, she'd had an amazing time.

"The city really is beautiful."

"So this isn't a date, huh?" His voice was soft.

"No. Um, I . . . I guess . . ." Flustered, she tried to find the right words. "I mean . . ." She let out a heavy sigh. "You know what I mean."

"Do I?"

She frowned. "Are you upset?"

"No, I'm not. But I have a question. If I kissed you, would you push me away? Because I've been thinking about your mouth all night."

She exhaled slowly, willing the butterflies in her belly away. *Will he always make me feel so hot?* "We're in public."

"So? Answer the question."

She peeked around him to see if anyone could see them.

"Come here." His voice, low and dangerous, and 100 percent sexy. *Ooh wee.* His words . . . part command, part plea. Those two words were always her undoing, because she could never tell him no. She could never resist the call. He made her want to give him whatever he asked, whenever he wanted.

She inched forward a tiny step, not too close, but close enough to feel the warmth emanating from his hard body.

"Zara?" he whispered.

She gasped when he tugged her to him. Leaning in, he kissed her temple, her eyelids, her nose, and finally her lips. But it wasn't a long, deep kiss. It was so soft, so sweet, she thought she'd imagined it. He buried his face in her neck, kissing the sensitive spot below her ear.

Soft jazz, the night air, the view of the Detroit skyline, and X. All elements of an explosive cocktail—one that threatened to take her out, it was so intense. As they swayed to slow music, bodies pressed together, she couldn't stop thinking about how he felt against her, how his presence seemed to eclipse everything and everyone.

"You're so beautiful." His breath tickled her ear and she dug her nails into his shoulders. "So mine."

"There is a label here." Skye's words echoed in her head. "X, I—"

"I don't think I can stop," he whispered.

She didn't know what that meant, but her heart leapt in her throat. *Stop what? Stop talking? Stop dancing?*

"Don't make me." He kissed her jaw.

Zara held her breath, waited for him to make a move, to say something. *Anything.* But he didn't budge. He only stared, like he was seeing through her, like he already knew the answers to questions she'd been asking herself since this *thing* started.

As the silence stretched on, she fidgeted under his heated gaze. Eventually she couldn't take it anymore. "X, please."

"Please, what?" He brushed his lips over hers.

"Kiss me," she pleaded.

"Are you sure?"

She caressed his face, searched his dark eyes. "I'm su—"

His lips were on hers, his tongue was stroking hers, before she could finish her sentence. And she realized she didn't care about her rules, she didn't care who saw them, she didn't even care about blog posts and trending hashtags and public perception. She just wanted him.

I just love him.

Chapter 16

"Open your eyes, baby."

X peppered Zara with kisses, over her face, over her neck, down her chest. Lips, soft and firm, circled her nipple. His tongue circled the puckered bud. His teeth tugged gently until she moaned.

"I can't," she whispered.

They'd spent the night in her hotel room, wrapped around each other, making love until she'd collapsed with exhaustion. And that morning, he'd taken her from behind, his hands on her breasts and his fingers against her clit. The remnants of the orgasm she'd just had still coursed through her body.

"Zara." He hummed against her skin. "I can't get enough of you."

She ran her fingers through his hair. "I think you broke me."

The tremble of his laughter made her stomach flutter and her pulse race.

"I broke you?"

"Yes."

She finally opened her eyes and smiled. He kissed the tip of her nose.

"I have a plane to catch."

"You don't have to go now," he coaxed, brushing his mouth over her stomach. "You can stay a little longer with me."

"I have work to do, meetings to prepare for."

"Or we can just lay here and waste time together."

"I have to go."

"No, you don't."

He kissed her core before he licked her clit, and she arched off the bed.

"Oh, you're killing me."

"Good," he said, before continuing his ministrations, winding her up again until she released against his tongue.

It took a minute for her to catch her breath, but when she did, she laughed. "I don't know what you've done to me. I've never been sexed so much, so good."

He rolled over on his back, and she burrowed into him. "I'm here to serve," he answered.

"Why do you think that is?"

Cocking a brow, he asked, "Why what?"

She perched herself up on an elbow, searched his eyes. "Why now? We've known each other since we were kids. I've seen you with girlfriends, you've been around when I've had boyfriends. And we've never done this, never even close."

"I don't know. I guess I never thought about it before."

"How can you not? A year ago, we'd never even hugged each other full-on. Only side hugs."

His eyes flickered with amusement. "Stiff side hugs."

"Awkward, stiff side hugs."

The corner of his mouth lifted into a sexy smirk. "If I had known how good you feel against me, I might have tried it sooner."

She grinned. "It's probably a good thing you didn't." If she was having a hard time with them now, there was no way she'd been able to handle it then.

"Yeah, you're right." He peered up at the ceiling. "Maybe it was always there, but dormant, lying in wait for the right time."

Zara thought about it for a moment. "You think so?"

"It's possible." He shifted to his side, facing her. "Think about it. The things that we went through, the people we met, shaped us and made us who we are today." X brushed a piece of hair out of her eye. "And if we didn't have those experiences, we might not have reacted to each other the way we have."

"But what changed?"

"Nothing. Everything."

"In other words, you don't know."

He chuckled. "I know that I've hurt people. I've made stupid, impulsive decisions. I've made so many mistakes, but this isn't one of them."

"You're sure?"

"Honestly, I don't know why you're not."

She couldn't figure out why, either. He filled her empty spaces, the tiny parts of her that felt lonely or sad, the pieces that longed for a connection. He'd saved her time and again, made her feel safe when the world was scary and dark. But every time she opened her mouth to tell him what he meant to her, how she felt about him, what she needed from him, nothing came out. She couldn't say it.

Xavier picked up her hand and placed it against his chest, over his heart. "Feel that," he said.

The steady beat of his heart beneath her palm matched her own. "Yes."

"That's for you. I love you."

She gasped.

"I want you."

Words escaped her. But it felt like she should say something, because he'd just bared his soul to her. He'd taken the first step, every step. And she owed him bravery; she owed him the truth. He deserved to know that she loved him, that she could power the world with the love she felt for him. It was so real, so potent, she thanked God for the chance to feel it, to experience something so good.

"X, I—"

He placed a finger over her mouth. "Don't. Don't say it if you don't mean it. And don't tell me 'thank you,' because that's not . . . Just no. I know you're not ready, and I accept that. But the thought of walking around pretending that you're 'just my friend' is unacceptable. I can't do that anymore."

"I think . . ." Once again, she struggled to find the words she needed to say. Because the fear in the pit of her stomach took over and she said, "I think I can catch the later flight tonight."

He smiled and wrapped her in his arms. "That sounds like a perfect idea."

"I have to admit"—Phil Whitney leaned back in his chair, finally relaxed after being mostly tense throughout the pitch—"I'm not a man who's impressed often, but I have to hand it to you, Jax. The proposal is solid."

"Thanks, Phil." Jax grinned. "Rest assured, we have a top-notch team ready to jump in and make the transition smooth."

Xavier eyed Zara out of the corner of his eye. They'd spent the last several hours trying to convince the Whitney Agency to consider their offer. Presentations from several departments were spread out during the meeting: everything from the official announcement to the handling of current Whitney Agency clients to compensation for Phil's sons, should they choose to stay on, had been covered.

Phil glanced at Zara. "I must admit, having you in on this allayed some of my earlier reservations."

Nodding, Zara smiled back at the older man. "Thank you, Phil. It would be a pleasure to work with you again. I hope you take the time you need to review the proposal more in depth. The projections Xavier provided should also go a long way to easing your mind."

That's my baby.

Pride swelled in his chest as she continued to point out specific pages in the packet that would be going home with them. He'd always known she was good at what she did, but watching her in action . . .

She's exquisite, he thought.

For the most part, they'd run the meeting together, working the room like seasoned pros playing a complicated game against a longtime rival. His father had only interjected when asked direct questions, which was his way. And Xavier appreciated it, because they had it. Where he fell short, she soared. And if she threw the ball in his court, he caught it and made the slam dunk. In business, like in their budding personal relationship, they fit together.

When they returned from Detroit, he didn't bring up his confession of love to her again. It didn't make sense, but he knew she cared for him, even though she hadn't said it. And he was okay with that. Really. He'd told her not to say anything, and had basically given her permission to keep her feelings to herself. In hindsight, that wasn't the best move, because he didn't even give her a chance to tell him she loved him, too. But he knew her. She had to tell him on her own time, in her own way.

And not because he had said it first. He wouldn't want her to do that, anyway.

Her silence after his declaration of love didn't bother him as much as her commitment to keep their relationship private. The more time they spent together, the more it frustrated him that she wouldn't just be with him the way he knew she wanted to be with him. Nothing much had changed. She didn't flinch when he touched her at dinner or duck when he went to kiss her in her office—when the door was closed—or jump away if someone approached them while they were out, but they hadn't "gone public" yet. Their interactions had mostly remained behind closed doors. Which pretty much sucked. And he had no intentions of letting the status quo continue.

"The media tends to paint a narrative that is often misleading," Phil said. "Xavier, I want you to know that you've done impeccable work on this proposal and with the company."

"I appreciate that," X said. "I hope we will be able to work together on this new venture."

"I had some reservations, considering we were in negotiations with Ethan Porter."

No matter what he did, Xavier couldn't escape that punk. "I understand. Mind if I ask what happened with that deal?"

Phil explained the problems with the proposed contract from the beginning. Apparently, Ethan had demanded Whitney take a lower commission on everything, and had thrown a temper tantrum when they'd balked at his requirements.

"It's one thing to advocate for yourself, but to expect your agent to do the work and not get a reasonable commission is outrageous," Phil continued. "When we ended the talks, he stormed out and made some threats."

"What kind of threats?" Jax asked.

"He threatened to sue us for stringing him along, saying it was breach of promise."

Laughing, Jax shook his head. "That's definitely not how this works."

"I hear he's suing your agency." Phil leaned forward, resting his elbows against the table.

Jax glanced at Xavier, before turning to Phil. "I can assure you, the lawsuit will have no bearing on any agreement we reach today or in the next few weeks. My legal team is handling everything, and we have a top-notch team."

"I don't doubt that." Phil assessed X for a minute, then looked at Zara. "Porter also insinuated that he had plans to talk to you about representation."

Zara choked on the water she'd just sipped. Recovering quickly, she straightened her back. "Excuse me?"

"Yes, he mentioned setting up a meeting with you."

Xavier's stomach tightened. They'd spent most nights together, and she'd yet to bring up possibly taking Ethan on. *She wouldn't do it.* But as he watched her assure Phil that she hadn't heard from Ethan, he wondered if he'd misjudged her. After all, she'd already told him that she needed to be focused on work. Representing Ethan Porter would definitely be a boost to her career, open up new doors. Especially since Atlanta had competed in—and lost—their first NBA Finals since 1961. And the city residents loved him, even though he was a sorry-ass muthafucka.

A knock on the door interrupted the conversation. His father's assistant, Megan, poked her head into the room. "Mr. Starks, Ethan Porter is here to see you."

Jax nodded and stood. "I'm sorry, Phil. I have to handle this."

Phil shook his father's hand. "I'll be in touch, Jax."

"Round of golf?"

"Perfect."

Jax exited the conference room. Xavier and Zara spent a few more minutes answering questions posed to them by the Whitney family. They scheduled a follow-up meeting for a few weeks away and showed Phil and his sons to the door.

The Whitney crew members weren't out of the building for two minutes before Ethan emerged from an adjacent conference room. "Well, well, well," he said, "if it isn't the lovebirds."

Xavier cocked his head. "What are you doing here?"

"I have business with your father." Ethan shrugged. "Last time I checked, *he* ran this company. Not you."

Shaking his head, Xavier waved a dismissive hand.

Losing his temper again wouldn't bode well for him, and he wouldn't give Porter the satisfaction. He started to walk away, but Ethan couldn't let it go.

"That's right. Walk yo punk ass away. I don't have shit to say to you."

X opened, then closed, his fists several times, grinding his teeth so hard he'd probably have a headache later.

"It's just as well, fool," Ethan continued. "I need to be alone with Zara, anyway."

The man touched Zara on her shoulder. Obviously uncomfortable, she retreated backward. "Don't touch me," she warned.

"Keep your fuckin' hands to yourself," X bit out.

"Why? Worried another one of your women will choose me?"

And X snapped, advancing forward swiftly, intent on knocking some sense into the small forward, but Zara intercepted him.

"X, no!" She planted her hands against his chest, pleading with her eyes for him to think about his next move. "Not here, not now. You have too much to lose."

He swallowed rapidly. "If you think I'm going to stand here and let him disrespect you, you don't know me at all."

"I understand that, but I can handle myself. And you can't do this here, X."

Throwing his hands up, he backed up, away from

her. "Then handle it. You've made it very clear that you don't need me."

She stiffened visibly. And he felt like shit for hurting her. He moved toward her, but she raised her hand, signaling he needed to back up. Without another word, she turned to Ethan. "Mr. Porter, I don't know what you think you're doing. But this is a place of business. You will not approach me in a disrespectful manner, and if you put your hands on me again, I will kick your ass myself."

Ethan opened his mouth to respond, but Jax's voice boomed over the whispers in the immediate area. "Back to work, everyone. Porter, follow me."

Xavier glanced at his father, noted the disappointed look on his face, and walked away. He stormed into his office a few minutes later and paced the small space.

"What the hell was that?" Zara stalked in, shutting the door behind her.

He froze. "Zara, don't."

"Don't what?" she asked.

"Don't start with me on this."

"Or what? You're going to embarrass yourself again in front of all of our colleagues. Embarrass me?"

"Look, I don't care what people think of me."

"*Now.* You don't care *right now* because you're angry."

"No, I just don't care. I'm not some robot without emotions. He put his hands on you, and I'm not supposed to react?"

Her eyes softened. "X, that's not the point."

"What is the point? Oh, I know what it is. You're worried that people will figure it out, that you're more to me than a colleague. And you can't take it."

"That's not . . ." She sighed. "I wasn't worried about people knowing about us. I was worried about you. There is a pending lawsuit against you already. I didn't want you exacerbating the situation."

"What's going on, Zara? Is there any truth to what Phil said? Are you planning to take Porter on as a client?"

"No. That's the first I've ever heard of that." She inched closer to him until she was standing so close, he could feel the heat of her body through his shirt. "Baby, Ethan is nothing to me. But you are everything."

Xavier wanted to believe her, but he'd been burned before. And he loved Zara. If she did what Naomi did to him, he'd be wrecked, destroyed. Could he take the risk? Especially since they weren't even together "officially"?

He leaned down, resting his forehead against hers, and letting her pull him into her arms. They stood like that for a while, holding each other. When she pulled back, she smiled. "But we have something to celebrate."

Frowning, he asked, "What?"

"I'm ninety-nine-point-nine percent sure we're merging with the Whitney Agency. They ate that presentation up."

A smile tugged at his lips. She was right. The

follow-up meeting was just a formality at that point. By the end of July, contracts would be signed. "True." He held up his hand and she gave him a high five. "We definitely kicked ass today."

"Yes, we did. Can we just celebrate tonight? I don't want us to be angry or brooding. I want to have fun," Zara said.

"Together?"

"What kind of question is that? Of course."

"At home? Or are we still hiding?" Yes, he was being an ass, but he didn't care. He wanted all of her—at home, at work, at the bar, on a bench in the park.

"X, why are we still having this conversation?"

"Because I want to know."

Jennifer peeked into the office. "Zara?"

She dropped her head and let out a heavy sigh. "Yes?"

"Patrice called. Mr. Starks is looking for you."

"Thank you," Zara said. "I better . . ." She pointed toward the door.

"Do what you have to do?"

She hesitated for a brief minute, before she walked out of the office.

"Congrats, cousin!"

Xavier clinked bottles with Skye, Duke, and Garrett before taking a gulp of his beer.

Skye beamed. "I'm so excited for you." Once his cousin found out they'd nailed the meeting, she'd arranged an impromptu happy-hour excursion to the bar down the street from the office.

"Yeah, bruh," Garrett said. "That's dope."

"Yes, it is." Duke twisted his bottle. "But what isn't dope is how that clown Porter keeps showing up to shit."

"Right?" Skye agreed. "I know you were mad."

"Mad" wasn't the right word. "Livid," "incensed," "murderous"—all better adjectives. He snorted. "You have no idea," he grumbled.

Skye glanced at her watch. "Where is Zara? I texted her a while ago and told her where to meet us."

He shrugged. "I don't know. Dad called her into a meeting. Haven't heard from her since then." And, no, he didn't check his phone three times since he'd arrived.

Skye blew a piece of hair out of her face and slid onto a bar stool. "I need y'all to stop playin'. Everybody at this table knows you're together. What's the problem?"

"Hell yeah," Duke agreed. "We're not idiots."

Garrett nodded. "Exactly."

"My relationship with Zara is not up for discussion. Period. Now drop it."

His cousin shrugged. "Fine. But let the record show that we're not fooled." She grinned and waved toward the front door of the bar. "There she is."

Xavier turned and locked eyes with Zara. She offered a small smile before approaching them, never breaking contact.

She stopped right in front of him. Peeking

around him, she greeted their friends and turned her attention back to him. She moved even closer still, stepping between his legs. "Hey."

"Hi." He rested his hands on her thighs, waiting, longing for her to make the move. Then she did.

Zara gripped his jacket in her hands and pulled him to her, right into a kiss. And it wasn't a soft, chaste peck. It was hard, demanding, possessive. She was trying to tell him something; she was staking her claim. In public. His hands fisted in her hair, holding her to him, but letting her control the kiss.

Too soon, she broke the kiss. He wanted to pull her in for more, but Skye, Garrett, and Duke stood up and clapped, snapping him back into the present.

"It's about damn time, bruh," Duke murmured.

"Right!" Skye screeched. "Finally!"

Zara placed her hand against Xavier's chest, over his heart. "The excuses I made for how I feel when I'm with you don't make sense anymore. They never really did. Because I love you. Sometimes I think I've loved you since you saved me from that big-ass bee that day in the park."

Stunned, he felt his mouth fall open.

"Xavier, what we have matters. It matters so much. I was drowning before, but you gave me life, you make everything better. And if you're ready to jump, I'm jumping in with you."

He pulled out his wallet and dropped forty dollars on the tabletop. "Come here," he commanded.

She smiled, wrapping her arms around his shoulders. "I'm here. I'm with you."

He kissed her, ran his finger down her cheek. "Love you. Let's go home."

Arching a brow, she asked, "Your place or mine?"

"It doesn't matter."

Xavier hopped down, threw up the deuces, and walked out, hand in hand, with his girl.

Chapter 17

"I'm in love." Zara fell back on the four-poster bed of their beachfront villa.

Surrounded by tropical gardens, the Nanuku Auberge Resort, off Fiji's southern coast, was a serene slice of heaven. Zara had traveled to various tropical destinations, but this ranked in her top five. Lush views, white sand, beautiful blue water, made her want to explore.

Their luxury villa, situated on the east side of the resort, offered stunning views of the ocean, a separate living area, a private pool, and an outdoor shower, which she wanted to use in two-point-two minutes, soon as she could pry herself off the soft mattress. The soothing sound of waves filtering through the open windows made her feel at peace, calm.

Xavier tipped the Itokani butler. "With me or with the resort?" he asked jokingly.

Zara rested on her elbows and winked. "Both."

After over seventeen hours in the air, a five-hour layover in L.A., and the short direct transfer flight from the Nadi International Airport to the resort's private airstrip, Zara was exhausted. It was eight o'clock in the morning, and she could definitely use a nap. When they arrived, they received a warrior welcome. Their Itokani gave them a coconut and placed a *teki teki,* or flower, behind her ear. A wedding host greeted them and provided them with the details for the wedding weekend.

He crawled on the bed. Bracing himself above her, he placed a kiss to her chest and then rolled over on his back. "Want to sleep or eat?"

She sat up and climbed over him, straddling him. "Neither."

His hand swept up her legs, under her dress. Cupping her behind, he pushed his growing erection against her core. "I'm down for that, too." He sat upright, lifting her dress up and off. With his eyes on hers, he slipped a finger under the band of her panties and stroked her clit leisurely.

Her head fell back as warmth flooded her body. "Yes," she whispered when two fingers slipped inside her heat.

Xavier continued to ply her, to love her, whispering heated, dirty words in her ear as she rode his fingers, climbing higher and higher, until she exploded, climaxing long and hard.

He kissed her down, murmuring sweet declarations of love against her neck, her shoulders, her breasts. When the last tremble subsided, the urge to give him something, to pleasure him in the same way he'd pleasured her, took over.

Zara pushed him flat on his back, unbuckled his

belt, then slid it off. Sliding his pants and boxers off, she smirked at him before she gripped his erection and took him in her mouth. He gripped her head, pumping his hips slowly as she sucked his length. A low curse burst from his lips.

"Zara," he groaned.

She swallowed around his head, hummed around him.

Another curse pierced the air, and before she could protest, he tugged the back of her head gently, whispered her name. "Stop."

She released him and sat up. "Hm?"

"Come. Here." He beckoned her with his finger.

Zara climbed over him, deliberately slowly, and screamed with delight when he pulled her the rest of the way, sat her on his lap, and pushed himself inside her. Hard. Soon they set a pace, pushing and pulling, nipping and sucking, kissing.

"I'm so crazy about you," he said. "I'll always want this. I need you. You're mine."

She cried out as her orgasm sliced through her, pulling him with her, and leaving them both breathless and spent.

She cracked one eye open, then another, to find him watching her, a smirk on his lips. Covering her face, she groaned. "What?"

He smoothed a hand over her back. "Nothing. I just love looking at you. You're so beautiful."

Dropping her hand, she kissed him. She loved the way he looked at her; she loved the way he loved her. Hell, she loved everything about him, about this. She'd be devastated if she couldn't see him, hold him, just be with him.

"You know what?" he asked.

"No, what?"

"You never did tell me what you were talking about with Rissa that day in your office."

She tried to remember what he was talking about. Frowning, she asked, "What are you talking about?"

"Your first day in the office, you were on the phone with Rissa. I overheard you saying, 'There will be no X.' You stopped when you saw me."

Oh, God. The rowing-machine dream. Zara felt heat creep up her neck and she dropped her head on his shoulder. "No, don't ask me."

He tickled her sides, and she burst into a fit of giggles. "Come on, baby. Tell me."

She looked at him. "You're going to crack up."

"What is it?"

"I can't believe I'm even considering telling you."

"Just say it."

"Okay." She blew out a nervous breath. "I had a dream about you."

His eyes widened. "*Me?* We were just friends then."

"Friends with some strong-ass chemistry."

A sexy smirk crossed his lips. "True. After the holiday party, you haunted me."

Her mouth fell open. "I did?"

Nodding, he said, "Oh yes. But don't try and change the subject. I want to hear all about this dream."

"Fine. I won't give you details. I'll just tell you it

involved me, you, and a rowing machine—in the office gym."

He lifted a brow, the corner of his mouth quirked up. "Hm. A rowing machine, huh?"

"See! It's crazy, right?"

"I'm thinking of a way I can make this work."

She nudged him. "Stop."

"Seriously. Now I'm curious."

"I think it would be hard to work it, although we had no trouble in my dream." She remembered it was so hot, she'd awakened soaked in sweat and horny as hell. She had to jump in a cold shower.

"We might need one of those expensive rowers, one that wouldn't break," he mused.

"You're really talking about this?"

"Yeah. If you dreamed about it, I want to make it happen." He stared at her again and she wondered what he was thinking.

"X, you're staring. What's going on in that brain of yours?"

"Just thinking." He brushed his thumb over her chin, then kissed her softly.

Cradling his face in her hands, she ran her thumbs over his cheeks. "I love you. I love this."

"Love you, too."

Her stomach growled and she giggled. "Now feed me!"

Laughing, he said, "Okay. We'll order food, shower, and relax. In that order."

After breakfast and a short nap, X told her they were going on an adventure, to enjoy the beautiful weather. He'd rented an off-road vehicle and the two of them set off to explore the island. Fiji in July was absolutely gorgeous, not too hot, as it was the "winter" season in the country. After a nice scenic drive through the mountains, they took a short hike through the rain forest to a beautiful waterfall.

"Oh, my gosh, this is stunning." Zara pulled her shirt off and rubbed sunscreen over her arms. She'd decided to wear a two-piece suit so they could take a dip in the water.

During the tour, she'd been captivated by the scenery, the lush greens surrounding them, the blue sky above, the sound of the water in the distance. But up close, the falls were magnificent, nothing that she had ever imagined in her mind's eye.

Xavier set the picnic basket down. Their butler prepared a simple lunch for them to enjoy during the excursion. His gaze swept over her slowly and she shuddered.

"It is," he agreed.

"You're staring."

"I love the view," he said, shrugging.

"You're so corny, X."

Wrapping his arms around her waist, he said, "Only when I'm with you." He kissed her.

Pulling back, she pushed her shorts down and threw them at him, laughing when they hit him in the face. "I can't wait to get in the water." Turning to walk away, she stepped onto a rock and turned back to him. "Are you going to get in with me?" She stepped into the warm water, and kicked some his way.

He lifted his shirt off and followed her in. As

they waded farther into the water to the falls, she thought about all the movies she'd watched where the half-naked couple made out as water fell on their heads and wondered when she became the girl who wanted to experience that.

"I have to get away from you," she muttered.

"Why?" He caught up to her easily, tugging her to him. He brushed his lips over her ear. "I like you with me, not away from me."

"Your corniness is rubbing off on me."

"What's that supposed to mean?"

Pointing at the falls, she said, "I just imagined kissing you under the falls. I imagined getting my hair wet and making out with you, like in a sappy romance."

"Movie or book?" He laughed when she smacked his arm.

"Ha-ha. It's funny now, but when I'm begging you to kiss me in the rain, not even caring that my outfit is ruined, it won't be a laughing matter. I might get my boss card snatched away. And that just won't do. You're making me soft."

He flashed that sexy-ass smirk.

"And don't do that."

"Do what?" He shrugged.

She waved her finger in a circle in front of his face. "Look all hot and make me bothered."

"You're silly." He traced the band of her bikini bottom, then hooked a finger under it.

"I'm only half serious, though." She hugged his waist, stepping up on the tips of her toes and kissing his chin. "You can make out with me whenever and wherever you want."

He rested his arms on her shoulders and dipped his head down. "Like I told you this morning, I'm here to serve." The simple press of his lips to hers turned heated, intense in seconds. His lips. *Lord.* His tongue stroking hers. *Yes.* The kiss lit a fire in her, one that threatened to consume her from the inside out.

A chorus of laughter snapped them out of the moment and she glanced to her left, just in time to see a group of ladies entering the area. And not just any ladies. Naomi and her crew.

Oh, boy.

X dropped his head to her shoulder. "This is not what I had in mind."

"It's okay," she said. "We're fine."

The moment the bride squad spotted them, all of the giggles and girly shenanigans stopped. The five women surveyed them, some with suspicious glares and some with indifferent glances. And there was one who eyed them—well, X in particular— with a mixture of guilt, adoration, and desire.

"Hi, X," Naomi said, sauntering over their way. "You're here. I'm so glad."

X folded his arms over his chest. "Naomi."

Zara wanted to throw a blanket over him. *Because those amazing, firm pecs are mine.*

"Hi, Zara. Good to see you."

The saccharine-sweet tone in her voice and tight smile on her face let Zara know that her hello was less than genuine. The popular actress probably couldn't stand Zara. *Feeling's mutual.*

Naomi beamed at X. "I had no idea you'd be here. I thought your father would attend."

"Unfortunately, he couldn't make it," he said. "But he asked me to come in his place. As a client of Pure Talent, we want to congratulate you on your upcoming nuptials."

He deserves a high five for that. And Zara couldn't help but smile at the calm, professional way he'd handled himself. Especially since she knew he didn't want to attend the wedding or even talk to Naomi or Ethan while they were there.

The bride-to-be couldn't keep her eyes off of X, which was anything but professional. It seemed the future Mrs. Ethan Porter had no shame in her game the way she was ogling him, raking her gaze over X's washboard abs, strong arms, and even his . . .

Oh, hell no.

Zara didn't appreciate that shit. No, she hated it. Unable to take the slow perusal and awkward silence any longer, she stepped in front of X. "Congrats on the wedding, Naomi. Are you ready for Saturday?"

The ceremony was scheduled to take place in three days, at noon, which Zara liked because she and X would get it over with and spend the rest of the day together. She wanted to make the most of their time on the beautiful island.

Naomi answered her question, but Zara didn't

care enough to pay attention. So she nodded and smiled.

"I'm sure there's a lot to do to prepare for that walk down the aisle," Zara said. "But I'm glad you were able to get out with your girls." She vaguely heard X's low chuckle behind her, but didn't dare acknowledge it. "We'll let you enjoy your day." She turned to X. "Let's go."

"Bye, X," Naomi said.

"Yep" was his response, which was perfect in her opinion. He headed toward their picnic area, and Zara gave a half-ass wave and followed him.

"What was that?" He picked up his shirt and put it on.

Zara slipped on her shorts and shirt quickly. "I was just congratulating her on her big day."

"Is that what that was?" He reached out and buttoned her shorts.

She glanced over at Naomi and her squad, which were watching them with interest. Still. "Yes, what else would it be? I said 'congrats.'"

"Hm. I could've sworn it was something else. You sounded and looked a little jealous."

"You're imagining things, seeing stuff that's not there."

"Oh, I'm seeing a whole lot of things. And I'm so honored to make the list."

Frowning, she asked, "What list?"

X picked up the picnic basket. "The list of men you would fight for."

She shoved him playfully, cracking up. "Shut up. You just keep imagining that."

"I'm having flashbacks to homecoming."

Zara brushed past him, heading toward the entrance to the falls area. "You wish. Let's get the hell out of here."

"After the wedding, I thought we could spend the day on the beach." Xavier toweled off after a long shower. The wedding would start in a few hours, and he was looking forward to it being over.

They'd spent their days enjoying Fiji, kayaking on the Middle Navua River, scuba diving in the Beqa Lagoon, and sampling the local food. They'd even had lunch in a tree house. He was glad they'd decided to stay an extra night and would leave on Monday, instead of departing on Sunday, the morning after the wedding obligation.

"Maybe we can take the sunset cruise the butler told us about?" he suggested.

When Zara didn't respond, he called her name. *Where the hell is she?* He slipped on his boxers and went off in search of her. After checking the living area, he peeked outside. She wasn't on the patio. Stepping outside, he scanned the area.

He heard her before he saw her. She was talking to someone, and she didn't sound happy. Following her voice, he spotted her in front of the covered terrace. She didn't look happy, either, judging by her jerky movements and the deep-set frown on her face. She paced back and forth, switching between running her free hand through her hair and waving it in the air.

"I just don't know," she grumbled. "I know. But I . . ." She let out a heavy, frustrated sigh. Her shoulders fell. "Okay. I'll be in touch later. After I talk to him."

"Talk to who?"

She jumped, nearly dropping her phone. "X." She placed a hand over her heart. "You scared me." Speaking to the person on the line, she said, "Thanks. Bye." She ended the call and turned to him. The smile plastered on her face didn't reach her eyes, letting him know it was for his benefit.

"Is everything okay?"

Nodding, she said, "Yeah." She averted her gaze, fiddled with the belt of her robe.

"Are you sure? Because you look upset."

She met his gaze again. "Oh, I . . . Work stuff. You're done in the shower?"

"Yeah. Who was that on the phone?"

"Skye," she replied.

"What did she want?"

Bracing her hands on his shoulders, she kissed his cheek. "I told you. It's work."

She's lying. And not because she couldn't look him in the eye for long, but because he was close enough to hear a male voice on the other line. Jealousy was a foreign emotion for him. In the past, he just never cared enough about anyone to feel the emotion. But he heard him. And then she lied.

"I'm going to get dressed." She brushed past him and disappeared into the house.

The overwhelming urge to call Skye reared its ugly head and he grumbled a curse. Shit, when did

he turn into a person that felt the need to check up
on a woman. Even with Naomi, he never cared who
she was talking to. Not really. And it had come back
to bite him in the ass in a huge way. Zara wouldn't
do that to him. *Would she?* Not after he'd opened up
to her. Not after what they've shared.

But as he stood outside in the morning air, re-
playing the entire interaction in his head on a loop,
he realized he was more than jealous. He was hurt.
Because one of the things he appreciated about
Zara was that she'd never lied to him. *She'd* set the
rules—that they would tell each other the truth,
even if it hurt. And to have her tell that bald-faced
lie didn't sit well with him.

"X?" He turned to find Zara standing in the
doorway. "I'm sorry. That wasn't Skye. It was Jax."

He released a breath he didn't know he was
holding. "My father? What did he want?"

She stared at him, as if she wanted to tell him
something important. "It's work. Client stuff. I
don't know why I told you it was Skye. I shouldn't
have lied." She stepped outside on the patio and
inched closer to him. "I must have been thinking
about her because I have to call her to handle something for me."

He studied her face. He'd memorized everything about her, the lines of her face, the beauty
mark above her lip, her smell. And he knew when
she was happy, when she was sad, when she was
hurt. There was a sadness in her eyes, one that
made him want to hold her. At the same time, he

couldn't shake the feeling there was more going on. And that it had something to do with him.

He decided to drop the subject for now, though. Wrapping his arms around her waist, he kissed her forehead. "Okay. We're running behind. We should get dressed."

"I decided to wear the pink dress. Not so formal that I have to change. What do you want to do later?"

He repeated his ideas for the day as they walked back into the villa. "But we can decide after the wedding and reception. I don't want to stay long."

She agreed and they spent an hour or so getting dressed. A golf cart arrived to take them to the ceremony and they made small talk about the island. But he *knew* her. Something wasn't right.

The "happy" couple exchanged vows on the Club House lawn, overlooking the beach. Warrior drummers surrounded Naomi as she walked down the aisle. Perfect for the many pictures he was sure she wanted. Except she'd barely smiled, not when the guests stood upon her entrance, not when she looked at Ethan, not when they shared vows, not even when they were pronounced "man and wife." But he didn't miss the coy smile she'd sent *his* way during the recessional. And judging by Ethan's tight jaw and sour expression, the basketball player had noticed it, too.

He leaned over, brushed his lips against Zara's ear, not missing the way she'd tensed. He eyed her. "Are you okay?" He must have asked the question twenty times since he'd overheard her conversation earlier. And the more she said she was fine, the more he was convinced she was not.

"I'm good." She offered him a smile.

Standing, he reached for her hand. They followed the rest of the guests to the reception area. The brunch reception was intimate. Guests were seated around long tables, talking about everything from the resort itself to weather back in the States. Naomi had opted to have a private party later in the evening, so there was only a quick first dance and father-daughter dance.

Resting his elbows on the table, he peered over at Zara. "Ready to go?"

She'd barely touched her food, confirming that she wasn't *okay*.

She hooked her arm in his and leaned on his shoulder. "Yeah, I think we're done here."

Nodding, he asked, "Let's go for a walk?"

A whisper of a smile crept over her lips. "Sure."

His phone buzzed and he glanced at the screen. It was Skye. He glanced at Zara, who was looking at her own phone.

"I need to take this," he told Zara, before he stood and walked out of earshot. If Zara wasn't going to tell him what was going on, maybe his cousin would.

"What's up, Skye?" He ducked around a tree. "Everything okay?"

"Hey, X, I'm sorry to call you while you're on vacation. Not that seeing Naomi marry Ethan's ass is pleasurable. I'm sure it's like hell on earth."

He chuckled. "It's okay. What's up?"

She cleared her throat. "Sorry. I'm calling because there's a problem."

"Is it Zara?"

"No, isn't she there with you? Wouldn't you know if she had a problem?"

Apparently not. "What is it?"

"It's Hill."

Xavier straightened. "What happened?"

"There was a shooting at a nightclub, and—"

"He was shot?" Xavier swallowed past a lump in his throat. "Is he dead?"

"No, X. Let me finish. He wasn't shot, but he was with the person who fired the shot. They arrested him."

"Shit," he mumbled. "Did his mother call you?"

"I just got off the phone with her. She's so distraught. I told her you were out of the country, but that I would let you know what was going on."

Skye told him an abbreviated version of the events. "I called the director of the movie he's shooting, let him know that Hill won't be on set for a few days."

"I bet he's not happy about that."

"He's fine. I agreed to go out on a date with him."

Shaking his head, he said, "Thanks, I guess."

"Don't worry. I'm doing everything I can. But I figured you'd want to know."

"Thank you. I appreciate the call. Keep me posted. When I get back, I'll take over."

Ending the call, he sent a quick e-mail to Jennifer, asking her to set up a meeting with Hill's parents for late Tuesday afternoon. "Time to get the hell out of here," he mumbled.

He walked back to the reception area and froze. Off to the side, Zara was talking to Ethan. *What the hell?* As he approached them, he noted the hushed tones, the body language. They were standing entirely too close, huddled together like they'd talked like that many times.

"Don't you think you need to tell him?" Ethan asked.

Dread in the pit of his stomach, rage coiling through his veins and taking over him, made him want to hem Ethan up and throw him somewhere. Preferably off a cliff, but he would settle for the pool. Because the newly married player didn't need to say X's name for him to know they were talking about him.

"I'll handle my business," Zara hissed. "Make sure you handle yours, Ethan."

Ethan spotted him first, but didn't say anything to him. "I will, Zara. I promise you." He eyed X again, smiled, and said, "I look forward to working with you, as your client, as your partner. I know we'll do big things together."

Chapter 18

The Lord must have really been working on him, because he hadn't pummeled Ethan in the middle of the reception—he hadn't even confronted them. He'd only interrupted the conversation with two words: "Let's go."

Zara hadn't argued. Instead, she simply followed him out of the reception. The entire ride back to the villa was filled with tense silence as he waited for privacy to say what he needed to say. When the cart stopped in front of their villa, he slipped out, tipping the driver. Now they were alone. Now he could unleash the torrent of emotions that had threatened to choke him from the moment he'd seen them.

"X?" she called to him after they entered the villa. "Can we talk about this?"

"What the hell was that?" he roared, slicing a hand in the air.

"Please calm down."

"Don't!" he warned. "Don't talk to me like I'm the problem." He pointed at his chest. "Respect me enough to tell me the truth."

"If you'd just let me explain," she pleaded, "I can tell you what that conversation was about."

"Fine. Explain to me why you agreed to represent that fool. Explain to me why you lied to me."

"I didn't lie to you, X."

He snorted. "Oh, you lied. When you acted like you knew nothing of those rumors Phil told us about, when you told me you weren't going to rep Porter. And you lied this morning, first by telling me you were talking to Skye, and then every time I asked you if you were okay."

"I told you it wasn't Skye. I apologized for lying about it then."

"But you still lied. You've *been* lying."

She dropped her head, took a deep breath. "I'm sorry."

"I don't accept that 'sorry.' Because *you* set the rules. Truth, no matter how much it hurt. Remember that?"

"Xavier, I . . ." She gripped her throat and her eyes filled with tears.

Xavier hated himself for making her cry because he knew she hated it. He'd hurt her, but he couldn't stop. Because he was hurt, too. And he needed it to stop. "Were you really talking to my father? Or to Ethan? You're pretty cozy with him. How long have you been working together?"

"Today," she answered. "I agreed to represent him today."

He peered up at the ceiling. "Why?"

"That's why Jax called me. He asked me to do it."

Xavier took a reflexive step back. And the hits kept coming. Now he had to contend with his father, pulling strings, playing chess with his life.

"Your father said he needed a favor," she continued.

"And you couldn't say no?"

She smacked her palms against her thighs. "What was I supposed to do, X?"

"Tell him no. It's not that hard, Zara." He tapped his chin. "Unless you didn't want to. Maybe you realized that this would be huge for your career, maybe you figured it would seal the deal on the department head."

"I don't care about that damn job. You can have it."

He let out a humorless laugh. "Whatever. You say you don't care, but you fell in line."

She gasped. "Stop."

"You did what my father asked. Never mind what I think, or how I feel." X paced the floor like a caged animal that needed to escape. "He freakin' sued me!" he shouted. "And you're going to help him succeed, help his career. You're giving him a piece of you!"

"Stop yelling at me!" she blared.

Silence stretched on, both of them glaring at each other now. A soft breeze floated through the room, through open windows. It felt surreal, to be arguing with her in paradise. Irony at its best.

"X, just stop. I know you're hurt, and I'm sorry

for hurting you. Because I hate seeing you like this, and I hate being the cause of it."

He closed his eyes, allowing his mind a brief glimpse of the past, allowing himself to be transported back in time. Memories of them together, of long walks, quiet games of checkers, shared joys and deep sorrows. There were no explicit promises to never hurt each other, but there *was* a history of respect and unwavering support that had assured him of her loyalty.

That's why this wrecked him, why it felt like she'd cut him off at the knees. To some, it might not feel big, but to him . . . she'd basically chosen her job over him. She'd chosen the corporate ladder over their relationship.

"I never wanted you to find out like this," she said. "I was going to tell you after the reception."

"Of all people, you should understand why I'm angry. You should get it."

"I do, X. I get it. But I'm doing this for you."

He blinked. "What the hell does that even mean?"

"I can't tell you. I told your father I'd wait until he could talk to you."

"Always the professional," he murmured. He wanted her to catch the sarcasm in his tone. He wanted her to feel it in her bones. "You'd rather destroy my trust in you than ruin your reputation with my father."

She reeled back as if he'd slapped her. "That's not true."

"How am I supposed to deal with this? What do

you suggest I do? Hell, what would *you* do in my position?"

She opened her mouth to respond, but he held up a hand.

"Don't answer that. Because I already know what you'd do. No need to add more lies to this argument."

"Okay. Well, I guess now I have some answers to my own questions." She sucked in a deep breath, then let it out. And when she met his gaze again, her eyes were hard. The emotion swimming in them only seconds earlier was gone. "Obviously, you don't trust me. You're incapable of listening or even giving me the benefit of the doubt. You're so angry I can't recognize you right now."

"Don't turn this around on me."

"I'm not. I messed up. But I'm not going to stand here and keep begging you to listen, to hear me. To forgive me. I made one mistake. *One*." She held up a finger. "Out of a lifetime of friendship. I didn't tell you right away about something that I knew would upset you. I was wrong. But you're already putting me in the same category as Naomi. You're already lumping me in with all the people who've hurt you and lied to you before. You're forgetting everything that we've been to each other."

"I spent months in a relationship, being lied to on a daily basis."

"And now you can't trust me at all. So, as far as I'm concerned, there's no point in going any further. I'm done."

His temper flared. "*You're* done? Oh, okay. Is this

the part when you tell me you knew this wouldn't work out between us? Because I'm angry when I have a right to be?"

"No, this is the time when I tell you I'm going to get some work done."

He needed a break from her. He needed time to process things, to let his anger simmer down. "I'll take the couch tonight."

"That's exactly what I was thinking." She walked into the bathroom and turned to him. "At least we still agree on some things." Then she slammed the door.

The rest of the day was spent on opposite sides of the villa. He'd heard her, walking on the ceramic floors, talking on the phone to someone. Sometime after seven o'clock, she left without a word.

When she didn't come back for hours, he was tempted to go find her. She could be anywhere, all alone on the island. He should've been with her, but his pride wouldn't let him. But concern for her had won out, and just as he was getting ready to go look for her, she came back. And ignored him for a few more hours until he just went to bed.

Sleep evaded X that night. He'd tossed and turned, replayed every scenario in his head, until he couldn't take it anymore. He needed air, so around four o'clock in the morning, he'd dressed and went out for a run.

As he jogged along the beach, trying to outrun his emotions, he realized he wasn't angry anymore. Not really. But he still had valid concerns about their relationship. Everything was different. She wasn't just Zara. She was *his* Zara. There was a whole subset of emotions at play that hadn't been there six months ago.

They'd wasted an entire day because he'd overreacted. And he'd lashed out at her because he was hurt. And he never wanted to hurt her. He never wanted to be the reason she dropped a tear. She was right. She'd made a mistake, and he'd drilled it into her head until she shut down. It was no wonder she didn't want to talk to him. He was an idiot. And he would make it right. He had to make it up to her. Because spending the night near her, but not with her, was as unacceptable to him as just being her friend.

Decision made, he turned around and ran back to the villa. He opened the door, called out for her. No answer. She wasn't the type to sleep late, so he checked outside by the pool first. No Zara. He knocked on the bedroom door.

"Zara, we need to talk. Baby, open the door."

Sliding the barn door open, he peeked in, expecting to find her perched up on pillows, typing on her tablet, or asleep. But she wasn't there. His stomach tightened as he poked his head in the bathroom to find it empty. He walked in the closet. *Damn.* All of her clothes and her suitcases were gone. She had left him.

Zara opened her front door. "Mom, you came." Regine held out her arms and Zara walked right into her embrace. And cried.

Half an hour later, Zara was still crying, but at least they weren't standing in the doorway anymore. Now they were in her bedroom. Her mother was sitting next to her, resting her back against the headboard, a box of Kleenex in one hand, and Zara lying on her lap.

"Babe, it's going to be okay." Regine ran soft fingers through her hair, like she'd done so many times before. It was one of Zara's favorite things as a child, so soothing.

"What if it's not?" she said, sobbing. "Look at me, I'm a mess."

"Yes, you are," Regine agreed. "But you're allowed one hot-mess day."

Zara laughed. "Thank you."

"I promise I won't tell your sister."

"Thanks for that, too."

When Zara decided to take an earlier flight—their original Sunday flight—she'd called her mother and told her she would be in L.A. the next morning. Instead of boarding the connecting flight to Atlanta, she went home.

In hindsight, it wasn't the most mature thing to do—leaving the way she had, or even wasting an entire day in Fiji on a stupid argument. She'd left without a word, a good-bye, a letter, or a short text. And every time she imagined the look on X's face when he found out she was gone, she sobbed even harder. They both had overreacted, whether it was out of fear, hurt, or just plain stubbornness. Too bad she didn't realize that until she was somewhere over the Pacific Ocean, at thirty-five thousand feet in the air.

"I messed up, Mama." She wiped her nose with a tattered piece of tissue. "I should have talked to him, but I just couldn't. I was so angry. Hurt."

She'd told her mother everything in the form of a long run-on sentence, while they were standing at the door, before her mother insisted they go inside and "stop giving the neighbors a show."

"He'll probably never forgive me."

"I doubt that, babe. He loves you. When people are in love, they tend to overlook a lot of things."

Finally Zara sat up and glanced at her mom. "But what if being together isn't the right thing? Look at us. We could barely stand to be in the same room."

Regine waved a dismissive hand at her. "Girl, that's just how it is." She shifted, turning to face her. "I realize I've done you a disservice."

Zara's eyes widened.

"I don't think I've set a good example for you and your sister."

"Don't say that, Mom. You did the best you could do."

Her mother shook her head. "No, I didn't." Placing her hand on top of Zara's, she said, "My relationship with your father failed spectacularly. For many years, we couldn't be in the same room. We couldn't talk because he'd hurt me so much. And I mourned the life I could have had, if I hadn't given up everything to be with him."

Zara had often thought about her mother's choice to leave her career behind to marry her dad and raise them. And every time she did, she was struck by the sacrifice her mother had made. She could never imagine leaving her job for a man.

When she'd envisioned a romantic relationship or marriage in the past, she'd always envisioned a mystery man who was okay with her drive. Her ideal man would even encourage it, because he would be strong enough *not* to let her success make him feel like less than a man. Now she just envisioned X. Because she was desperately and dangerously in love with him. And she'd be devastated if she couldn't see him, hold him.

"But maybe I just showed you the bad side of the divorce. I didn't let you see the other side of the pain. Joy. After everything was said and done, all the court dates, all the years of watching him traipse around the world with the newest flavor of the month, I realized that I don't have any regrets."

Zara's chin trembled as she watched her mother's wistful look. "You don't?" she asked.

Regine gripped Zara's chin, tilting her face to look into her eyes. "Not a single one."

"Why? He hurt you. He left *us*."

"So? That doesn't negate the good years we had. It doesn't change the fact that I have two beautiful, successful daughters who are carving their own way in the world. I had an amazing son. I can't regret that, babe."

Zara lowered her gaze, ran her fingernail over the edge of the blanket. "I'm scared. I hate feeling vulnerable."

"That's real. Remember, I told you arguments

were part of this. Fear is as well. Vulnerability is strength, Zara. It's uncomfortable, yes. But it's an authentic emotion. Embrace it."

She'd always associated vulnerability with being weak. It would be work to reset that definition in her mind.

"I'm not telling you that you won't lose sometimes. Pleasure and pain are two sides of the same coin. Can't have one without the other. And you wouldn't want to, because the pain makes you work harder, hold on tighter, love with everything in you." Her mother brushed tears Zara hadn't realized were falling from her cheeks. "Opening yourself up is always a risk. But doing so can provide your greatest victories."

Heartbreak was part of love. She'd felt it before, and it nearly ruined her life. But that was nothing compared to what she felt for X. He filled all of her dots, crossed every one of her *i*'s, almost like God molded him just for her. And she would be a fool to let that slip through her fingers. Still . . .

"Zara, it's okay to love him."

A sob burst through Zara's lips.

"It's okay, babe." Regine embraced Zara again, smoothing her hands over her daughter's back, comforting her in a way only she could.

"I love him so much, Mom."

"I'm not surprised." Regine chuckled when Zara pulled back, brows raised. "I always knew there was something there."

Zara bit her bottom lip. "How?"

"Girl, from the first day you met him, I told Ana he was courting you."

She tried to remember that first day and laughed because she recalled the way X had held the door open for her and shared his Gummi Bears with her. "Mom, you're funny."

"Of course, you were so young, it morphed into an enduring, lasting friendship. One that has lasted through time and distance. That's something right there."

"True."

"Now you better stop all this crying, pull those big-girl panties up, and take your ass home. Work this out. Trust me, it will be worth it."

Zara took a deep breath. She knew what she had to do. But first, she needed to fix this Ethan mess. She grabbed her phone and dialed a familiar number.

"Zara, hi," Larry said. "I've been calling you. I'm glad you finally called me back."

"Hi, Larry." She made sure to keep her voice calm. "I won't keep you long."

"I've missed you. Are you in town? Can we talk?"

"The only thing I want to talk to you about is what you're going to do for me."

Silence.

"Larry, you know what you did. *I* know what you did. Up until now, I thought I would just move on with my life, would let it go. But you owe me. And I'm calling to collect."

Chapter 19

"What the hell is this?" Skye snapped the piece of paper in her hand and shoved it in X's face. It was a screenshot of the latest Page Six headline, which included a pic of him emerging from the airport, looking like shit. It read: XAVIER STARKS DEVASTATED AFTER ZARA REID WALKS OUT. WITH ETHAN PORTER.

Right under it, there was a subtitle: NAOMI WANTS X BACK.

Growling a low curse, he turned and stumbled back over to the couch, where he'd been since he walked in the door from the airport.

"Are you drunk?" Skye asked.

"Not yet." He plopped down on the couch and finished off his second beer of the morning.

"I need to be a damn police officer so I can arrest every damn person guilty of driving while stupid," Duke said, walking into X's condo. "Sick of these nondriving assholes."

His best friend scanned the living room, which was in disarray because X didn't care enough to pick his shit up off the floor after he'd trashed the living room in anger. Throw pillows were scattered throughout, broken glass littered the floor, and his suitcase remained where he'd left it—right in front of the door.

Duke's gaze locked on X. "I would tell you to get your shit together, but looking at you now, I just can't bring myself to throw salt in that open wound."

"What do you want?" X yelled.

"I have a better question." Skye stepped over Zara's coffee mug, the one he'd bought her a couple weeks ago—the one that had *I'm allergic to stupidity* printed on it—the one that he'd hurled to the wall when he realized she wasn't in Atlanta. His cousin stopped in front of him, narrowing her eyes at him. "What did you do? Why is Zara in L.A.? And "—she scrunched her nose as if she'd tasted something disgusting—"why are you wearing the same clothes from this picture?" She held up the paper.

"I didn't do anything. Except be an asshole. I guess she's minding her own business. And I can wear whatever the hell I want, because *I'm* at home. You don't have to be here."

"X, when is the last time you took a shower?"

He opened a third beer, took a large gulp, and burped.

Duke laughed. "Man, you're dumb as hell for that." His friend grabbed one of the beers from the six-pack sitting on the coffee table and popped the cap.

"Duke!" Skye folded her arms and glared at them both. "You're supposed to be helping, not encouraging him."

"Shit, I'm thirsty." Duke shrugged. "I'm not used to being up at the butt crack of dawn, and I'm definitely not used to performing interventions on my boy."

"X, you look like shit. And you're crusty."

"I just took a shower. Monday." As in Monday morning, before he boarded the plane to come home—alone. It was now Wednesday morning.

She sighed, picked up a shirt and a pair of pants off the floor, and then set it on a chair. "X, you can't do this. You have clients, you have responsibilities."

He closed his eyes, rested his head against the back of the couch, and kicked his feet up on the table, inadvertently knocking an empty beer bottle over. "I'm on vacation."

"You're hiding. Which is not like you, cousin. Come on, what happened?"

After Zara left him in Fiji, he'd dived into a bottle of liquor and hadn't come out. "She left me." And every hour since she'd been away from him felt like hell on earth. He couldn't breathe, he couldn't think.

Skye's gaze softened. "X, why?"

Because I'm an asshole. "Don't you already know?" He would bet money that Skye had already talked to Zara. There wasn't much they didn't know about each other.

She sat on the edge of the sofa, right next to him. "We talked, but not for long."

His chest tightened. She probably wouldn't have responded to him, either, if he'd called her. But he didn't. Not because he was still angry, but because he wasn't. And that made the entire argument stupid. He'd overreacted and she'd bailed.

"Rissa told me that she didn't say much to her, either," Skye said.

He swallowed hard.

"It couldn't have been *that* bad, X."

Closing his eyes, he said, "Skye, just let it go. Things didn't work out."

"But why? You two were happy, in love. In public. How did you go to one of the most beautiful places in the world and break up? This isn't right, you—"

"She left me!" he roared.

Skye froze, turning to him. "X, tell me what happened."

"Go somewhere, Skye," Duke said.

Sighing, Skye walked away, picking up trash and muttering Tagalog curses under her breath.

"Dad asked her to represent Ethan and she told him yes," Xavier said. "I saw them talking at the wedding and I blew up, accused her of keeping shit from me and choosing her career over me."

With a heavy sigh, Duke set his beer down on the end table. "Skye told me about Ethan."

X looked at him. "And you didn't say anything?"

Shrugging, he said, "Bruh, you were on the other side of the world. How was I supposed to know you were going to act like a damn fool? Plus, this just happened. She wasn't keeping this from you for months. It was, like, a day."

"She wouldn't even tell me why she did it. Just

that Dad asked her and she agreed." But he'd watched her demeanor throughout the day. Hell, he'd even seen how distraught she seemed during the call. She didn't want to do it. He knew that now, but he'd let his own issues cloud his judgment.

"The lawsuit," Duke said. "Ethan agreed to drop the lawsuit *if* Zara agreed to take him on as a client."

X clenched his teeth together, irritated with his dad for once again considering Pure Talent over him. "I said some crazy shit to her, man. She'll never forgive me."

"I doubt that, bruh."

"You didn't see her." Xavier shut his eyes, willing the image away. "And you know how I get when I'm pissed."

"I do. But Zara does, too. She knows who you are, and she still took a chance on yo ass. Go figure. God is a miracle worker."

X chuckled. "Shut up, man."

"Hey, I call it like I see it."

"I can't even be mad at her anymore because it seems so small now. I ruined everything because I'm an asshole. I lashed out." *I made her cry.* "And she walked away. Without even telling me."

Skye appeared in front of him, a broom in hand.

"She changed her flight and left while I was on a run." He'd rushed to the airport, but it was too late. The plane had taken off fifteen minutes before he got there.

"Oh, X." Skye set the broom down and sat down on the armrest. "I'm sorry."

He finished the story, telling them mostly everything. He left out the part about her telling him she was done. Because if he said it out loud, it might be true. She might have meant it, and the thought of life without Zara was too much for him right then. Every time he'd closed his eyes, her voice, the way her chin trembled slightly, the pained expression in her eyes, haunted him.

"Is she okay?" X asked. "Is she moving back to L.A.?"

"Not that I know of," Skye said. "But—"

"You wouldn't put it past her."

She offered him another sad smile and nodded her head. "I know her."

He knew her, too. Which was why he should have believed her, he should have given her the benefit of the doubt. But he'd let his anger get the best of him, he'd let his past destroy his present.

"You were wrong. But you can't just give up!" Skye shot to her feet.

"Okay, real talk, bruh." Duke turned off the TV. "I'm just going to tell you what I think you should do. And after this, I'm going to need something stronger than beer." Duke took a long gulp and slammed the bottle down on the table. "All this talk about feelings is getting on my nerves. But, anyway, I've been around both of you for years. I've watched you over the past few months. And what I see is a chance, for you and her to be happy. I wouldn't be your brother if I didn't tell you to get your head out of your ass. Don't let this be the end of the story."

"Exactly," Skye agreed, tugging his arm. "Get your ass up. *Now.*"

X stood reluctantly. "What am I supposed to do?"

"You're going to get your rank butt in the shower while I finish cleaning up around here. Then you're going to see Hill. He needs to see you."

The reminder that he'd let another person down made him feel worse. Instead of going straight to him when his plane landed, he'd wallowed in filth and beer.

"And I'm going to get you on a flight to L.A. today," Skye continued.

He stared at her.

She shoved him. "Go."

"You heard her." Duke stood and snatched the broom from Skye.

She smacked him. "Move. I can handle a broom."

"Go do something else, Skye. I'll sweep."

"You're going to stop telling me what to do!" Skye shouted. "You get on my nerves."

X shook his head and jogged up the stairs as Skye and Duke argued about who would sweep and who would wash the dishes.

Two hours later, he was sitting across from Hill. The young man had been released from jail Monday morning, and had been laying low at his parents' house.

The normally talkative Hill had only said two words since he'd arrived: "Go away."

Xavier couldn't help but laugh, because that was something he would've said when he was seventeen. Only he would have added a few expletives in there, made it more colorful.

"What happened?" Xavier asked. Hill shot him a look, then turned his attention back to the television. "You know you can tell me."

"Why should I?" Hill crossed his arms.

"Because I'm here for you. I'm going to do my best to make sure your career survives this."

"I don't care about my career!" Hill shouted.

The conversation was eerily similar to one he'd had with his dad when X was seventeen. The only difference was, when he'd told his father he didn't care, X actually meant it. But X knew Hill loved being an actor. The young star loved the spotlight, sure, but Hill loved the craft. He spent hours studying it, attending classes, and working to improve.

"I know you don't. Today. But tomorrow you will."

Hill's eyes filled with tears. "No one sees me. They only see what I can give them. It's all about my money, my fame."

The way Hill's life paralleled his own was striking. Which was why he'd agreed to represent him in the first place. He didn't want the young guy to make the same mistakes he did. More important, he didn't want him to feel alone.

"I see you," X said.

"You don't. You're here to save my career, because I make you money. That's it. That's all."

X knew how hard being in the spotlight really

was. It could be fun and exciting, but it could also be lonely and dark. But he'd had friends and family that supported him. *I had her.*

"I don't have anybody, no friends or siblings."

"Man, that's not true. Having parents that love you and support your decisions puts you ahead of most."

"That's why I was at the club." Hill wiped angry tears from his face. "Someone from my high school told me about the party and I used my name to get us all in. I had no idea he had a gun, until he pulled it out and shot at some girl."

Seeing him cry twisted something in his gut. As much as they were alike, they were different. Hill wasn't like other young stars. He didn't act like X did at that age. He wasn't a fighter; he didn't walk around with a chip on his shoulder; he didn't live to bed girls or go to VIP events. He was just a geeky kid, who liked comic books, video games, and technology. He didn't deserve what happened to him.

"Okay. It's okay, Hill. Your lawyers are handling it."

"You talked to them?"

On his way over, he'd talked to Hill's parents about the case. According to the court documents, they booked him on aiding and abetting, but the lawyers thought they could have the case thrown out due to the fact that Hill is the one who called the cops on the shooter. Xavier was pretty sure the arrest was a political move. Arrest one of the top actors in the country, come off as hard on crime—no matter who the criminal is.

"I talked to your mom and dad," X told him.

"Am I going to prison?"

He shook his head. "No. Not if I can help it."

Hill nodded his head. "Maybe you can come to court with me?"

X clasped Hill's shoulders. "I'll be there."

"Thank you, X. I appreciate it, man."

"No problem. And Hill? I don't care about the money. I'm here because I care about you. You said you don't have any friends, but you have me. I'm going to make sure you get through this, and I'm not going to let you buckle under the pressure."

"Thanks, man. Wanna play *Madden*?"

Xavier stood. "Not today, man. But let's set something up for next week." He walked to the front door. "Call me if you need anything. I'm going to L.A. for a few days, but I'll make myself available if you need me."

Hill gave him a quick hug. "You're like my big brother. I'm glad you're on my team."

"And when you get to be my age, pay it forward."

"I will."

Xavier said his good-byes to Hill and his parents and headed to his next destination. If everything worked out, he'd be in Zara's arms by dinner.

Zara entered Jax's office after Megan gave her the go-ahead. The older man was sitting at his desk, scribbling something on a piece of paper.

"Hi, Jax."

He glanced up and smiled. "Zara, give me a second." Once he finished what he was doing, he set the pen down and stood, walking around the desk. He motioned to the empty seat. "Sit."

She did as she was told, and he sat on the edge of his desk in front of her. "What can I do for you? How was Fiji?"

"It was good. Until it wasn't."

Jax tilted his head to the side, assessing her. "Care to elaborate?"

"Xavier found out about Ethan. He's not happy."

"Okay, I knew he wouldn't be. I'll deal with it."

She shot him an incredulous glare before she could even think about it. "You'll 'deal with it'? I think it's a little late for that." She stood, trekked to the other side of the room. She needed to steel herself for what was coming next. "Over the years, I've watched you. I've modeled my career after yours. I made sure I put on my game face before I walked into meetings, negotiated with confidence, and I never let a client see me defeated or even unsure. All things you taught me." Her voice cracked, and she paused.

Jax didn't only teach her about work, he'd taught her that life was basically a game of basketball. He told her that in order to win the game, she needed to maintain self-control, keep her eyes on the ball, show initiative by setting up her play and not rushing a decision to shoot, and bounce back even after missing the shot. And he'd told her to remember the game couldn't be played alone, she needed a squad.

"You're like a father to me," she admitted. "You've been there for me when my own father was too selfish to show up." She blew out a deep breath. "But you were wrong."

Jax's eyes flashed to hers.

"You put me in a bad position when you asked me to represent Ethan."

"Zara, you could have told me no. You don't have to represent Ethan if you don't agree with me. I've always told you that no one can make you do anything you don't want to do."

That was true. Another lesson he'd given to her after he found out a boy in the neighborhood had tricked her into playing hide-and–go-get-it. Of course, her father wasn't around when she'd kicked Trevor Coleman in the nuts and ran for her life, straight to X's house. Only X wasn't there. Jax was. And he'd walked right to Trevor's house and threatened both him and his parents with bodily harm if he ever put his hands on her again.

"Yeah, I know." Her voice was a whisper. Shame rolled through her in waves. Because she knew better. She knew what taking Ethan on would do to X. But she'd done it, anyway. Partly because Jax had asked her, but mostly for X. "You knew I would, though. You knew I'd say yes when you presented the option as a way to make the lawsuit go away."

"Zara, my son needs to know that sometimes in life you have to work with people you don't want to work with, for the greater good."

"Yes, that is important. But not Ethan. He shouldn't have to work with a man who has made it a full-time job to make a fool of X. The man cheated with Naomi while she was with X, proposed to her, knowing they were still together. Ethan goaded him time and again. He delighted in it, gloated every time X lost his temper. When X hit him, it gave Ethan the leverage to manipulate him."

"Perhaps, but maybe it's time for Xavier to stop giving people ammunition against him."

"With all due respect, X isn't the same person he was in his teens. You know that. You even told me as much. Isn't that why you're grooming him to take over? He's committed to being a better person, but he's still human. I don't know many people who would walk away in the same circumstance. I know I wouldn't."

Jax sighed, stared ahead as if in deep thought.

"There's something else," she continued, flattening a hand over her stomach. "By dangling the carrot of dropping the lawsuit in front of you, Ethan knew it would put a strain on my relationship with X. And you let him. He made it contingent on *me* representing him. *Only me.* And I let him."

He raised a brow. "You have a relationship with Xavier?"

Her throat burned, her heart hammered in her chest. "Yes, there *is* a relationship. More than friendship, more than coworkers."

"I'd say I'm surprised, but I'm more shocked that you admitted it."

Her mouth fell open. Now it was her turn to be surprised. "You knew?"

"I suspected for a long time. Didn't know for sure, until I heard a rumor about a kiss in the middle of a bar."

Zara let out a slow breath. "Okay." She nodded, readying herself for confession number two. "I love him."

His eyes widened, and a slow smile crept across his lips.

"I'm in love with your son," she continued. "It's not a fling, it's not an office romance. It's real. And . . ."

This is harder than I thought. Not because she didn't mean what she'd said, but because she'd never imagined baring her soul to Jax before. She took another cleansing breath. "And I love him more than I love this job. I love him more than I love being an agent. If I have to choose, I choose him."

Shit, did I really just do this? Yes. Yes, I did.

The room descended into silence, so still she could hear faint sounds from the street below. She fidgeted a little, wondering if she should say anything else or just give him what she came to give him.

Unable to take the long pause, she pulled an envelope out of her suit pocket and handed it to him. "I took the liberty of calling in a favor. Larry Boston at Huntington Sports has agreed to represent Ethan."

After Larry had begged her to come back, and even declared his love for her, she'd told him to go to hell and take *his love* with him. But not before she told him what she needed him to do for her. Initially he'd balked at her request, letting her know that it wasn't illegal to steal someone's ideas.

His entire tone changed, however, when she threatened to tell everyone that he'd fathered a secret child with one of his client's wives—if he didn't agree to her terms, which included telling Ethan he'd represent him under the condition that he drop the frivolous lawsuit against Xavier and Pure Talent.

Good thing basketball players like to gossip, too. One of her clients couldn't wait to tell her about the rumors his wife had told him, especially after he'd heard what Larry did to her.

The conversation with Larry was pretty much over after that ultimatum. She wanted to end the call with a cheery "good luck, don't ever call me again," but had chosen to just hang up.

"You'll probably hear from your lawyers today on the lawsuit."

Jax opened the envelope and read the letter. When he met her gaze again, he asked, "You're resigning?"

"Yes, effective immediately."

Jax chuckled, which seemed odd.

"I'm sorry this didn't work out, but if I want to have a lasting relationship with X, perhaps it's better that we don't work together."

Jax stood. "You want to know what I think of this letter?" He tore it in half. "Sit down. Let's talk."

Chapter 20

"Mom, don't cry." Xavier handed his mother a Kleenex.

She sniffed, dabbed the tissue under her eyes. "Trust me, I don't prefer ruining my makeup, son. But I'm just so full right now."

They were seated at the café in the lobby, each of them nursing cups of coffee. He'd stopped by the office to grab some work, which he could take with him to L.A., when he ran into his mother. She'd promptly smacked him with the magazine she had in her hand and demanded he tell her what was going on with Zara.

Why his mom broke down in tears when he'd admitted he loved Zara, he'd never know. But apparently love made everyone emotional. Not just him.

"I'm so proud of you, babe." Ana placed her hands on top of his. "You've become the man I've always known you could be."

"I wish Dad would realize that."

"He does, sweetheart." She squeezed his hands. "He sees it. Trust me."

"Why would he do that?"

X had told his mother everything, from the unexpected attraction to Zara at the holiday party to Donutgate to Detroit, and, finally, to Fiji. He'd left out the sex parts of the story, because she was still his mother.

I'm sure she's grateful for that, too. Even though she always told me, I could talk to her about anything.

"Sometimes your father thinks 'big picture' so much, he tends to miss the smaller details that matter. I don't think he thought of it as hurting you. In fact, I know he only wanted to help you."

"He didn't help, though."

"But you didn't have to react the way you did, son."

Touché. One of the hardest parts about this entire situation was realizing that he'd been just as culpable as anyone, maybe more. He'd set everything in motion by beating Ethan to a pulp at the holiday party. And he was the one who'd lashed out like a crazed jerk. In the process, he'd hurt the one person he never wanted to hurt.

"You're right, Ma. I'm the one who started all of this. Doesn't mean Dad was right, though."

"He was definitely wrong. And I plan to tell him next time I see him."

They sat in silence for a few minutes, before he asked, "If I lose her, I—"

She patted his hand softly. "You won't."

He hoped not. If he did, he would be done, because she would walk off with his heart in her palm.

"How do you know?"

"Because I just do. Do you want to know why I invited her to dinner?"

He frowned. "I thought it was because you just missed her and wanted to spend time with her."

"That's absolutely true. But I also invited her because I had a feeling things were different between you two. I read the blogs, you know. I wanted to see for myself."

And he'd told Zara she was thinking about it too much! He chuckled. "Mom, you were scheming."

"I wouldn't put it so harshly. I just wanted to see for myself."

"And?"

"It was exactly what I thought. I saw her face when your father told you to attend the wedding. I watched her calm you in the midst of your anger, in a way no one has ever done before. Not me, not even Skye. Then there was the fact that I listened to a tiny bit of your conversation outside. Just a *tiny* bit." She held up her thumb and forefinger, indicating how *tiny* her eavesdropping was.

Xavier cracked up. "Mom, really?" He thought of their romp on the trampoline.

"Don't worry. I left before you reached the trampoline."

He cleared his throat, averting his gaze. "Yeah, let's not talk about this again."

She laughed. "It'll be our little secret."

"Like your 'tiny' snooping?"

Ana held her hands against her cheeks. "Oh, boy. Don't make me laugh anymore. Anyway, I could see the love even then." She cupped his chin in her hands, much like she used to do when he was a kid. "And the way you love her . . ." A tear fell from her eyes. "It makes me so happy to see it. One of the most important things in life is the gift of love—giving it freely without condition and then feeling it shining down on you. It is transformative, son. And that's what I've always wished for you. Once you have it, you won't be able to live without it."

Zara once asked him how he knew Naomi wasn't the one. They were interrupted before he could answer, but he doubted he would've known the answer then. But now, the answer was clear. Naomi wasn't the one because she wasn't Zara. She wasn't the woman X couldn't live without. Zara was.

X had been around the block many times, but no other woman had filled him up, emotionally and physically. She'd inspired him, made him want to be better. And he'd tell her as soon as he saw her.

"It will work out," she said. "I'm done crying for the day. Now I have to fix my face. And don't tell your father about the eavesdropping."

"No worries on that front."

She sighed. "You need to talk to him, babe. He needs to hear from you. Tell him how you feel."

"What good will that do, Mom?"

"You'd be surprised."

He doubted that. "I'll think about it. Right now, I have to get ready to catch a flight." His phone buzzed and he pulled it out. He showed it to his mom. It was his father.

Twenty minutes later, he stepped into Jax's office. "You wanted to see me?"

It had taken a few tries for his mom to convince him to talk to his father, but when she demanded he "take his ass up to the office," he knew she wasn't playing around. Still, he wasn't sure it was a good idea.

Jax stood. "I did. I wanted to talk to you about something."

"I'm actually running late. I need to be at the airport soon."

Jax gestured toward the couches near the window. "Drink?"

"No, thanks." Confused, X followed his dad and took a seat, while his father veered off toward the minibar in the office.

"Where are you headed? Client business?"

"I'm going to Los Angeles," X said slowly, still trying to understand what was going on, "to see Zara."

"It's a good thing you came here first, then." His father poured a glass of cognac, which he kept in the office for clients. It was old-school, but, hey, it was his company.

"Why is that?"

"Because she just left my office not even"—he glanced at his watch—"an hour ago." His father walked over to the couch and sat.

THE WAY YOU TEMPT ME

"She was here?"

"Yes. We had a good conversation." Jax chuckled, shaking his head. "That girl. I'm so proud of her. Boy, she let me have it."

X blinked. "What?"

"Zara," Jax said, as if he'd missed something. "She came in here upset with me. Then she quit."

Jax laughed then, muttering something about deal makers and negotiations and . . .

Wait a damn minute. "She quit?" X stood.

"Yep." His father leaned back against the cushions and sipped his drink. "I didn't accept her resignation, though."

"Dad, what is this?" X asked, frustrated at the whole conversation.

"What do you mean? Zara came here, quit, and I gave her the sports division."

The hell? "You gave her *my job*!"

Jax met his gaze, all hint of amusement gone. "No, son. I gave Zara *her* job."

X sucked in a deep breath as everything clicked. "You were never going to give me the job, were you?"

Jax shook his head. "No. I wasn't."

All of his fight was gone. He couldn't argue anymore. If his father couldn't see that he deserved the promotion, then he didn't know what else to do to convince him. Or if he even wanted to, at that point.

"Okay," X said.

"Don't you want to know why?"

"Not particularly. But I'm sure you're going to tell me, anyway."

"You're right. I am. Son, leading Pure Talent Sports is not your job."

"How many times—"

Jax cut him off. "Leading Pure Talent is your job."

X's eyes flashed to his dad's. "Wait . . . what did you say?"

"For a while, I've been watching you. You think I don't see you, but I do. I've seen you stay in the background and let others shine. I've seen you command a room, lead a team. I've seen you focused on Pure Talent, not on what Xavier wants or needs. Those are all qualities of someone that I want to succeed me when the time is right. So, no, I'm not giving you *that* job. I'm giving you *my* job."

Unable to even begin to process this latest development, Xavier just sat there and stared. His father wanted *him* to run the company? Not just the sports division or audio, but the entire agency?

Stunned, X murmured, "You're leaving."

"I'm not going anywhere soon. But when I'm ready to leave, you're it. And I know you'll take this company in an exciting direction, to places I haven't even thought of. You and Zara."

"Me and Zara? What does that mean?"

Jax smiled. "You already know what it means."

He shook his head. Because he didn't know shit. He'd obviously misjudged . . . everything. "Can you please enlighten me?"

"I'm going to make you a partner. You'll work

under me, report to me, from now on. I'm in the process of developing my succession plan and I want to work with you on it. Who better to help me than you? Since you'll be the head of the company, once I'm done. Running the agency is a lot more than just one department. You'll need to have your hands in everything." He patted X's back. "You're already off to a good start, having been in on the groundwork for both sports and audio. But there's a lot more to be done."

Nodding, X said, "Okay."

"We'll talk about it next week."

"'Next week'?"

"Yeah, you're off for the next few days. Didn't you just say you were headed to L.A.?"

X looked around the office, sure someone would hop out and yell, "Psych!" He felt like he was being Punk'd. "But you said Zara was here."

"She is. You should probably go see her. You two have a lot to talk about. Your first order of business is promoting her to junior partner."

"I thought you just gave her the job."

Jax shrugged. "I did. But I didn't make her a partner. I figured it would be best if you did that, son." His father squeezed his shoulder. "I've never been prouder of you than I am at this moment. You've risen to the occasion, against adversity and me. And you managed to find love along the way. That's all your mother and I ever wanted for you." He stood. "Now I have a meeting on the golf course." He set the empty glass on the counter. "You better get out of here. You can take the rest of the week, spend it with Zara, go to another island, since I ruined your last trip."

Standing, X approached his father. "Dad, I—"

"I'm sorry, son. I should have never asked Zara to take Ethan on."

"What about the lawsuit?"

"Done. I just heard from the attorneys. Porter dropped the suit."

"Seriously?"

"I don't lie about money. Like I said, you have a lot to talk to Zara about."

Before X could ask more questions, his father pulled him into a tight hug. And X let him.

"So, have you talked to him?" Skye asked.

"Not yet." Zara pulled her clothes out of her suitcase and tossed them in her hamper. Then she picked up her toiletry bag and started putting her things in her cabinet.

"Zara! He has a flight to L.A.!"

"That you told him not to get on."

Zara hadn't intended to talk to anyone before she talked to X, but Skye had sent a simple text stating how X was on his way. Immediately Zara texted Skye back to tell her that she was in Atlanta. Skye drove right over then, after she'd sent X a text telling him not to get on the plane.

"Still . . ." She picked up one of Zara's bracelets. "This is nice. You should gift me with it." She set it down.

Zara shot her a sidelong glance. "Yeah, no. I

paid too much money for that." It was a gift to herself when she signed her first client as an agent of Huntington Sports.

"Anyway, when are you going to call him?"

"I will, Skye. I'm going to call him when you leave." They needed to talk, alone. She didn't want to be interrupted, and she wanted to be able to speak freely.

"Oh?!" Her best friend laughed. "You're trying to get rid of me."

Zara put her makeup in her drawer. "Not at all. I love you, bestie."

"I love you, too," she grumbled. "It's because of my love for you that I want the best for you and X."

"You're so dramatic."

"I'm living vicariously through you. Which is pitiful."

"It's not, babe. You're good."

"When he finds out what you've done for him, what you were willing to walk away from . . . Oh, my God, he's not going to be able to take it."

"You're such a sap for romance, Skye." Zara picked up her phone and sent a text to Rissa. Her sister had threatened her with bodily harm if she didn't call her in an hour. She'd just told her that she'd call her tomorrow. Because when she did see X, she planned to go off the grid until they agreed never to let another sun set while they were angry with one another.

There were so many things they needed to talk about: her new job, his job, Pure Talent, Fiji, Ethan . . . everything. But what they had was worth a hard conversation. She wanted to make sure he knew that she chose him. And she would choose him every day for the rest of their lives.

A few minutes passed and Skye hadn't said another word. Zara stopped putting her earrings away and turned. Her friend was sitting on the edge of her bed, staring at some point on the blank wall.

"Skye?" She walked over to her. "Are you okay?"

Skye glanced up at her and smiled. "I'm fine. Just thinking."

"You're sure?" She sat down next to her. "What's going on?"

Her friend sighed. "It feels like my entire life is an overthought. I spend so much time thinking about everything that I'm missing my life."

Zara knew the feeling. She'd wasted so much time running, thinking about all the what-ifs of every situation.

"I'm almost at the point when I want to just say forget it," Skye continued. "Obviously, my life isn't bad. I'm not struggling financially, I have a home. What do I have to complain about?"

"Those are just things, Skye. They fade away or depreciate. The things that matter have heartbeats. Fortunately, you also have friends and family who adore you."

Skye rested her head on Zara's shoulder. "You won't come over at night and hold me." She laughed and Zara joined in.

"I would. I actually have. Just like you've come and held me." Their friendship had endured through the years, and she wouldn't trade her best friend for anything. "That's what we do for each other." She squeezed Skye's hand. "And as your friend, as your sista, I'm going to tell you that you need to let go of the anger. I believe that's keeping you from your happy place."

And from Garrett.

"Maybe," Skye mused. "Or maybe I'm just horny."

"Hey, I'm dispensing sage advice here, so you have to listen."

"Only if you call X now."

"If I call X, will you try to move past this? Because I hate to see you like this."

Skye bumped shoulders with Zara. "Okay, I'll make an effort. But only because I'm proud of you for stepping out there, for letting yourself fall, no matter how scary the descent was."

Zara did fall—so hard that she didn't know if she'd recover if it didn't work. "I can't help it. He's everything." X brought out the best in her. When she was near him, she was the woman she wanted to be. "My mom said we've been courting since the first day we met."

Skye giggled. "Ha! She's right. Remember the Gummi Bears? I wanted some of those and he wouldn't share with me. But you come and he just hands them over."

"She brought that up, too." Zara hugged her friend. "It's going to be okay. We're going to be all right. All of us. Even Duke."

"He's going to make some woman very happy. As soon as he stops talking so much shit."

Zara burst out laughing. "Right?"

The doorbell rang and Zara stood. Skye followed her down the stairs and into the living room. She swung the door open and . . . X looked so good standing there, in dark jeans and a cream shirt.

"Hi," she breathed, leaning against the door.

He gave her a once-over, a slow smile forming on his lips. It felt like he was undressing her, peeling off every layer, seeing her.

"Hi," he answered in turn.

"You came." She hadn't called him yet, so she wondered how he knew she was there.

"I did. Dad told me you were home." He rubbed his forehead with his finger. "Then Skye texted and told me not to get on the plane. So I figured I'd come by and take a chance, and I saw Skye's car out front."

"Good. I was going to call you."

"Good."

"Come in." She stepped aside and let him pass.

"Hey, Skye." X gave his cousin a hug.

"Hi." Skye pointed toward the door. "So I'm out of here." She rushed to the door, stopping to give Zara a hug along the way. "Deuces."

Then she was gone, and they were alone.

They stood there for a moment, staring at each other. Zara wanted to take him in. It had only been a few days, but it felt like a lifetime.

"Xavier, can—"

"Zara, I—"

They both laughed. She gestured to him. "You go ahead," she said.

"I overreacted. I lashed out and said things that I regret. And I'm sorry."

Zara swallowed past a lump in her throat. "*We* overreacted. I should have just told you the truth. I don't know why I didn't. I just know I was wrong. I broke the rules, and you had every right to be upset."

He brushed his thumb under her eye when a tear fell. "I missed you, baby."

"I missed you, too. I'm so sorry." Zara wrapped her arms around his waist and hugged him. She felt his arms wrap around her, cocooning her in his warmth.

He kissed the top of her head. "I don't want to spend another night apart."

Pulling back, she searched his eyes. "Me neither."

"No more running. You walked away, you left me."

Zara felt gutted by the pained expression in his eyes. It was raw, palpable.

"The first hour, I was angry, but then I went numb. If we're going to do this, you can't run anymore. You have to know that we'll argue and say things in the heat of the moment. But you can't leave. I can't take it."

She caressed his face. "I know. I'm sorry. I should've stayed. I promise I'll do better."

He rested his forehead against hers. "I promise, too." He placed a lingering kiss to her lips—one that made her want to weep, it was so sweet.

When he pulled back, she brushed her fingers

over her mouth and opened her eyes. *That was hot.*
She let out a deep breath. "X, today I quit my job
because you're more important to me than getting money and making deals." His eyes darkened
and she rushed on. "So I resigned, fully intending
on going somewhere else so that we could be together. I'm serious, I don't want to let this go. If that
means I have to—"

Before she could finish her sentence, she was in
his arms and his lips were pressed against hers.
With his hands fisted in her hair, he kissed her so
long, so deeply, so intensely, she felt weak in the
knees. Someone groaned. But she didn't care who
it was, because she needed this. She needed him.

When he broke the kiss, he stepped back. "We
probably should finish talking." He rubbed his
palms over his pants.

"Really?" She didn't want to talk anymore. She
just wanted to make love to him.

He nodded. "Yes."

"Okay." Her shoulders fell. "X?"

"Yes?"

"Can we sit down? I wore the wrong shoes today."

He laughed. "Okay."

She slipped her hand in his and led him to the
couch. He sat down first, and she followed suit, sitting right next to him, thigh to thigh. That didn't
last long, though, because he promptly pulled her
onto his lap. She laughed. "X."

"I need contact, baby. It's been a minute."

They sat still for several minutes, holding each

other. There was no kissing, no words. Just them, together.

"I negotiated a deal for Ethan to be represented by Huntington Sports, in exchange for him dropping the lawsuit," she told him.

"Really?"

She sat up and searched his eyes. "I had to make it right."

He smirked. "Thank you."

"But when I gave your dad my resignation, he—"

"Gave you my job."

She bit her lip and nodded.

"Do you want the job?"

"I do, but I want you. And I'm not sure we should work together *and* be together."

"It's up to you. You don't have to take that job. But I do want you to think about taking this one."

He lifted up and pulled an envelope from his back pocket. She'd been so engrossed in him, she didn't even notice the piece of paper sticking out of his pocket. She opened the envelope and scanned the document.

Her eyes flashed to his. "An offer letter! For junior partner!"

He grinned. "If you want it."

"Oh, my God, of course I want it." She hugged him. "Jax gave you this? I just saw him, and he didn't mention anything about partner."

"That's because it's my first official task as full partner of Pure Talent."

Her mouth fell open. "You made partner!" Jax

finally went ahead with his plan, and she couldn't be happier. "Are you excited?"

"I am. But I need you with me. Always. So take the job."

She beamed. "Of course, I'll take the job!" She kissed him, once, twice, three times. Then more. He leaned her back against the cushion, unbuttoning her blouse and kissing her everywhere. The boom of a loud knock jolted them out of their heated make-out session. She groaned. "Don't answer it."

He kissed her nose. "I'm expecting something."

She closed her shirt and followed him to the door, peeking around him when he opened it and signed for a large package. The burly deliveryman brought the tall box into the house and set it down in the middle of the floor. She turned to X, waiting for him to tip the guy and close the door.

"What is it?" she asked.

"Take a look."

She walked around the box, until she noticed the picture on one side. Gasping, she said, "You bought a rowing machine!"

He patted the box. "Told you I'd make something happen."

Zara jumped into his arms, wrapping her legs around his waist. "You're hilarious. I can't wait to try it."

"Another day, baby. Right now, I need you."

"Need you, too." She kissed him.

"I'm obsessed with you." He pushed her shirt off, brushing his lips along the column of her neck.

"Me too." She tilted her head back, letting him

work his magic as he carried her upstairs to her bedroom.

"I'm in this with you. Forever."

She moaned. "Yes! I feel the same way. Stop talking. Start doing me."

Chuckling, he lowered her to the mattress, peered in her eyes. "Love you."

Her stomach growled, and her eyes widened. "Oops. I haven't eaten much in three days. You have to feed me."

"I'll feed you. Later."

Zara laughed. "Sounds like a plan. And X?"

"Yes, baby."

"Love you, too."

Epilogue

Five months later

Zara walked into the Starks home and scanned the room. There were several people in attendance, as usual, at the holiday party. People she hadn't seen in years milled around, laughing heartily and sipping on cocktails.

Her family was in attendance this year. Rissa and Urick stood near the bar, talking to Paityn and Bishop. Her mother—who had officially enrolled in Le Cordon Bleu, in Paris, with the intention of realizing her dream—was over near the piano talking to all the other mothers. Skye was in the corner laughing with Duke and Garrett. And X? She frowned, searching for him in the crowd. *Where is he?*

Strong arms wrapped around her from the back. He kissed her cheek. "Are you looking for me?"

She turned in his arms. "Yes. I missed you."

He leaned down and brushed his mouth over hers. "I can tell."

The past five months had flown by as they'd settled into a rhythm with each other. She let her rental go and moved in with X. It was a struggle to get him to agree on a décor change, but a few well-placed kisses ensured that she'd get her way. Xavier had settled into his new position in the agency, and had hit the ground running with a slew of innovative ideas that invigorated the staff and made Jax confident enough to take more time off.

Zara assumed her role as head of Pure Talent Sports, right as they finalized the deal with the Whitney Agency. They launched officially on October 1. Since then, things had been hectic for both of them. Travel, meetings, contracts. Wash. Rinse. Repeat. But Zara wouldn't change it for the world. Because she was happy. She was in love. And she never wanted that feeling to end.

"Want to get out of here?" she asked, arching a brow. "Escape to the tree house outside?"

"I'm definitely down for that. But I have something to do first."

Confused, Zara asked, "Do what? What's more important than tree house action?"

"This." Xavier pulled out a tiny blue box.

Gasping, Zara stepped back several steps. "Oh, God," she whispered. "X, what did you do?" Just then, she realized that no one was talking. In fact, everyone was watching them. "X?"

He smirked. "Come. Here." His voice was a low, heated whisper, one that settled into her belly and bloomed, spreading warmth through her body.

Damn. He'd pulled out the big guns and she melted as she always did when he said those two little words.

Swallowing, she scanned the faces of everyone she loved and noted the tears standing in several eyes. *They knew about this.* Taking a deep breath, she took a step closer and he pulled her the rest of the way.

"A long time ago, I met this girl and immediately wanted to give her my candy."

Zara covered her mouth as a smile tugged at her lips.

"One year ago, that same girl walked into my parents' kitchen and proceeded to nurse my spirit back to health."

"And your hand," she added.

He chuckled. "And my hand." He ran his finger over her ear. "Since then, I haven't been able to stop thinking about her. I haven't been able to stop falling in love with her. With you. I love you, baby. I love our life. I want labels."

She held his hand to her, reveling in the contact. "X, I love you so much. You rescued me, saved me from a lifetime of excuses. You saved me from myself, even though I didn't realize I needed to be saved."

"A year ago, you asked me how I knew Naomi wasn't the one." He brushed tears from her cheeks with his thumbs.

She remembered the conversation last year at this very party. It was the first time she'd felt *more* for him. "I remember."

"I couldn't answer you then, but I can now. She wasn't the one because *you* were. I just didn't know it. When I was giving you my Gummi Bears and protecting you from every bully or asshole in school, I never knew that one day I would be in love with you. I never expected to feel so much for you. But I do. And I don't want to go back to a time when I didn't."

"I know the feeling."

"And I want to make it officially official. I want you to be mine forever. Marry me."

"Shit, I'm going to cry. And it's going to be ugly."

He laughed. "So hurry up and say yes, so I can take you to the tree house."

"Yes!" She wrapped her arms around his shoulders, kissing him deeply.

She was so wrapped up in the moment, in him, that she almost forgot where they were. Reluctantly she broke the kiss, wiping her lipstick from his lips. People swarmed around them, offering congratulations, and all she could think about was the tree house.

After she'd given out hugs to her favorite people, bawled with her mother and with Ana, and took selfies with her sistas, she glanced at X and leaned against him. "It's time."

Before she could say anything else, he was carrying her out of the room. He didn't put her down until they were in the tree house. Only then, did he set her down on her feet.

"X, you are crazy!" She laughed. "But I wouldn't

change anything about this moment. I love you, baby. I can't wait to be your wife. Now"—she unbuckled his belt and slid it off, tossing it somewhere behind her—"let's get this party started."

He smacked her ass. "I'm ready when you are." He kissed her slowly, thoroughly. "I love you, too."

Coming soon from Elle Wright . . .

Book 2 in the Pure Talent series

The Way You Hold Me

Dazzling, demanding mega-stars.
Tabloid drama. Brilliant, unpredictable creators.
Viral rumors. Ambitious, gifted newcomers.
Internet-breaking crash-and-burns.
The Pure Talent Agency team manages it all—
even risking scandals of their own . . .

Skye Palmer puts out the biggest publicity
fires for Pure Talent's top names.
But when an A-list Hollywood actress's
dream marriage proves anything but,
Skye has to do nightmare damage control.
Even worse, her ex-lover, attorney
Garrett Steele, is crisis manager for her client's
powerful director husband. Now for Skye
and Garrett, containing this disaster—and
keeping their reignited passion in check—
may be mission impossible . . .

Troubleshooting is what Garrett and his elite
firm does best. But saving his client from
career-killing bad news means battling the one
woman Garrett's never gotten over.
And when joining forces with Skye leads
to one steamy night together—followed by
another and another—both their reputations
are on the line. Yet now that they've turned up
the heat, can they put a new spin on their future?

Published by Kensington Publishing Corp.

Connect with

Us

Visit us online at
KensingtonBooks.com
to read more from your favorite authors, see books
by series, view reading group guides, and more.

for sneak peeks, chances to win books and prize packs,
and to share your thoughts with other readers.

facebook.com/kensingtonpublishing
twitter.com/kensingtonbooks

Tell us what you think!

To share your thoughts, submit a review,
or sign up for our eNewsletters, please visit:
KensingtonBooks.com/TellUs.